Mask of innocence

As Richard Patton, an ex-Detective Inspector enjoying early re-
tirement, well knows, wills can arouse strong passions. The
reading of them alone can be sheer murder. But he and his wife
Amelia nevertheless escort their friend, Mary Pinson, to Penhavon Park without too many misgivings. Her inheritance as a
former maid and nanny can barely affect the situation, it is
thought. The intriguing question is why Sir Rowland Searle,
Penhavon's squire, should have remembered Mary at all.

The answer to this is apparent as soon as they arrive, and in
fact is a pleasurable discovery. But very soon all pleasure dis-
solves into violent disagreement. The will of the late Sir Rowland is, to say the least, contentious. Even the manner of his
death is cause for concern to Richard, and an anticipated short
stay is soon extended by violent murder.

There can be no doubt that the loss of Charles Pinson is nothing
but a gain to the general populace. Nevertheless, murder is
illegal, and the police descend on the Park. The basic problem is
simple: not the locking of the front door of the cottage, nor the
lack of an obvious weapon, but – why wasn't the key returned to
its usual place, under the flowerpot?

Richard manages to find the answer after a stressful trip
through the emotional backgrounds, and a left foot where a right
should have been.

Master storyteller and ingenious plotter, Roger Ormerod has
once again produced a riveting puzzle to intrigue and satisfy the
most jaded palate.

MASK OF INNOCENCE

Roger Ormerod

Constable · London

First published in Great Britain 1994
by Constable & Company Ltd
3 The Lanchesters, 162 Fulham Palace Road
London W6 9ER
Copyright © 1994 by Roger Ormerod
The right of Roger Ormerod to be
identified as the author of this work
has been asserted by him in accordance
with the Copyright, Designs and Patents Act 1988
ISBN 0 09 473080 6
Set in Linotron 10pt Palatino by
Pure Tech Corporation, India
Printed in Great Britain by
St Edmundsbury Press Limited
Bury St Edmunds Suffolk

A CIP catalogue record for this book
is available from the British Library

1

The letter lay on the kitchen table, unopened. Nervously ignoring it, Mary was making a major operation of brewing a pre-breakfast pot of tea. Yet the letter was addressed to her. Miss Mary Pinson, The Beeches.

'There's a letter for you, Mary,' I said cheerfully, as though she hadn't realised. But ignoring it wasn't going to send it away.

I knew what was worrying her, the fact that it had come from a solicitor. There it was, printed in the top left-hand corner: Russell & Co., Solicitors, Penhavon Magna, Salop. This had to be a long-established and venerable firm, clinging still to the traditional county name.

There was nothing involved, surely, for Mary to worry about. But it was legal, and therefore had to be treated with nervous apprehension, though the possibility of Mary having become involved with legal iniquities was absurd.

Amelia was suddenly there at my shoulder. My wife is very astute about this sort of thing, sensing atmospheres, deciding on the action to be taken, and taking it with bland confidence.

'Letter for me? Oh no . . . it's for you, Mary. And there was I, thinking all sorts of exciting things! How you can let it lie there . . .'

Mary shook her head numbly. I said I would open it for her, and slit it with my penknife, then placed it back on the table. Mary put down the teapot, absently stirred, vacantly popped the cosy over it, and stood there, staring at her letter. I noticed that her fingers were shaking.

'It won't bite you, Mary,' said Amelia.

Mary reached out, withdrew the letter, glanced at it as though covering the complete contents with one wink, and put it down firmly on the table. Then she looked across at Amelia. She was alternating between pallid and flushed. 'What does it mean?' she whispered. 'Have a look at it, please.'

Amelia then skimmed through it, raised her eyes to mine, and said, 'Richard knows more about these things than me, Mary. May I read it out loud?'

'Of course,' Mary said.

I went and leaned against the wall. The two dogs, Sheba and Jake, came to snuffle at my fingers, aware that it was time for their morning run, and reminding me. I crouched, one hand to each head, pulling their ears.

'You're not listening, Richard,' said Amelia.

'Oh yes I am. And anyway, it's Mary's letter. Possibly private. I'll go out, if you like.'

I smiled up at Mary. She pouted at me, and gently shook her head. Then she returned her attention to Amelia, who had read quickly through it once more.

'Is it . . .' Mary hesitated, frowning heavily. 'Is it serious, Amelia?' She stood there stiffly, the tiniest quiver to her lower lip.

'Not for you, Mary. On the contrary. Listen. "Dear Miss Pinson, You may not be aware of the death of Sir Rowland Searle, who passed away on the 23rd of September. I am sorry to bring you this news, and regret that it has taken so long to locate you, but I can inform you now that he had not forgotten you." '

Amelia looked up, smiling. 'Well now! Isn't that nice? *Sir* Rowland, too. Sorry. There's some more. It goes on: "In accordance with his instructions, I have arranged a formal reading of his will on the 16th inst. If, as I hope, you can be present, I am sure you will not find your journey wasted." Inst, Richard? What does that mean?'

'It's Latin for "this month". Short for instant. The day after tomorrow, that'll be. Doesn't give us much time, does it?'

I straightened as I said it, and ran my hand down the back of my neck, this to hide the wink I gave to Amelia. My mind had been racing, and I knew that Mary, who had her own little car, would nevertheless dread the idea of a forty-mile run in the weather we'd been having lately, anything from pouring rain to fog, to early-morning frosts. So it was necessary to take the initiative from her, and present it as a settled fact. We would take her. I knew roughly where it was – the far side of Shropshire.

'Oh . . . but I couldn't! she cried. 'Oh no. The trouble for you! And I don't want anything to do with it, anyway.'

'Surely that tea's brewed now,' said Amelia with concern.

'Oh yes . . . yes . . .'

And Mary seemed genuinely relieved to turn her attention to a familiar and homely task, such as lifting the cosy and giving the tea a stir.

'We'll take my Granada,' decided Mary.

I agreed. 'Of course. My Stag . . .' I shook my head, smiling. It had been an adventure we'd all three shared. 'Remember Sweden, Mary? Now, wasn't *that* a time?'

She turned, biting her lower lip, but her eyes were shining with the memory. She had enjoyed it. Now I was offering the present situation as another adventure. 'How can I forget it?' she murmured.

'So it'd better be the Granada,' I insisted.

'But I haven't decided . . .'

'Now come on, Mary,' I said. 'If you don't go, they won't be able to read the will.'

This was quite untrue, but if she had the idea that her absence would cause difficulties she would break her neck in order to get there.

'There's more,' said Amelia. 'You're requested to be at Penhavon Park . . . Park! That sounds a bit grand. Requested to be there at twelve noon for the reading, when you will hear something to your advantage.'

'Advantage?'

It was a little too much for Mary. She sat at the table, and made no comment when Amelia began to set out the cups and the milk and the sugar, but twisted her hands together and gazed fixedly at them. She was not a stranger to wills, as she'd been a beneficiary in Amelia's Uncle Walter's will. Mary had been his housekeeper and he had made certain she would always have a roof over her head by leaving her part of The Beeches, Amelia inheriting the rest. It was fortunate that we had become friends, though Mary had never cured herself of her housekeeper habits, and looked after us meticulously. We didn't protest; it gave her pleasure.

Amelia poured the tea. This had become a custom, an early pot of tea, after which I would take the dogs for a walk, and return to find breakfast on the table.

'And what', asked Amelia, 'is your connection with Penhavon Park, Mary? Did you work there?'

Mary's eyes became somewhat vacant, the past capturing her. 'Oh yes,' she said at last. 'That was how it was. The girl from the

7

village, that's what I was. Fifteen when I went there, as an under-maid. I don't suppose they have such creatures now. Creatures! I wonder why that word came to mind, though I suppose that's what we were, me and the others. There were two sons . . . then. Jeremy, he was the elder boy. He'd have been about three, and little Paul one. When I started there.'

She was silent for a few moments, trying to recapture her youth, not much more than childhood, if she'd been only fifteen.

'I can't remember exactly when,' Mary eventually went on, 'but somehow or other my duties seemed to change, and I became sort of a nanny. Living in, then. Oh . . . the mistress was all fuss with them, and happy-like, when there was only Jeremy to look after, but young Paul was growing into a bit of a handful, so there I was . . . still in my teens, and the three . . . three children to look after, eventually.' She looked down at the table, where her hands were kneading themselves together.

'Three, Mary?' asked Amelia.

'Jennie. The little girl . . . my lovely. Why – they'll be all grown up!' Now she had a cup poised in front of her mouth, and she seemed not to be aware of it. She was gazing fixedly at the opposite wall. 'Oh yes,' she whispered, 'they'll be all grown up now. Yes. Jeremy – oh, he'll be well into his middle forties, and Paul not much younger.'

'Two years, Mary,' Amelia murmured. 'You said that.'

'I'd never recognise them,' Mary decided, nodding her head. 'Meet them in the street, and walk straight past.' And there her voice faded, and she stared blindly at her memories.

'But you won't be meeting them in the street, Mary,' said Amelia softly. 'You'll meet them in the setting you all know.'

'Yes, yes.' There was a catch in Mary's voice. 'I don't think I can . . .' Her voice tailed off. We had to guess what she couldn't do, which, clearly, was to face them, the children she had loved.

The fear, I knew, was that they would not remember her, that they might even resent her presence. My experience in the police force had so often brought me into contact with the violence that can arise from a will, that I was a little uncertain myself. Money has a lot to answer for, but there was no reason, in the present instance, to suppose that Mary's inheritance would be large enough to upset anyone's expectations. Nevertheless, the situation might prove to be traumatic, and in that case our presence beside Mary would certainly be necessary.

8

Then, abruptly, the cup clattered into Mary's saucer and she put her hands over her face. 'Oh . . .' she whispered. 'Rowley, poor Rowley.' Her shoulders were shaking.

I caught Amelia's eye, and she nodded. Time to take out the dogs. I reached for my old anorak, hanging from a hook on the kitchen door, and the dogs began to dance. We went out, and I closed the door behind us.

That morning it was our turn for frost. It made the steep paths down to the Severn quite treacherous, though the two boxers seemed unaware of it. Twice the grip per pound of muscle, they had over me. Jake was now fully grown, and already a little bigger than Sheba. But he clearly appreciated who was the boss around there. You could see the little glances he cast to her – for her approval, for her permission.

When we got back, Mary seemed to be her usual self. She was chattering excitedly, and I came in at the middle of a sentence.

'And dear little Jennie. She'll be quite grown up. So pretty, so lively, she was.' She hesitated. There had been a slight catch in her voice. Then she cleared her throat and reached out a hand in my wife's direction. 'Heavens – do you realise, Amelia – Jennie could be married now, and have children of her own. Only . . . how old . . . oh, six months old when I left – came away from there. But I could see it, even then. Oh yes, I knew she was going to be quite lovely. If only . . .' She stopped, gazing at the wall.

But there was emotion distorting her voice and she kept her face averted. It was, indeed, going to be very difficult for Mary. I was beginning to believe I'd made a mistake in almost forcing her into this return to her former life. I could possibly have saved her the experience with a quiet few words on the phone to G. Russell, who had signed the letter.

Too late, though, now. Mary was firmly embroiled in a state of joy at the prospect of reunion, though it was shaded by apprehension at what she might find there.

The trip required very little organisation. In the intervening period Amelia and I refrained from discussing the peculiar fact that Mary, a servant amongst other servants, most likely, had been selected for hearing something to her advantage. But of course, she had the small distinction of having been a sort of nanny, as she put it. Nevertheless, I would have thought that a simple letter from G. Russell, Solicitor, would have covered it.

On the morning we set out the weather wasn't ideal, heavy clouds scudding around, but the worst we could expect was rain, I thought. I calculated an hour for the trip, having consulted my map, though it would be polite to arrive somewhat early, to allow for introductions.

When we found the village of Penhavon, far off the nearest main road, it was typical of any other Shropshire village – dominated by the river. The Severn, here, was much closer to its source, and might even have been one of its tributaries. We came down to it along a winding lane, the banks high each side. Just before we reached the river bridge, humpbacked and thus hiding the fact that the road shot off to the right abruptly, in order to lay out its shops and cottages with their backs to the river, there was a small and almost squat Norman church, so close to the water that it could well have been a mill at one time. Once over the bridge and into the main and apparently only street, the cottages, the Red Lion, the shops all seemed, to my eye, to be not quite upright. It could have been an optical illusion, as I was lining them up with the church tower beyond. It was possible that the church itself was the one to be leaning.

The street seemed to be deserted.

'Could we stop a moment, Richard?' asked Mary, leaning forward. She was in the back with the dogs.

I drew up. She continued to lean forward. 'There,' she said, her voice uncertain. 'Between the Red Lion and the post office, that little lane. It was up there I used to live. I was born there.'

'Want to go and have a look at it?' I asked.

'Oh . . . no!'

'No relatives?'

'I'm sure not. Another family moved in when my parents died. There was a flu epidemic. Terrible, it was. My brother Charles, he'd moved out. Gone and married a girl from Pen Magna. Older than me, he is. He could still be . . .'

She paused. Amelia said quietly, 'You haven't kept in touch?'

'No . . . no . . .' She cleared her throat. 'It was a bad . . . a difficult time. Can we move on, Richard? I . . . no, stop! Please stop.'

I jerked to a halt again. 'Mary?'

'It can't be,' she murmured. 'But I'm sure . . . Look, that man there. He *looks* like Charlie . . . I don't know . . . Just come out of the post office.'

10

She was now in a flutter. How many years since she'd seen him? Forty-two, perhaps? Then she was out of the car as the man rolled towards us. I would have guessed he was drunk, and, just in case, I slid out from behind the wheel and stood quietly beside the car. He came on, apparently not having noticed us, but he was now moving more slowly. I saw, then, that the roll was probably habitual, as he was definitely bandy-legged, and those legs carried a six-foot-two, eighteen-stone man who'd been hardened by the elements and a lifetime of heavy work. Then he stopped, ten yards short of Mary.

'Charlie?' she whispered.

'By God, it's Mary,' he cried, his voice gruff, harsh. Then he came forward rapidly and put huge hands on her shoulders, kissed her on both cheeks, and clasped her close, almost crushing the breath from her. At last he held her away from him, the better to consider her, to assess the changes wrought by the years.

'Y' never kept in touch,' he said gruffly.

'How could I, Charlie? After what you said. What you did.'

'Well . . . I was pressured, see. Pushed. An' that's where you're heading, I reckon. The old bugger's dead.'

'Hush, Charlie, hush. It's a long time back, now. I've come about his will.'

'Ha!' He threw back his head. His face was permanently flushed by the north winds that must howl relentlessly down this valley, his eyes the same grey as Mary's, but his head was nearly bald. I would not have cared to argue with him. 'Remembered you, has he? I'd reckon so. They're not going to like that – up there. You can bet.'

'Now, Charlie . . .'

He suddenly grinned. It transformed his face. 'Oh – I'd love to be there.'

'Well, you're not going to be. Behave yourself.' She slapped the back of his hand.

He released her and stood back. 'Y' know where to find me, Mary. Don Martin's place, up Corrie Lane. Any trouble, an' I'll sort 'em out for you.'

She hesitated for a moment, then shrugged. 'You always were a fool, Charlie. I'll have to be getting along. Look after yourself.'

'And you.'

I held open the rear door for her, using the other hand to restrain the dogs. They were grumbling in their throats. Mary

11

got in, bringing with her the smell of cattle. I started the car. She might have glanced sideways at her brother; I detected the movement of her head. In the rear-view mirror I could see that he'd raised an arm in salute, and he hadn't moved when I rounded a bend, which cut him off.

'It's a turn on the left,' said Mary. 'Just along here.' Her voice was unsteady.

We had left the village behind, empty apart from Charlie. The road surface was wet, so they'd been having some rain. They proceeded to have some more when I turned into the rising, erratic curves of the minor lane, rain that lashed the car, with scatterings of sleet in it. Mud ran down from the banks each side, and the wheels shuddered over the broken, pot-holed surface. We climbed and climbed. If anything had approached from the opposite direction, we could not have passed each other.

'Round the next bend,' whispered Mary. She was becoming tense, I could feel, leaning forward and almost breathing into my ear. Then, 'Right here, Richard.'

It was no more than a gap between reaching, weeping trees, with a sign nailed to a tree-trunk: Penhavon Park. Now the roadway was more level, but we were on private property, deprived of the benefits of tarmac to surface the winding track; it was not much more than that.

'I don't remember it so narrow,' said Mary, her voice dead.

To the left, abruptly, the trees fell away, and there was a low hedge running beside us. A shadowy shape stood back, a dark and apparently deserted building.

'That's the old gamekeeper's lodge,' said Mary, a dismissive tone in her voice. 'I always thought of it as being a bit spooky.' She paused. Her tone changed and softened. 'Not always, though. The next bit's quite tricky, Richard, as I remember it.' But she was using a memory in which she would have been on foot.

I had been under the impression that it was already tricky, but nothing is ever bad enough that it can't get worse. For midday, the light was poor, with a heavy, black layer of cloud obscuring the sun. Now that there were no trees lining the drive, the dense woodland having retreated down the slope to the left, there was barely any guide to the track's width. I put on the headlights, but strangely they appeared to be less bright than in complete darkness. But now, ahead and way down below, I caught sight of the building that was our objective. It looked grey and miser-

12

able against a background of sodden fields and threatening clouds.

The sleet became splots of snow amongst the streams of rain. Then the track settled down to become a nearly-straight line, but not directly pointing to the house, so that it seemed, if it continued like this, we would miss the building altogether, and find ourselves nose-down in the stream that surely had to be there, down in the bottom of the valley.

I slowed. The pot-holes now were severe.

'But it looks smaller,' murmured Mary. 'Perhaps some of it's fallen down.' She sounded as though that would in no way surprise her.

The drive had been heading towards the left of the house, as though determined to ignore it, but now, just beyond the inevitable wooden bridge, over which the wheels juddered, it turned right, levelled off, and projected us on to a surface that at least had received some attention, though only to the extent of a scattering of gravel. It opened out. The grey, sombre building faced sideways, and we were now at its front.

There was no imposing façade to offer to visitors arriving down that track, no compelling aspect whichever way you looked at it, so that to offer a blank end of the building to arriving guests would at least suspend the expectation of possible grandeur. If that had been the intention, the eventual realisation would have been a disappointment, though with no time left to brood on it and retreat. The total aspect was completely flat. True, there were steps up to a terraced entrance, and a solid front door, but the overall design was drab. They must have searched far and wide in order to discover all that grey and depressing stone. And in the event, they had found rather too much of it, so that it was only with reluctance that a window had been put in here and there, each of which was rather too small, allowing the stone to dominate. The frontage was flat, the roof a simple peak of Welsh slates. It was no more than a grey unsubtle block with holes in it for the windows. Penhavon Park.

'But it's so small,' said Mary breathlessly.

I wouldn't have said that. They'd imported a lot of that stone, and they'd continued building until it was all used up. It could, with very little alteration, have been converted to its apparent true identity, a prison.

13

'We'll have to run to the porch,' said Amelia. 'If you can't get any closer.' The rain battered the roof.

Vehicles were scattered between us and the door. Other visitors had realised the problem. A red van was parked nose-in beneath a window. A large Mercedes was right across the front steps, and beyond it loomed something that could have been a Citroën 2CV.

'It's as close as I can get.'

So we ran for the porch, after I'd assured the dogs we wouldn't be long. But there was no porch, no cover at all to protect that solid dark-oak door with the tiny stained-glass panels. I pushed the bell button, and we waited. Now the sleet hurled itself at our backs. Clots of snow slid down the door. We had brought no spare clothes, no macs or umbrellas. I'd been stupid, not envisaging the necessity.

Then the door opened.

'Come in, come in. Don't stand out there in the rain.' As though we'd had a choice.

He was tall, elderly, elegant, with a dove-grey waistcoat beneath his black jacket, a watch-chain draped across it and no doubt a half-hunter in the pocket. The trousers too were grey, his concession to informality, as the jacket almost demanded pin-striped trousers.

We stood inside the hall, shaking ourselves. It was deliciously warm within those grey walls. Built to keep the elements out, I thought. Practicality rather than elegance.

'I am Geoffrey Russell, Sir Rowland's solicitor. You'll be Mary Pinson,' he said confidently, smiling at our Mary. 'Don't deny it. I can see you are.'

With this puzzling observation, he stood aside, raising bushy grey eyebrows. I introduced us.

'This is my wife, Amelia, and I'm Richard Patton. We thought we'd run her here for the reading.'

We shook hands politely. Amelia was frowning at herself in a tall mirror on the wall, Mary dabbing at her face with a tiny handkerchief. Amelia touched her hair, frowning even more deeply. I allowed myself to look beyond them, observing what now faced us.

In defiance of the lack of taste and style presented by the exterior, the interior compensated with overpowering grace. The actual hall entrance was narrow but it opened up into a grand, panelled hall, with a wide fireplace on one side and a wall bearing four doors on the other. From a landing facing me above, a staircase swept down, this alone being enough to catch me on an indrawn breath. It began as a relatively straight stair at the top, but widened steadily as it swept downwards, though with fanned, curved banisters. The stair treads, therefore, formed the shape of a trumpet profile, an exponential curve that resulted in treads of gradually widening and deepening curves towards the bottom. The staircase dominated the hall. And the two glorious banisters themselves . . . I looked more closely later, to confirm my original impression, and yes . . . each banister rail began as narrow at the top, a mere four inches, and gradually broadened, as it curved, to a width of more than a foot at the bottom, where it was surmounted by a decorative ball. And search as I might – as I did later – I could find no join, no hesitation in the grain. Each had been carved from one solid trunk of an oak, and they matched exactly. It must have been a huge task, a triumph for a long-dead and probably unsung master carpenter. And the whole house was filled with beauty from the two same hands, I later discovered. This was the true Penhavon, not the travesty promised by the outer skin.

And Mary had lived here. But had she been required to use the back stairs, the servants' stairs?

It was as though this thought had inspired a vision, for there, it seemed, was our Mary, descending the noble staircase. A younger woman, though, in her mid-thirties, was tripping down with agility, her left hand sliding down the rail. But due to its construction, the stair treads themselves being bowed so that they butted on to the curve of the banisters accurately, the effect was that she gradually turned slightly from us, so that a full face of her, seriously concentrating on a staircase that could be difficult to navigate, became gradually a three-quarters side face, as though she pirouetted on a pedestal. As well she might, this young woman, because beauty was there on display, slim beauty. Dark brown the hair, dark grey the eyes as at last, the stairs safely behind her, she lifted her head, and her face flushed with a wild, almost frantic joy.

'Nan!' she cried out. 'Oh . . . Nanna!' Then, feet now safe on the parquetry, she ran straight into Mary's arms, and they hugged each other frantically, as though it could be a vision that might slide away if inadequately applauded.

15

But now, close up, I could see that I'd been deceived by this woman's slim, youthful figure, by her vivacity and the sparkle in her eyes, and that she must have been close to forty, if not actually nudging it, and Mary's indecision and reluctance were displaying their reason. Her position in the family group – her inclusion in Sir Rowland's will – all this became clear in an instant.

Mary must have realised that there had always been a chance that the child would grow into a resemblance of the mother. As she had. A little taller than Mary, slimmer, but with the same features, the honest and trusting eyes, they were all there.

This had to be Mary's child, the child she had called Jennie.

2

Mary had perhaps realised what she might expect – but had Jennie known? She had greeted her as 'Nanna'. But she had been too young when Mary had left there to recognise her as her nanny. This, then, was her version of 'Mother'. It was a compromise. That, at least, implied an expectation. If there had always been a photograph in the house that included Mary, then Jennie could well have grown into the knowledge as she achieved the likeness. In any event, she had to realise it now, and if it in any way disturbed her there was no sign of it. Excited and delighted her, yes. Disturbed – no.

'But you're all wet,' cried Jennie. 'Come on up to my room, and I'll find you something.'

'Ridiculous child.' Mary glowed.

And so absorbed were they with each other that no introductions were made. We might not have existed. They walked away and up the stairs, Jennie's arm around Mary's shoulders. 'But you never came to visit,' I heard her murmur.

Russell cleared his throat. I had forgotten he was there. 'So you're Mary Pinson's friends?' he asked me softly.

'Indeed we are,' said Amelia, whose eyes were shining, and whose lips were moving towards an outright laugh or possibly tears; in either case, joy.

'Then you no doubt realise why I had to make it an official reading of the will.' He was heavily solemn.

'An out-of-date procedure now, surely,' I said. 'But in the circumstances . . . you'll be able to control the situation this way.'

'I can but try,' he said, a little doubtfully, staring at his feet. Then he looked up quickly. 'Mary Pinson may need her friends.'

'We'll be close,' I assured him.

'Good. It would seem strange if her only support came from the testator's solicitor. But heavens! I do beg your pardon – you're both wet. We'll have to do something about that.'

And he rushed away into the nether regions, calling out, 'Tessa, Tessa!'

This led to Tessa, who was clearly the widow, escorting us upstairs, where she took Amelia into her own room, and ushered me into that of the late departed, directly opposite. I was supposed to help myself.

I sat down on the edge of his huge double bed, with the feeling that we were not going to get away from there very easily. We were being drawn into a situation that threatened to be distressing, and I was expected to wear a dead man's clothes in which to tackle it.

Hell! I thought. Bloody hell!

But I was wasting time. I was not really very wet, though the jacket seemed damp to my shoulders and the trousers were sticking to my knees. There was no alternative but to resort to Sir Rowland's clothes. If we were anywhere near the same size, that was the point.

I was reasonably lucky. The slacks that I found were a little short for me, the waistline somewhat loose. They would have to do. And for now – around the house – a V-necked cardigan would suffice. I stretched, feeling better, opened the window, and stood there as I lit my pipe and blew smoke into the cold, wet day. The rain had ceased, but the air was restless and chill. Then I prowled the room, knowing that Amelia would need more time, my natural curiosity leading me on. It was by no means a search, just a look around.

The room was large for a bedroom, by my standards, and there had been attempts made to absorb some of the space with heavy, dark cupboards and wardrobes, small tables, and the double bed, all of the woodwork delicately carved, the proportions perfect. The same master carpenter?

On every available surface there were framed photographs, all of them records of the growing family. In some was Mary, smiling, a trim and younger Mary, so strikingly like Jennie was now that it was breathtaking. But Mary was in there with the boys, always, hands resting on or snugly around shoulders. Mary, Mary. But not one photograph included the mother, Sir Rowland's wife, Tessa. One or two featured Sir Rowland as well, a well-built and placid man, though in all cases it was with the two boys. It was possible that he had not wished to go on record as being intimately connected with a child so clearly Mary's. By this time, it seemed more and more certain that he had to be the father. Had he not remembered her in his will – a young woman in a menial position in the household?

It was even, I realised, likely that Geoffrey Russell knew the truth about that.

But I'd wasted enough time. I went out into the corridor, strolled towards the head of the stairs, and glanced at my watch. Twelve twenty. Already we were late for the reading. But there was no hurry, though I was concerned a little about the dogs, shut away in the car.

Below me, I saw Russell walk out of one of the doors into the hall. He too looked at his watch, flipping it out of his waistcoat pocket. I walked rapidly down the centre of the staircase, and he looked up.

'It's not really safe,' he said quietly. 'Down the middle.'

'What isn't?'

'Coming down the centre of the stairs. It's all very fine using curved treads to match the curved banisters, but it *can* be confusing. The curved vision – the perspective.'

'I didn't realise that.' But I did realise he was leading, delicately, to something.

'Even dangerous for people used to it.' He nodded sagely. 'It was how Rowland died, running down the middle and turning his head from side to side.'

He stopped, his eyes on mine. It was my turn to take it on. 'And why was he doing that?' I asked politely.

'He was, apparently, trying to detect where the shouting was coming from. And who, I suppose. Or so the doctor decided. He'd had experience of those stairs. In any event, the Coroner didn't think an inquest was necessary.'

He was explaining more fully than he needed to have done, and to a virtual stranger.

'Shouting?' I asked. 'Do you mean quarrelling? Disputing?'

'If it matters.' He shrugged, his bony shoulders lifting high. 'Jeremy and Paul were always going on at each other. If it matters,' he reflected, more emphatically now. 'We're going to be late.'

'Does *that* matter?'

He became abruptly severe. 'Rowland broke his neck. That's what matters.' He seemed determined that I should have this information.

'I meant, does it matter if we start late?'

He looked surprised at this suggestion. Russell was a man fixed in his life patterns. 'Well, no. I suppose not.' Then he smiled weakly. 'Though I must admit I'll be glad to get it over and done with.'

As he turned away, I looked back at the staircase. The whole effect was startlingly beautiful, but, as the banisters were graded in their curves, from almost straight at the top to a much tighter curve at the bottom, this meant that the stair treads also curved in tighter arcs, and were wider towards the bottom. It was a most bewildering effect as you walked down.

I had concentrated ahead, and found no difficulty. But the significant fact was that Russell had used the explanation awkwardly, as an excuse to tell me this. His legal training, I had to suppose, precluded any direct statement of the facts. But he was clearly concerned.

'And why would they have been fighting?' I asked.

'What else but over a woman? Or so I was told. You'll know that it's the most usual reason for violence.'

'I believe the statistics would indicate that.' I could match his formality.

'Know from your own experience,' he said softly, almost sadly.

So that was it. He'd wanted to establish my background.

'You know I'm an ex-policeman?'

'I guessed. I was once involved – I rarely touch criminal work – but I was involved in a burglary case. A Sergeant Richard Patton was the police officer making the charge.'

I couldn't help grinning at him. 'Then why the devil didn't you just ask?'

He looked severe. 'I have a reputation to protect.'

'For what?' I raised my eyebrows at him. 'Deviousness?'

He didn't even blink. 'Discretion.'

'Your reputation remains solid,' I assured him.

'Thank you. Ah – here they are now.'

Amelia and Tessa were coming down the stairs, Amelia leading, each with a hand on a banister. I had found little difficulty with my sartorial change, but Amelia had clearly been difficult to fit. Slim Amelia, at five foot six, and rather plump and colourless Tessa, at five foot ten. There was a certain amount of tuck-ing-in here and there, a belt to the waist, and rather more leg showing beneath the skirt than was usual for Amelia, as they'd clearly rolled up the waistband, but rather too far, keeping on the right side of decision and future eventualities.

'The youngsters are in the library,' said Russell. 'Shall we join them?'

It was clear, as we approached the library door, that the young-sters, who turned out to include Mary, were certainly not quietly reading. The chatter was loud, and at the moment it was friend-ly. They were, it was clear as we entered, indulging in a nostalgia trip. D'you remember the time . . . That sort of thing. However, as is usual, the memories did not always produce the same images. The arguments were fierce, but amicable.

At our entry there was an abrupt silence. Almost shocked silence. At once they had to rearrange their minds. Friends a second ago, now potential disputants.

They were facing each other across a long table down the centre of the library. The smell was of musty and unruffled books, and of wasted learning. The shelves were packed with it. Mary was sitting beside her Jennie, oblivious of the fact that their relationship was now revealed so openly.

The two men were sitting side by side, facing them. I had to assume they were Jeremy and Paul, the sons, Jeremy the elder. His seniority was obvious, though there was no more than two years between them. He looked more mature than Paul, more fixed in his ways, more severely concerned with life's fortunes and misfortunes. From the moment that their mutual nost-algia trip was interrupted by our entrance, he almost visually thrust from himself any hint of frivolity, and sat back, stern, presenting a figure of strict rectitude. He was smartly dressed, and there was a distinct air of authority about him. He might have been at a board meeting; his bearing was that of a senior director. The Mercedes out there at the front could well have been his.

Paul affected no such dignity. His air of casual patience seemed to smooth his features, so that he looked much younger than his actual age. Designer jeans and a T-shirt sufficed for Paul, and a discarded denim jacket was over the chair-back behind him. The brothers shared the Searle nose, beaky, but in Jeremy's case I felt it would probe suspiciously, whereas in

21

Paul's it was a questing nose, quivering with the scent of adventure and excited exploration.

I inclined my head slightly to Amelia, who knows my every gesture and understands why I make it. She took the seat beside the two men, so that I could face them and be beside Mary, with Jennie the other side of her. It was then that I noticed that Mary, too, was in jeans and a T-shirt, and a neat little cutaway jacket. They looked like sisters, she and Jennie. Mary had shed twenty years in twenty minutes.

By this time Russell had settled at the head of the table with his back to the end window, and was going through his papers, the impression being that this could be his first sight of them. He was frowning, as though he didn't quite understand the legal phraseology that he'd drafted himself.

Tessa was now the only one not present. I had to assume she intended to make an entrance befitting the bereaved widow. I stared above the heads of the two brothers, at the books ranked facing me, and allowed my eyes to focus on them. If anything – if I'd given it any thought – I would have expected to see the usual collection to be found in neglected libraries, uncut leather-bound collections of sermons from the past and similarly uncut memories of the House of Lords by peers who'd never stood up and opened their mouths. But no. A former baronet of this house had possibly measured the available shelf space and ordered eighty-seven yards of books from an anonymous bookseller. What else could one put in a library?

At this point, Tessa entered the room quietly and with no comment to anyone, no glance to confirm that everybody concerned was present. She took a seat at the far end of the table, facing Geoffrey Russell and with her back to the door. She was looking severe and morose. I could detect that at one time she must have been quite personable, in a grand and overpowering manner, but at this time a puzzled sternness seemed to be what she intended to project, or could not hide, though it might have been habitual. Her features were permanently moulded into a mask of dissatisfaction, of a timeless and ingrained insecurity. She placed her linked hands on the table, and stared down at them. Her fingers were shaking. From this angle, I could detect that her cheekbones were high, their line ruined now by a certain flabbiness beneath, and that the sons' noses, aristocratic, were inherited from her, not perhaps from Sir Rowland.

'Now,' said Russell, 'as you all know, we are here to read the will of Sir Rowland Mansfield Searle. I'll just mention that it is no longer usual for wills to be read in this manner, but I thought it best to have you all together – and this was Rowland's wish, anyway – if only because there are one or two legal points that might need elucidating.'

'Can we get on with it, Geoffrey?' asked Tessa, her voice tone-less.

'But of course. This is the last will and testament —'

'We know it is,' she put in.

'Of Sir Rowland Mansfield Searle,' continued Russell, his tone unchanged, uninflected. 'As is usual, the smaller legacies are listed first, to clear the field, one might say. First: I bequeath to my elder son, Jeremy Clive, the oil paintings in my art collection, which he has always admired. To my younger —'

'Is that *all*?' demanded Jeremy, his voice flat and forceful. 'You said "smaller". It can't be *that* bloody small.'

'Language, Jeremy, please!' said his mother, without notice-able emotion.

'That', said Russell, peering over the glasses he'd just put on for that precise purpose, 'is the exact wording. I wouldn't ven-ture to use the word "small" myself, as you've always admired them, and I'm sure they are what's known as old masters.'

'No, they're not,' put in Paul, grinning sideways at his brother and nudging him. 'I always thought they were rubbish, and now I know. Rubens, my foot. Gainsborough? Tcha! Reynolds? Fid-dlesticks! They don't just stick a brush in your hand and tell you to paint, y' know.'

I gathered that Paul had to be an art student.

'So what does that leave *you*, then?' demanded Jeremy, a flush to his face now, the probing nose positively red, and with some-thing close to panic in his voice.

'I was just about to come to that,' put in Russell. '*If* you'll let me continue.'

Jeremy sat back in his chair, lower lip jutting, and waved a hand in dismissal. 'I can't wait.'

Russell peered at him again over the glasses, and looked round for silence. At last: 'May I go on? Thank you.' He consulted the will, lifted his head. 'To my younger son, Paul Stephen, I bequeath the remainder of the contents of my art collection.'

'Yip!' cried Paul.

23

'Is that *all*?' asked Jeremy, not quite concealing a hint of satisfaction.

'That is all,' said Russell.

But Paul was clearly delighted. 'The masks,' he said. 'I get the masks.'

'Those rotten old stone things?' Jeremy laughed. 'You're welcome.'

'Thank you,' said Paul. 'But y'see, they're Olmec. Did you know that, Jerry-lad? Olmec, and there're nineteen of 'em. Lovely.'

'Ugly as sin.' Jeremy dismissed them.

'And I get the watercolours,' Paul added.

'Oh no, you don't. They're paintings. That makes 'em mine. Mine.'

'No, it doesn't. It says: oil paintings. Isn't that so, Mr Russell?'

'It is specifically stated, in Jeremy's bequest, oil paintings,' agreed Russell. His eyes were bright. This was one of the points he'd expected to have to clarify.

'Well . . . the other four are watercolours,' said Paul, waving an arm expressively. 'A Cotman, two David Coxes, and a Turner. Watercolours. So they're not yours, Jerry. The Turner alone'd buy you a few Rolls Royces. How d'you like that, then? Eh?'

'I'll see a solicitor –'

'There's one right here,' Paul pointed out. 'Ask him.'

'I'm afraid he's quite correct,' Russell said gravely.

'Tcha!' Jeremy had lost faith in Russell.

His head was now down, and he was staring at his clenched fist on the table. It opened. It closed. Then he looked up.

'I want a copy of that will.'

'You shall have it,' Russell promised him quietly.

'Now! I want it now.'

'I can hardly —'

'There's a photocopier in the gallery. We can use that.' Jeremy held out his hand, but Russell clutched the will to himself possessively.

Paul laughed. 'No, you can't, Jerry. The remainder of the contents, it said. The copier's part of the contents, so it's mine now.'

'Damn you, Paul.'

Paul thumped him on the shoulder. 'Oh, come on, Jerry. Of course you can use it. But later. Let the man finish. You can have the masks, too, if you like.'

24

'You can stick 'em.'

Paul shrugged. 'Well . . . I offered.'

'Can we get on with this?' Tessa demanded, her voice still unemotional. All through the dispute, she had remained unmoved.

'If I may,' agreed Russell. 'Where were we? Oh yes, here we are. To my daughter, Janine Marie —'

'Adopted daughter,' put in Tessa. At last a little emotion had crept in. And clearly this was Jennie, who was really Janine Marie.

'In law,' said Russell, 'an adopted daughter is equally entitled, and is correctly addressed as daughter. To Jennie, then, to make the identification clear, is left the gamekeeper's lodge, and the enclosed land measuring three acres.'

Jennie put her hands to her face. She was making a small keening sound.

'And', pursued Russell, 'the sum of £10,000, for necessary modernisation.'

'Eek!' said Jennie. She lowered her hands. Her face was shining, tears on her cheeks. 'We'll be able to get married. He knew!'

'You're engaged?' asked Mary, delighted.

'Sort of, Nan. Kind of living together. He's renting a little bitty cottage, and I'm over there as much as here, now.'

'A situation', said Tessa in a flat voice, 'of which I can't say I approve.'

Mary seemed to ignore this. 'Then you must tell him your good news as soon as possible, love.'

'I'll just pop out —'

'What?' demanded Tessa.

'He's waiting outside in his car.'

'You left him outside? You foolish girl.'

It seemed to me that she'd have made much the same criticism if Jennie had brought him in.

'After what you said last time, he didn't want to come in.' So I'd guessed correctly. Jennie, though, was showing a little spirit. 'And we didn't think it would take this long.'

'Then go and fetch him in,' said Tessa with dignity. 'And no more argument from you, my girl. Surely a mother – even though you're legally a grown woman – has a chance to give approval to this engagement, or withhold it.' Tessa clearly still thought of Jennie as a young girl.

25

'Her mother', said Mary gently but firmly, 'hasn't yet had the chance. Fetch him in, Jennie love.'

I caught Amelia's eye as Jennie ran out of the room. She raised her eyebrows. This was a Mary we had never seen before. No more the retiring and quiet Mary, but one in whom confidence had bloomed. The ragged strands of her life were coming together, weaving into a strong fabric.

We waited. For a few moments there was silence, until Paul, lifting his head from what seemed to have been a deep and morose contemplation, cried out, 'But you can't do that!'

'Do what?' asked Russell cautiously, His worst expectations were proving to have been inadequate.

'That gamekeeper's lodge. You can't give it to Jennie.'

'I am not giving —'

'I live there.'

This wrangling is getting out of hand,' declared Tessa, slapping both hands on the table surface. 'What does all this matter? Who gets what! So paltry – piffling. You don't *live* there, Paul. You live here, and you use the gamekeeper's lodge for your ridiculous painting. It's quite simple. Jennie moves to there, and you take over her room here as a studio.' She looked round the table, her face shining with smug satisfaction. 'Such a fuss! Heaven knows we've got enough empty rooms, anyway.'

'But the light wouldn't be right,' Paul explained. This was a quiet, reasonable statement, by no means a complaint. No doubt experience had taught him that his mother never really understood anything, simply because she never made the attempt.

'Light!' she said. 'Really, you children baffle me.'

'Nowhere', complained Paul, 'in this damned place is there enough natural light. Piffling little windows. Hell!'

'Then', she said, 'you'll have to knock a bigger hole in a wall, and put your own window in. Won't you?'

'But I can't . . . oh, never mind.'

'You see,' said Tessa placidly, 'it only takes a little thought.'

He shrugged, then looked up as the door opened, and Jennie came in, drawing behind her, her hand clasped round his wrist, a rather bulky man of about her own age. Both hands clasped, I saw, as he had a thick wrist. There was quite a lot of him inside an old grey overcoat that came down over his calves, and a great woolly muffler round his neck, above which was a rather battered and flushed face. In his free hand he held two dog leads.

'Whose're these dogs?' he demanded.

It was Sheba and Jake. I got to my feet. We were just about level, eye to eye. He released the leads, and then Amelia and Mary had to help me, or they'd have had me on my back. Tessa was screaming. 'Take them away! Take them away!'

'This is Joe,' shouted Jennie through the turmoil.

And Joe stood just inside the door, leaning back in order to balance his bulk, his face beaming until he closed it down, and glared.

'You oughta be ashamed of yourself,' he told me. 'Leavin' 'em like that, in a car that's freezin' cold.'

By now they had settled, but were still slightly quivering with excitement, Amelia and Mary having one leash each. I walked up to Joe, face to face.

'Are you telling me you went and opened our car door, with two boxers inside?'

'Yeah. Sure. They were whimpering. You ain't fit to —'

'You damn fool, they could've taken chunks out of you.'

'Nah!' He shrugged. 'I didn't try to get in, only opened the door, and out they come. Y' don't know how to handle dogs, that's your trouble. I just talked to 'em. Kind of friendly like. Crouched down . . .' He demonstrated, crouching, looking now a little like a spreading, damp shrub, with one big blossom of red face sticking out of the top. He made a sound with his tongue. Sheba and Jake pushed forward to reach him. He grinned at me. 'Y' see?'

Then Jennie crouched too, or rather kneeled, and took one head under each arm and kissed their noses. I glanced at Amelia, who was close to laughing out loud, possibly at my expression, and at Mary, who wasn't even looking at the dogs, but at Joe. Jennie glanced back and up at her, and Mary inclined her head slowly, smiling softly. He'll do.

'Joe breeds Dobermanns,' Jennie explained.

'He's not going to do it here,' said Tessa, nodding her head vigorously, in total agreement with herself.

'At the lodge,' said Jennie soothingly. 'That'll be where.'

By this time, poor Geoffrey Russell was close to a state of despair. 'May I finish this?' he asked feebly, slapping his palm on the will.

Nobody took any notice.

'I would like to finish reading this will,' he stated, more firmly.

There was silence. No one seemed interested in taking his or her former seat, and we all stood around, or crouched, or knelt, as the case might be. Only Jennie paid him any direct attention.

'Say it again,' she pleaded. 'For Joe.'

'Very well. To my daughter, Janine Marie, I leave the game-keeper's lodge, and the enclosed land measuring three acres, and the sum of £10,000 for the necessary modernisation.'

'That you, is it, Jennie?' asked Joe. 'Janine Marie. Hey – that's classy.'

'And . . . ' Russell stressed it, to maintain continuity. 'To Mary Pinson, for her devoted services, the sum of £10,000.'

There was an abrupt silence. Mary had gone shockingly white. I moved to her side quickly. 'Richard!' she whispered – almost whimpered.

'Hey . . . ' Jeremy began something he didn't know how to finish.

'The remainder of my estate to my beloved wife, Theresa June. And that's it.' Russell scrambled to an untidy finish.

He sounded very relieved that it was all over and, in some hurry now, began putting away his papers.

'Hold on,' said Jeremy. 'Just hold on a minute. Let's have that will, and I'll photocopy it.'

Russell flushed. Then he shrugged. 'Very well. But bring me back the original.'

Amelia was at my elbow, we now had one dog lead each, and there didn't seem to be any need to stay any longer. She touched my arm. 'For her devoted services! I liked that, Richard.' So Amelia had realised, too.

Tessa, either with dignity or with wounded pride, rose stiffly from her chair and stood a moment, hesitating. She said, 'You must all stay to lunch,' in an empty voice, as though reading from a book on etiquette. Then she walked stiffly out of the room.

Jennie and Joe were whispering together at the far end of the library, Mary standing beside us, smiling in their direction, and no doubt wondering how best to spend £10,000 on them. Russell, his briefcase and papers gathered together under his arm, was waiting impatiently. And I was beginning to assess the difficulties that now assailed us, Amelia and me.

There had been that mention of lunch, and this offer must surely be accepted. The place was large enough to justify the employment of some kind of domestic help, so it wouldn't be any strain on Tessa herself. But it would be difficult to drag Mary away, if our stay became extended, and though the dogs required only one main meal in the evening they were nevertheless an embarrassment. Tessa had clearly registered a dislike of animals, and how would I dare to shut them away in the car again? Joe would surely give me a good talking to.

And, somewhere within those four walls, damp clothing was, I hoped, being dried for Amelia and myself.

No, we would have to stay, at least for a little while. We were only an hour away from home, after all.

To occupy Geoffrey Russell's mind, and relieve his impatience a little, I strolled over to him.

I nodded towards Jennie and Joe, smiling. 'They're already planning to move in.'

'Oh . . . but it'll take a little while. The probate and the conveyance . . . Some months, I would say.'

'Then they ought to be told that.'

'You'll be staying?' he asked.

'A short while.'

'Then you can inform them of the position – though I'll be in touch with all of them, in any event.'

'I'll do what I can. But tell me something.'

'Yes?' His eyes were on the whispering couple.

'How did you know he was swinging his head, one way then the other?'

'Pardon? Who? When?'

'Sir Rowland. If he died by breaking his neck – how was it known exactly *what* he was doing?'

'Oh . . . I see. It's all right. Tessa saw it happen, with her own eyes.'

'Then that explains it.'

'From the head of the stairs.'

'Then she would know.'

'Of course she would. You might ask her, if you get the opportunity.'

Not discretion, I decided. I'd been correct the first time. He was devious. He was also worried about it.

It was then that Jeremy and Paul burst in, one waving the will, the other a copy of it. This seemed to release Russell, who made certain he had the correct will, tucked it away in his briefcase, and after a vague comment about the weather, he left.

There was one of those silences, when the mainstream of conversation has gone away. It was broken by the door opening again. A tall, slim, and positively grim-looking woman stood there, seemingly counting us. She was wearing plain black, with white cuffs and a snow-white collar.

'Would you wish for lunch in the dining-room, or in here?' she asked. 'It'll be cold, I'm afraid . . .'

The voice had attracted Mary's attention. She turned. 'Why – it's Miss Torrance. Gladys!'

'Mary? Good heavens, it's Mary Pinson. How splendid! Come and eat with me, my dear. We'll have so much to tell each other.'

Clearly, Mary would have preferred to stay with Jennie and Joe, but there was something in Miss Torrance's voice, a yearning, a muted happiness, and Mary had never been one to offer disappointment.

'Of course. I'll love that.' She turned to the others. 'If that's all right – don't go away.'

And in the event, it was she who helped her friend to bring the lunch, on trays.

3

With Mary somewhere in the far reaches of the house, chattering to her friend Gladys Torrance, and Jennie and Joe whispering excitedly to each other in a far corner of the library, Amelia and I felt somewhat left out of it. Then, as I could hear raised voices from the next room, presumably the gallery, if that was what they called it, I thought it might be a good idea to stroll in there and keep an eye on things. So we went along to the next door, and opened it. I was, in any event, anxious to see what exactly was in dispute.

It was larger than the library, yet had only one small window, at the far end. All the lights were switched on – daylight tubes, which were humming. Their white light did little to alleviate the gloom of one whole wall of old masters, as Jeremy seemed to have believed them to be. But even to my inexpert eyes it was clear that no master's hand had been near a single one of them. They were all, apparently, ancestors, and they'd been a pretty gruesome lot to start with. One or two were robed in their official gowns or uniforms, a general here, an admiral there, a judge, I guessed, certainly someone who'd considered his place in the legal hierarchy to be a grim and miserable undertaking. The females were equally unlovely. A smile here and there would have helped. An attempt, at least, towards a flimsy delicacy in their gowns would have softened the clothing with silken femininity, but an unpractised hand had wielded the brush; many such hands throughout the ages. They were all hard, implacable females, seemingly encased in starched armour.

Amelia and I didn't need to exchange comments. The paintings were obviously worthless.

And behind us a heated argument proceeded. Voices were rising, and anger was exploding close to fury. Our presence was totally ignored.

31

On the end wall opposite the window, segregated, it seemed on purpose, from the ancestors, we found the four watercolours. No explanation of Paul's enthusiasm was needed. Oh . . . how they would have graced our living-room at The Beeches.

Two were labelled David Cox, the other two as John Sell Cotman, and J.M.W. Turner. I could not have made any guess at their value.

'You'll sell the bloody things for a fortune,' I heard Jeremy shouting behind us. 'What do *you* want with the money? A few blank canvases and your bloody paints, and you're as happy as a pig in muck.'

'Sell them?' demanded Paul.

Now they were at our shoulders, staring past us at the watercolour paintings in question.

'Not on your life,' said Paul. 'I'll stick 'em on the wall – wherever I finish up laying my head – and look at 'em. Just look.'

'Liar!'

'But I'll sell the masks. Oh yes, I'll sell those. They can stay here for now, but I'll get somebody from Sotheby's to come and have a look at 'em. By my reckoning, they'll buy me a little place somewhere, and I'll have my own proper studio. It's all I want. All I need.'

It might have been that Amelia and I were not there. We were ignored.

'But Christ, Paul, I need the money. Need it.'

'Bad luck. Sell the Merc.'

'Not *that* sort of money. Real money.'

There was a silence. No doubt they were staring at each other. Jeremy was pleading for help, considerable help, if a Mercedes didn't represent real money.

We turned to face them. It was as though we had suddenly become visible.

'Well – what do *you* think?' Jeremy demanded of me.

'Think? It's not for me to express an opinion. I'm an outside party. But I do know you're both in too much of a hurry. The will's got to be proved. Sometimes, that takes months. In the mean time, everything stays as it is. Nothing . . .' I waved an arm. 'Nothing can be sold until it's all settled. So you're both jumping the gun. It's possible to take the matter to court, I believe, if anybody wants to contest the will. But I'm only an ex-policeman. My line's criminal law. This is civil, so I can't advise.'

I thought that just about covered it. Jeremy's eyes were wild. I had the impression that he must have been in dire financial difficulties. Paul was only mildly angry, but my words had at least calmed him. He could see, now, that he would be able to continue working up at the gamekeeper's lodge for a little while, time enough for him to sort out his intentions. If the masks had any value at all, he could rely on those as a financial background to his future.

'What's your grammar like?' Jeremy suddenly demanded, looking from Amelia's face to mine, then back again. She had stiffened and was frowning. His demand had been ungracious.

'Passable, I suppose,' I said. 'Between us, we could string a sentence together.'

'Then come and have a look at this.' He turned away, and if I hadn't wanted to see the focus of his attention I would have told him to go to hell.

Down the centre of the gallery there was arranged a set of tables, five of them, some smaller than the others. It was on these that the masks were displayed, some tables bearing three, some four. Jeremy seemed to be indifferent to them. He might or might not have known their financial value, but he certainly did not afford them a glance of appreciation. He saw in them no artistic value. Collector's items, not enthusiast's. I could see his point. The stone from which they were fashioned was green, with flecks in it, not all the same green, and they were of differing sizes, some as large as an ordinary face, some half the size – a child's face. Kings, princes, princesses, children. And a long while ago. They were all masks of faces having thick lips, broad and flattened noses, and ears hard against their heads. Death masks, I supposed they would be.

Each one had its little walnut stand, in which it nested as though in a wooden egg-cup, with a brass plate giving details. Middle pre-classic, circa 1000 BC. That kind of information.

It was on one of these tables that Jeremy and Paul had spread the photocopy of the will.

'Look at this!' cried Jeremy, waving an arm and banging his knuckles on one of the heads.

Reaction forced me into clutching for it, but it was too heavy to have been displaced. My memory flicked back to my youth – the coconuts you shied at. But it gave me a feel of the mask, smooth and polished, almost with a slippery touch, as though the smoothing paste was still wet on it. I'd have guessed it to weigh about six pounds.

But Jeremy was pounding his forefinger at one specific sentence in the will – a part of that sentence. It was the one that read: 'the oil paintings in my art collection, which he has always admired.'

'So?' I asked.

'I've always admired *all* the paintings,' Jeremy claimed.

Paul pounced in. 'But it says oil. Oil! The *oil* paintings you've always admired. And he was right. Dad was dead right. Every time you've brought anybody to stay, haven't you stood here and shown 'em the old masters, as you called 'em?' Paul was going up and down on his toes in emphasis, almost jumping from the floor. 'So . . . right. They were the ones you admired.' And he was clearly enjoying himself.

'I admired the others, too!' Jeremy shouted. 'So it includes those. Now I ask you . . .' He turned to me. 'Doesn't it mean that, Mr . . . er . . . er?'

Amelia was staring past his head at me, her eyebrows rising up towards her hair, her lips compressed to restrain something, possibly a burst of laughter.

'But it does specify oil,' I pointed out. 'And the name's Patton. Richard.'

'Oil! Oil!' Jeremy flapped his arms. 'P'haps father dictated it. Yes. Dictated it, and he said "all", not "oil".'

'But dad signed it as it *is*,' Paul pointed out.

'I'm going to contest this.'

'All right. If you like. But that load of rubbish on the wall is all you're going to take out of here.'

'I'm taking nothing out of here,' said Jeremy, with a pitiful attempt at dignity. 'Not till Sotheby's have been here. Two jobs in one, then we'll see. Your masks, my old masters.'

'But I'm taking my watercolours,' Paul decided positively. 'I know what you're like, Jerry. You'd deliberately ruin 'em, simply because they're mine. Or will be. I know your temper. Know it. Smash the glass and throw a jug of water at 'em, that'd be right up your street. I'm taking them up to the lodge.' He turned to me. 'Would that be all right?'

I shrugged. 'I'm not a civil law expert. I told you that. You can't take them *away*, but I suppose, if the lodge is in the Penhavon grounds . . .'

'It is.'

'Then you won't have taken them away. But phone Mr Russell, I would. Be certain you're in the right.'

'I will. I will.'

And Jeremy exploded with fury. 'You're on his side,' he shouted, like a child.

'Nonsense.' I was short with him.

'Then he can take his bloody masks as well.'

'What?' said Paul. 'What'd be the point? They can stay here until they're sold. Which, if Mr Patton is correct, is going to be a few months, yet.'

Jeremy was flushed with anger, his hair untidy and his eyes wild. 'You get 'em out of here. D'you hear me? When the Sotheby man comes, I don't want any misunderstandings. Everything in this room, I'll tell him. Just that. No distractions. Everything. And none of your soddin' masks.'

Paul hesitated. He looked for help to Amelia, then to me. But we could offer nothing. Then he nodded. 'I'll take the watercolours when I'm ready, but I'm not humping that load of masks. And that's final.'

The masks would be safe from Jeremy, being stone. It would take a furious attack with a power saw to harm them. Yet, in Jeremy's present temper, I wouldn't have put even that past him.

It was, I thought, fortunate that we were interrupted. Joe put his head in. 'Lunch is on the table in there. Coming?'

Like a drowning man clutching at straws, Jeremy asked, 'You any good at grammar?'

Joe had shed his coat and muffler. He stood now in an untidy magnificence, wearing a roll-neck sweater, and jeans that had clearly encountered the worrying effect of puppies' playful teeth.

'Grammar?' he asked, and surprisingly added, 'Well, yeah. I took my degree in literature.'

'Then come and have a look at this.'

'The coffee's hot.'

'It'll only take a second.'

Reluctantly, looking warily from one face to the other, Joe advanced. Jeremy stabbed his finger at the offending phrase.

'Ah!' said Joe, after he'd read it a couple of times. 'The tricky bit about "which" and "that". It's all a matter of the defining clause. I see. The paintings you've always admired. If it'd been "that", it would've defined them. The ones that you admired. That's you, is it, Jeremy? Yes. The paintings you, Jerry, have always admired. But it isn't "that", it's "which", so the clause isn't defining. "Which", preceded by a comma. That makes it a simple observation. He's saying that he knows you always admired them – his oil paintings.' He glanced round at the wall. 'P'haps he meant it as a comment on your taste.'

He grinned at Amelia and me. 'Coming?' he asked.

We went with him. I was somewhat awed. What strange creature had Jennie found for herself? Did he teach his dogs correct grammar, or had he, as I suspected, taught himself dog language?

In the hall, he paused to say, 'It's a bit more complicated than I made it sound. Let the law argue about that and which.'

'The law is almost completely bound up in that and which,' I told him.

'That which is mine?'

'Precisely.'

He held open the door for Amelia.

I would have expected Joe to have taken a degree related to veterinary matters, he being so naturally inclined towards dogs. But perhaps he'd merely wanted to learn how to spell Dobermann Pinscher. Perhaps his BA(Lit) had been based on German, so that he could talk their language.

The library, at this time, was occupied only by Mary and Jennie, chatting away like magpies, catching up on the missing years.

'So here you are,' Mary said to us.

'Where have you been?' Jennie asked Joe.

'In the gallery, that answers both,' I said.

'They're fighting, aren't they?' asked Jennie.

'Arguing.'

'Oh . . . it'll be fighting soon. You'll see. It's always been like this.'

She didn't in any way sound concerned about it, being used to family quarrels. But the disputes she had witnessed couldn't possibly have been as serious as the situation we were now encountering. It had been desperation that I'd heard in Jeremy's voice.

On this issue, I tried a little probing, while we ate. There were sandwiches, cooked beef and ham and cheese and pickle, and warm mince pies and warm sausage rolls. I noticed, but made no comment, that Sheba and Jake, who knew we never fed them titbits, sat beside Joe, one at each knee, and he slipped them pieces of ham and beef, even a mince pie each. I would have thought it inadvisable, but I wouldn't have dared to argue with a breeder. He gave them each a saucer of the warm milk, which meant we had our coffee almost black. Again, I made no comment. Water, not milk, I'd always been told.

36

'I've got half an acre and a few kennels, the other side of the village,' Joe told us. 'Only six pups at the moment, and only four dams and two sires. D'you fancy a puppy?'

'Not really, thanks.'

'You've been listenin' to tales. It's how they're brought up, and I reckon you'd bring 'em up right.'

'Those two are a houseful, I can assure you.'

'They're beauties,' he said. 'Real beauties. Breedin' from 'em, are you?'

'Well, no,' said Amelia. 'Sheba's neutered.'

'That's cruel.'

'Before we even met her,' she told him. 'I inherited her.'

He waved a meatless sandwich. 'Inheritance! Y' never know what you'll get, do you? Take this thing now. Jennie never expected much. She's got her own little room here, but she's as good as living full time in the bitty old cottage I'm renting. Now . . . if I've got it right . . . there's three acres go with the lodge, and money to build proper kennels. I'll really be able to get going. Proper marriage and we'll start our own breedin'. *She* ain't neutered, I reckon.'

'Joe!' said Jennie, nudging him.

'Wassamarrer?'

'That's not nice.'

'Isn't it?' But there was just a flicker of his eyelid in our direction. A dry one, this Joe. 'Well, we can make it nice, any time you say. Get properly married, and stick it out at my cottage for a bit. Take a time, that will's goin' to do. What d'you say, Jen? We've got somebody proper to give you away, now.'

Mary flushed. 'Any time,' she whispered.

'I'll be glad to get away from here,' admitted Jennie quietly. 'Rows. Always violent rows. Jerry trying to persuade father to sell some land, and he refusing, backed up by Paul. Paul said it was part his. I suppose it is.' She paused, looking surprised. 'Part mine, too.'

'As it will be,' I told her.

Sheba and Jake had now come round to me for titbits, but I didn't want to get them into bad habits.

'Oh yes,' Jennie agreed. 'I was forgetting. The lodge and the land, and *all* that money.' As though she could have forgotten!

£10,000, she meant. To her, to Joe, it was a fortune. To Jeremy it would be pocket-money. And yet it was he who was panicking.

It had, though, been cruel of his father virtually to disinherit him. Legal action could put that right, I was sure. He would be entitled to something fair, though his mother, inheriting the balance of the estate, would no doubt rescue him from whatever was worrying him. No – terrifying him. More than money had to be involved, it seemed.

I was pouring coffee for Amelia and myself, my eyes on what I was doing. 'You mentioned violent rows, Jennie. When was this?'

'The really terrible one was back in the summer,' she said thoughtfully, searching her memory. 'Jerry and father. Summer, yes. July or August. A month or so before he had that dreadful fall . . . down the stairs.'

I replaced the pot, carefully, casually. 'I was really thinking about rows between Jeremy and Paul. At the end. On the day of the fall.'

'Oh no. He wasn't here, Paul wasn't.'

'And you, Jennie?'

'Me?'

'Where were you, on the day your father died?'

'Oh . . . me. Well, yes. I was over at Louella's place, the riding school.'

'And where was Paul, then?'

'What . . .' Her attention kept wandering to Joe. 'Oh, he'd gone away for a month, with his painting lot. Part time, he does, at some art school near Shrewsbury. They all went for a month in the south of France. Now wouldn't *that* be lovely? Joe! Wouldn't that be grand for our honeymoon? A month in the south of France?'

'What about the dogs? Couldn't leave 'em for a month. You could go on your own, though, love.'

'On my honeymoon, alone? Oh no. It wouldn't be the same.'

'That's so. Never thought of that.' Then he laughed, and leaned sideways to kiss her cheek. 'We'd put 'em in kennels. I've got a mate, Leominster way, he breeds Dobermanns. How'd that be? And I'd screw his neck if he breeds from my sires. How's that?'

'Apart', said Jennie, 'from the neck screwing, simply super.'

'That's settled, then,' said Joe placidly. 'When're you free for the wedding, Nan?'

She was his nan, too, I realised. 'Any time,' she repeated softly. Now she'd got somebody else to cherish.

I filled my pipe, then remembered where we were, and put it away again. 'A month, you said?' I asked Jennie. 'Not your honeymoon, love, but Paul's painting trip, I mean.'

'That's right.'

'So he wasn't here when your father died?'

'No. And oh, I did miss him!'

Yet Geoffrey Russell had said he'd been told that Paul and Jeremy had been fighting. It had distracted their father on his way down the curved stairway. But Paul hadn't been there. So how had the doctor come to accept this story? And why, if it had been accepted, had Jeremy said nothing at the time?

I realised then, my thoughts switching to the two brothers, that it had gone very quiet in the gallery, and they had not come in for lunch. Excusing myself, giving no explanation, I got up quickly and went from one door to the other, entering in a rush.

Jeremy was sitting on the floor with his back against the wall, Paul bending over him and slapping his face. 'Come on! Come on!' he was whispering.

I pushed him out of the way and bent over Jeremy, reaching for the pulse in his neck. It was weak but steady. I straightened.

'What happened?'

'The damn fool threw a punch at me. I hit him back and he went down, and banged his head.'

'You're both acting like stupid children.'

'And he'd got no reason. He owes me, and I owe him nothing. I even offered him the masks. But he said I'd gotta have the masks, because they're mine. Said he'd carry them up with his own hands.'

'Up?'

'Up to the lodge. He's a fool. Says he wants the watercolours. He can see the value there. Even he's heard of Turner and Cotman. Not Cox, perhaps. But he's a stubborn idiot. Always has been. Got himself in a right mess, he has.'

Jeremy groaned, and moved his head.

'Water?' I asked.

'I've got some. He's been out for ten minutes. More.'

I was silent for a few moments. Then I asked, 'What sort of trouble?'

'The deep and murky sort, that's what. He's an accountant. Posh offices in Shrewsbury. Investments, he's in. Stocks and shares. He's a sharebroker, or something deadly dull like that. Trusts. Only he's been playing around with other people's money. And along comes this recession – and he's caught. They all *need* their money – and he can't raise it. Or something like that. It's way above my head.'

'The young fool.'

Young, I thought. I wasn't all that much older than Jeremy, but his personality was years younger than his age. Or his morality was. But it's childish to take such risks, I've always thought. The 'last across' syndrome, where the danger is the lure. A children's game. Or at least, it used to be when I was a kid. This time, Jeremy had tripped, and the trailer wagon was almost on him.

'I offered him the masks,' Paul repeated numbly.

'They're not yet yours to offer,' I reminded him shortly. 'He's coming round now. When he can think a straight thought, try offering them again, but as a security for a loan, or something like that. If he can hold on. If he can't, then nobody can help him.'

Paul was shaking his head, trying to clear it, trying to think logically. 'It's how he's always been. Stubborn pride. Decided he doesn't want the masks, because they're mine, so he won't touch 'em. Damn fool, playing at being a martyr.'

I nodded. Yes, as a policeman I'd met them, had separated them when they'd been close to killing each other, and over paltry boundary arguments. Not give an inch, not take an inch, that was always the attitude. It had to be right. Nothing less would do. Right and proper and fair.

Quietly, I made a suggestion. 'Then offer him the watercolours. He claims they're his. He could possibly raise money on their value.'

'What?'

'Offer him the watercolours. He thinks he's got a right to them, anyway.'

'Not those. Not on your life. I want 'em to look at. And I told you, I don't owe him anything. It's him who owes me.'

'I think you possibly do, you know.'

'What?'

'Owe him. For the watercolours and the stone masks. Work it out, Paul. Work it out.'

I turned and went out.

But his voice followed me into the hall. 'What the hell does that mean?'

4

I could have bitten off my stupid tongue. It's one thing to juggle various thoughts around in your own mind, but quite different to bring them out into the open and flaunt them.

But I was becoming exasperated with all this wrangling, and Paul had managed to impress on me the fact that Jeremy was urgently in need of money. And the sudden end to Sir Rowland's life was very far from being satisfactorily explained. Fallen down the stairs, indeed!

Ridiculous, I thought. They weren't steep enough, and besides – the story of that death, as explained by Russell, was quite unacceptable. He had heard shouting – and his head had swung from side to side! As though *that* would have caused a fatal fall!

And that shouting had been attributed to Paul and Jeremy – when Paul had been in the south of France! At the very least, there had been some sort of cover-up, and it seemed that Jeremy had to have been involved in that aspect of it. Certainly, from what I'd heard, Jeremy wouldn't have been bereft at his father's death.

It seemed to me, thinking about it, that Jeremy had been involved in some sort of conspiracy of silence, and Paul did have his father's death to thank for his own inheritance.

'What did you mean?' Paul asked again, and I had to give him some sort of explanation. He'd followed me into the hall.

'Perhaps Mr Russell's got it all wrong,' I assured him. 'He had some idea that your father's fall was caused by the sound of quarrelling, fighting, or something like that. Shouting, in any event. The doctor seems to have accepted that, but the implication was that it was Jeremy and yourself doing the shouting.'

'I wasn't here.'

'I know you weren't. But Jeremy doesn't seem to have denied it – and he's obviously not told you about it. But what does it

41

matter now? Your father was distracted, and he fell. Leave it at that.'

He was staring at me, baffled. He shook his head. 'If it doesn't matter, why say . . . what you did say?'

I shrugged. 'Just a retired copper's twisted mind. Forget I said it.'

'How can I —'

'Your mother', I said gently, 'doesn't seem to have disputed the facts, and she, apparently, saw it happen.'

'You implied something, damn you. You as good as said that Jerry . . .' He didn't manage to finish it.

'It's a damned lie!' shouted Jeremy from the gallery doorway.

He was still white and unsteady, clinging to the door frame. 'There wasn't a bloody quarrel. Somebody shouting. I heard that. I don't know who . . . Oh Christ – my head!'

'See to him,' I said quickly. 'I was probably all wrong, in which case you owe him nothing. Except for the fact that he's your brother. Go to him.'

I turned away, cursing myself, but aware that there had to be deeper emotional issues involved than I could yet imagine. Sir Rowland's motivations for the framing of his will were certainly too complex to sort out with the information I had. But certainly, the photographs in his room indicated that he had been Jennie's father, and he had treated Mary generously in his will. An honourable man? It would explain his distaste for the basis of Jeremy's personal troubles, and his rejection of any sympathy in that direction.

It would, after all, be an honourable man who would have adopted his own illegitimate child, in order to free Mary from the burden Jennie would present.

But Mary wouldn't have thought of it in that way. She would not have parted with her child unless she'd been desperate. I was seeing Mary, now, with every passing minute, in a different light from the Mary whom Amelia and I had known more recently.

But I had no opportunity to explore these ideas, as the door to the library burst open, and the hall became full of movement and bustle.

'We're going to have a look at the lodge,' said Amelia. It was she now who had the dogs on their leads.

'Do you mind, Paul?' called out Jennie.

Paul had reached his brother, and had his hand on his arm. He turned. 'Help yourself.' He reached into his tight back pocket,

42

and tossed her a key, one of those large, old-fashioned deadlock keys. 'But don't touch the paintings.'

'As though I would.'

'We'll need something, in case it rains,' I said.

'The sun's shining, Richard,' Amelia told me. 'Haven't you noticed?'

I hadn't. As Paul had said, the windows were so small that very little of the outside weather made any impact.

Paul had taken his brother back inside the gallery and shut the door. I could hear their voices, though now they were not raised.

Outside, it was so. The sun shone. It wasn't a very encouraging sunlight, and clouds still lurked towards the west. I viewed it with suspicion, though it was a little comforting to recall that I was now wearing another man's clothes. Amelia, I could see, might have difficulty walking far. Already that skirt hem was creeping downwards, as the rolled waistband began to shed its load. Much lower, and she would be tripping over it. Mary, Jennie and Joe seemed unperturbed by either the terrain or the unpredictable weather.

Joe had left the Granada's door open. I went and shut it, retrieving the keys I'd left in the ignition lock. Then I caught them up. Sheba and Jake were now running free, madly excited.

'It must be quite a walk,' I said, catching up with the group, and remembering the length of the drive.

'There's a short-cut,' Jennie told us, striding free, a certain jauntiness in her steps. 'Nothing to it.'

'Then don't go too fast,' Mary told her, as Joe was clearly eager to inspect the lodge, and Jennie eager to display it.

First, we had to cross the stream, busy and noisy now. The wooden bridge we had driven over was strongly built, with a low railing each side. Then, at once, we turned away from the drive we had driven down, swinging right with the surface level here.

'There used to be a sunken garden up ahead,' Jennie called out. 'But father let it go. He said he couldn't afford a full-time gardener. It's gone a bit wild.'

We were walking a firm path, but with an uneven surface, pools of water lying in it. In single file, Jennie leading, we circled the puddles. A full-width stretch of water almost barred the way to the four stone steps we were approaching, five feet wide but encroached by a rough, unclipped hedge. We had to push through, backs to the hedge, to get past with reasonably dry feet.

At the bottom of the steps another pool, wider, awaited us. But now the hedges fell back. Having circled the water, we were again on a path, which was grass now, and at least somebody had run a mower along there.

Ahead of us, I could see that dense woodland closed in on the path from both sides.

I paused and looked back. The hedging we'd had to push past, and which had soaked my back, now almost hid the house. Only the roof and chimneys were visible. The path ahead turned to the left a little, then straight ahead again, and plunged into a tunnel of trees.

'It's only a little way,' Jennie called out.

It seemed to me that we had already covered a reasonable distance. I glanced at Amelia, who pouted. We could not have imagined when we left home that we would need waterproof trousers and anoraks and hiking boots.

'Are you going to manage, love?' I asked.

'Just about. I'll be able to tidy up at the lodge – perhaps.'

'Maybe we can borrow some jeans from Paul, if there're any up there.'

She looked at me with raised eyebrows. The others were well in front now, Mary matching them stride for stride.

But now, though the surface was becoming firmer, it was in that condition only because it had been protected by the trees, which loomed heavily and closely each side. They had lost most of their leaves, but if the sun was still shining, somewhere out there, it certainly wasn't forcing its way through the branches, or doing much to guide our feet.

'It's not far now,' called out Jennie.

Yet it was a steady climb, not too steep but winding, and, as far as I could guess, unending. The dogs were loving it, racing around, wet through and mud-spattered, barking furiously at the imagined wildlife that might be hiding behind each tree. Not far, Jennie had said. Already, I reckoned, we'd been plodding along for a good quarter of an hour, and I could detect no end to it.

There had been an implication in something Mary had said. What had it been? Something about the lodge being spooky, but not always. I was able to guess that Mary could have led us there, and knew that path as well as Jennie did; guess that it was at the lodge that Sir Rowland had contrived their clandestine

44

meetings. These would surely have had to be accomplished well away from the house, where they were master and maid. I could clearly visualise him marching out of the house in one direction, toting a shotgun – why else but for the game birds had there been a gamekeeper? – and Mary in another direction, ostensibly to collect flowers for the house from the now-barren sunken garden. She would have needed to walk only a few yards before becoming invisible from any window in the house. Then later she would return, flushed, bearing armfuls of flowers, and the grouse would live a little longer.

I was tired, that was why I couldn't control my imagination, tired and worried. Worried about the dogs. We would have to leave as soon as we returned to the house, as Tessa, clearly not an animal lover, would not be prepared to have them indoors, and Joe wouldn't let me shut them in the car, and if I had to show him a fist in order to persuade him on this point I would still have Amelia protesting about wet dogs clambering all over the seat upholstery.

The others had now disappeared from our sight. Amelia paused for a moment, panting. Then I heard Jennie up ahead. '*There* it is,' she cried, with blissful enthusiasm.

It had taken us, I reckoned, all of twenty minutes.

We walked out from beneath the trees on to a level surface, which had been paved, long ago, with blue bricks, now uneven and sunken in places. This, though it hadn't been apparent when we had driven past it, was the front of the lodge. There was a walkway round one side of the building. Walkways round both sides, I realised, at the same time becoming aware that these were two semi-detached cottages, now with only one in use. There were two front doors, side by side, with about a yard between them. The cottages were half-timbered, in that wood had been used liberally, the spaces in between being blocked in with housebricks. Yet this was not black, preserved wood, but scarred and partly rotted wood, the bricks now doing most of the work of holding up the roof, which was plain slating. One or two of the slates were slipping out of place, the roofs sagging a little in the middle.

The windows were small, and the impression was that it would be inadvisable to open them too abruptly or too far, or they might drop off, or crumble into dust and shards of glass. At the two opposing gable ends there were disproportionally high chimneys, one surmounted by a tall chimney pot, one without. This would have been necessary because of the back-draught caused by the proximity of the trees.

It was barely conceivable that, far in the past, families had lived in each house, children had played outside on the blue bricks, and no doubt huddled for warmth in the chill bedrooms at night, and that they had not considered they were in any way unhappy. Whereas the lord of the manor, down at the big house, had miserably contemplated his rolling acres and worried himself silly about upkeep, wondering whether he might dispense with the services of the gamekeeper and his head gardener, or – the last desperate measure – part with his foxhounds and resign as the local MFH.

The cottages now were sad, senile and sagging.

'So this is what you call the lodge,' said Joe, in a neutral voice.

He would, if he had visited Jennie often, if secretly, have driven past it, because this was the building we had seen, set back from the drive, when we had arrived.

'Isn't it lovely!' cried Jennie.

Joe put his arm round her. 'We'll soon put it to rights, precious.'

It seemed to me that Jennie would need all her £10,000 simply to make it liveable. Mary was standing, staring at it, and, unless my guess had been completely wrong, lost in a memory of those past, ecstatic years. To her, it probably glowed, bathed in warm memories.

Paul had said he didn't live here, only used it for his painting. I didn't suppose anybody had lived in it – them – for thirty or so years. Two families, at that time.

Jennie and Joe would have at least twice as much living space all to themselves, and room for a dozen or so Dobermanns around the fire.

I realised that he had wandered away from the group. I'd already decided that Joe was something of an individualist, pursuing his own personal plans. He had no doubt gone to check what I had guessed, that the driveway formed the rear of the property. Three acres, the will had quoted. Quite a decent bit of land.

Jennie had produced Paul's key. This was to the door to the left, as we faced the cottages. The keyhole had worn to a funnelled gap.

'The other door's nailed shut,' she told us. 'No way in there.'

Not for humans, perhaps, but I knew that the neat, smooth-edged holes in its bottom edge were evidence of the presence of rats. They would scatter into the woods when the Dobermanns took over, resenting their eviction.

'There's a spare key hidden under the flowerpot,' Jennie informed us, bending down to pick it up and displaying a rusty key.

This was the first place a burglar would look. No . . . he would first look at the property, and hurry away.

The door opened directly into the living-room. Immediately facing us was the lower end of an open stairway, which led up, through a hole in the ceiling, to dense shadows. On the far left was a black and rust coal range, with ovens each side of the fire. Otherwise the room was empty.

The smell of damp rot was very evident. Nobody commented. Joe, who was now with us again, was very silent.

'Kitchen through here,' Jennie told us, heading for a flimsy door facing us. This led into a narrow and cramped space dominated by an ancient wooden draining board, sullenly hanging its lip over a pottery sink. There was a single tap dripping into it, a rust stain where the drops fell. The rear door was beside it.

'This is the back,' said Jennie, reaching for the door in order to show us, and stretching up for the top bolt.

I leaned over the sink and peered through the smeared window. The immediate view was of a derelict patch of earth, stretching a matter of fifty yards to the low hedge beside the drive. Really, there was no point in Jennie opening the door, but she was a determined woman.

'The security's very good,' she told us, peeping back over her shoulder as she struggled with the rusted bolt. I assumed that a touch of humour was intended, as it seemed to me that the bolts, top and bottom, were the only supports to the door. If it could be called a door. It consisted of vertical planks held together by a Z of other planks on the inside surface. Chinks of light peeped through the slits. There was an ancient lock screwed to the inner surface, but no sign of anything into which the tongue might have slipped, even if it hadn't been rusted solid. Simple, tired hinges barely hung to the opposite jamb.

Joe could have walked through it without removing his hands from his pockets. Jennie submitted to defeat by the bolts, lowering her arms.

'In any event,' she assured us, 'there's only the two places along the back I wanted to show you.'

'Places?' murmured Joe.

'One with the water tank in,' said Jennie. 'There's an electric thing that switches the pump on. Real, genuine well water. But it's not been used for years. We're on the mains, now.'

She demonstrated by reaching over and turning on the tap. It accomplished no change. The tap continued to drip.

'And the other?' asked Joe, fascinated. 'The other place out there?'

'Oh . . . that's the loo.'

'Ah!' He nodded thoughtfully.

So . . . no bathroom anywhere. Such a luxury would have been asking for too much. Sheer pampering. I shuddered at the thought of a wash-down at that sink, so close to the slatted door, in January.

'Let's go and look upstairs,' suggested Jennie, bravely maintaining an enthusiastic tone.

'The dogs!' cried Amelia, who'd been very silent. The word 'upstairs' had reminded her. Dogs love to climb stairs, especially our dogs.

'Oh Lor!' I said, turning and dashing for the staircase.

It was narrow, intended for people slimmer than me. The opening at the top seemed no larger than a normal trapdoor to an attic. At the head of it was a corridor, sideways, right across the width of the cottage. There were no windows. You had to manage with what light filtered up from downstairs. But there was a slice of light to my left, a dog-sized slice of a door that had been nosed open.

'The paintings!' Jennie screamed from behind me.

I was not worried that the dogs could have done much harm, though they might have nudged over an easel. I'd heard no clatter. But dogs are nosy, and boxers have the nose for it, big and flat and wet. Paul, no doubt, worked in watercolour, judging by his enthusiasm for the Turner, the Cotman, and the two Cox's. Watercolour wouldn't react kindly to a wet nose exploring it. But past important discoveries have come about from random accidents. I was perhaps about to be introduced to a new watercolour effect: the boxer's nose application.

There was no easel in the room; nothing to knock over. But paintings were leaning all round the skirtings. At these, Sheba and Jake were snuffling.

'Heel!' I said sharply.

Promptly they came to sit one each side of my legs, looking up at me with pride at their discovery.

'Oh heavens!' said Amelia from behind me.

I was surreptitiously looking for traces of colour on the dogs' noses. There weren't any. I took a deep, relieved breath.

Then Jennie was there. She stood still, and looked round quickly. The paintings against the wall were all worked on thick card, supporting themselves without bowing. I wasn't looking at them as paintings, but for evidence of smears. Jennie detected my concern.

'It's all right,' she told me. 'No fuss. Those're acrylic. It's like oils, only you thin it with water. They dry pretty quickly, and you can paint over. Here're the watercolours, on the bench.'

I hadn't paid much attention to the bench. It ran right along the rear wall, a rough construction supported by four-inch square wooden legs, and slightly sloping.

Paul had probably constructed his own alterations; it looked, on closer inspection, to be a very amateurish job. He had also brought a Calor gas heater in here. It was tucked away beneath the bench. In the facing roof, there being no ceiling, Paul had inserted a wide window, almost absorbing the full width. This, therefore, had to be a north-facing prospect. The window seemed to be a more professional job than the bench, I noted.

'These're the watercolours,' said Jennie.

They were on a heavyweight paper, and stacked at one end of the bench. Jennie reached for a dozen or so, and spread them out on the bench surface. We all gathered together and stared at them. The paper was about sixteen inches by twelve.

'Isn't he good?' asked Jennie with pride.

I didn't know. Nobody spoke. Four of them were sketches, colour run rapidly on to the surface, all much alike, as though he was trying for some special effect. The fifth was the same, but more finished. It was completely finished, as he'd painted right to the edges.

I don't know much about art. I like pictures on the walls that I can look at with pleasure. These were ... well ... I stared at No.5. It was like Impressionism, but I got no impression from it, though unlike the modern art that I do not understand, and which seems to consist of random whirls of casual colour. Behind this painting of Paul's, or beyond it, as I stared at it, I saw a picture emerging. A woman – I thought there was a skirt – was riding side-saddle on a grey pony down a leafy glade, with the sun behind her. I could have lived with it. I could have returned to it time after time, to confirm it hadn't changed.

'What do you see?' I asked Amelia.

'Isn't it beautiful! I always fancied a holiday in Venice.'

'Eh?'

'It's a man poling a gondola under a bridge.'

'Ah.'

'He paints at the bench,' Jennie explained, 'with his paper sloping. Or the colour doesn't run correctly. He told me that. Showed me. That's why the bench slopes.'

Mary was saying nothing. Quietly, she was looking through the pile of watercolour paper.

From behind us, Joe remarked, 'Cosy in here. We could have the bed there, Jen.' Pointing towards the bench. 'Then we could look up, and be sleeping under the stars.'

It was a remarkably romantic observation from such a bulky and physical man. Jennie flicked him a smile.

'Poor Paul,' she said. 'I know he loves it here.'

'Yeah,' said Joe. 'Any more, are there?'

'Any more what?'

'Bedrooms, Jen.'

'Two more, one tiny, one bigger.'

'Well then.' Joe shrugged. 'Run the two cottages into one, then you'll have your own proper kitchen, an' six bedrooms. It'll be a while before we can fill six bedrooms, or five if one's a bathroom.'

'Now, Joe . . .'

He went on, regardless. 'So Paul can go on usin' this place. Pity to hoof him out. Yeah . . . go on workin' here, he can, and see how he gets on with the nippers running round his legs.' Then he made a loud sound, like a Dobermann barking. I assumed it had to be a laugh.

'You're a dear fool, Joe,' said Jennie. 'Isn't he a fool, Nan?'

'Oh, certainly.' Mary compressed her lips into a thin, concentrated smile. It was the only way to contain her happiness for them.

Then we all went downstairs. There would have to be something done about those stairs, I thought. But Joe would know. He was already planning it all in his head. We went outside, and waited while Jennie locked the front door. Then we watched as

Joe strolled round to find the boundaries to the property. These were only vaguely indicated by random stumps and ancient trails of barbed wire. Joe was already working it out. A long shed over there, a row of kennels here, lifted above the ground for dryness. Plenty of room for exercise. The full extent of three acres would include some of the woodland.

'I'm sure mother wouldn't mind if you exercised them in the Park,' called out Jennie. Then she frowned. Mary – at the moment called Nan – was now really mother. I would expect her to live out her life as Nan, but Tessa Searle would have to acquire another name. It was worrying Jennie.

The women remained behind, while I strolled around with Joe. He glanced at me, but said nothing. I was casually filling my pipe.

'I suppose you realise that you can't start any work here until it's all settled,' I said quietly, keeping this to the two of us.

'Sure,' he said. 'Don't worry. I'm just planning.'

'There'll be the proving of the will, and the conveyance of the property. It'll take a while.'

'I know.'

'And the cottages will gobble up Jennie's inheritance. Nothing to spare. You thought of that, have you?'

'I've thought of it. What's it to you, anyway?' He turned to stare at me. There was no expression on his face. It was round and placid, but his eyes were steady and blandly cool.

'We're good friends of Mary,' I told him. 'It would only be natural for Jennie to ask her mother for financial help, if help is needed.'

'No!' He bit it off.

'It would be natural, as your wife.'

'I wouldn't let it happen.'

I smiled at him. 'I think she's got a mind of her own, Joe.'

'We'll manage on our own.'

'Easy to say. But . . .' I pointed the pipe stem at him. 'But if I hear Mary's being pressured – you know what I mean – I'll personally come all the way here and push your teeth down your throat. Understand? No worry for Mary.'

He was still staring at me blankly. Then he gave his peculiar bark of a laugh.

'Big feller! Why'd I want to argue with you? I'll just tell you this, matey. Mary does what pleases her best. She might want her own improvements, if she's living with us. Then what?'

'No!' I burst out. 'Mary lives with us.'

'And if she changes her mind? I'll tell you this, friend. If I hear she's had any pressure from *you*, I'll come to your place and push your teeth right down your throat. Okay?'

I stared at him. He stared at me.

'Mary pleases herself,' I said.

'Mary decides.'

He grinned. I believe I grinned back.

'I'm goin' to breed the best damned Dobermanns in the country,' he told me.

'I hope you will.'

'And we'll have the neatest, bestest cottage in the county, if I have to rebuild the whole blasted place myself, from the ground up, with my own hands.'

I lit my pipe. 'I'll leave you my phone number,' I said. 'Ring me if you want any help. Okay?'

'Fine. I'll remember.' He looked at the wire trailing in the grass. 'Barbed wire! Disgustin'. Thanks, I'll remember,' he repeated, just so that I wouldn't forget.

5

The journey back to the house was naturally much easier than the climb from it had been, downhill now and rather more dry underfoot. I wasn't too uncomfortable myself, but clearly Amelia was wet and miserable, and the hem of her skirt was soaked and muddy.

We led the way, eager to get out of these clothes, and the others lagged behind, delayed by a warm argument about what was to be done with the cottages, and how. There was no mention of when. I was sure that neither Mary nor Jennie was truly aware of the legal fences yet to be climbed.

Gladys Torrance was waiting in the hall with the door wide open.

'Oh dear, you *are* wet. Do come in out of . . . oh, it's stopped raining. You'll find your own clothes all dry, up in your room. Then if you'll let me have those . . .' She stared at us, tutting to herself and shaking her head.

She stood aside. I tried to apologise. 'We went to see the cottages . . .'

'The lodge? Oh, I could have saved you the trouble. I was born in one of the cottages. Oh . . . so long ago, now. It was dreadful then, and if you ask me I'd burn them both down, and start again from the bare ground. Much the best thing. Oh yes.'

Then she stood, her head shaking and her lower lip protruding, and with her mind lost in the past.

'We'll just go and change, then,' I said.

'Oh yes . . . yes. And Mr . . . er . . .'

'Patton. Amelia and Richard.'

'Yes. Mr Patton, the mistress asked if you wouldn't mind having a word with her. When you're free, and dry.' She flicked us a little smile.

I felt Amelia's fingers on my arm. 'But Richard . . .'

Then I realised what she meant. Sheba and Jake, their leads in her other hand, were sitting quietly between us.

'The dogs,' I suggested, somewhat embarrassed. 'I can't . . . we don't know what to do with them.'

She smiled, and made a dismissive gesture. 'Give them to me. I'll take them to the kitchen and dry them off. They'll be thirsty, I reckon. And I'll see if I can find them some scraps. What're they called?'

'Sheba and Jake,' I told her, somewhat feebly. Amelia held out their leads.

'Come along with me, my lovelies,' Miss Torrance said, bending over them and making noises with her lips. They looked up at her with adoration.

I was a little disconcerted that strangers could handle them so easily. First Joe, and now Miss Torrance. She glanced back over her shoulder. 'We used to have foxhounds in the pen round the back. I know about dogs.'

We watched her walk them away. They didn't even glance back at us. I had the idea that she and Joe would be able to talk to each other in dog language.

'Oh . . . Miss Torrance . . .' I called after her.

She looked back.

'I don't know where to find Mrs Searle.'

'It's Lady Searle, really, but I don't suppose she cares. She's in her room, that's the one right opposite to the one you've been using. You might as well go on using it, if you like.'

'Thank you,' I said.

'I could have told you that,' said Amelia, as we walked up the stairs, up the side of the stairs with a hand to the banister, the curved treads being just as confusing going up. We didn't speak until we were in what, I now had to assume, was our room, the late Sir Rowland's room. The visit seemed to be assuming a somewhat embarrassing permanency.

There, our clothes were laid out on the bed, dry now, my slacks sharply creased, and Amelia's little jacket and her trousers pressed.

'Lady Searle,' she said. 'Does that make her late husband a knight or a baronet, Richard?'

'I'm not very well up on titles,' I had to admit, as I climbed into my slacks, feeling more comfortable every second. 'Either, I think. My professional life rotated around a different social level.'

'Does that make Jeremy a sir, then?'

I gave that a little thought. 'I think, only if it's a baronetcy, and we don't know about that. Anyway, I think it's safer to stick to Christian names for now. D'you want to come with me, love?'

She eyed me with consideration. 'There's something in your voice, Richard.' She tilted her head. 'An eagerness, shall we say? No. You go alone. It was you she asked for. Now go along. Don't keep the lady waiting.'

'Lady Theresa Searle,' I said, trying it on my tongue.

Then I crossed the corridor and tapped on the door opposite. 'Come in.'

I did so, turning to close the door before I cast my eyes around. It was a bedroom I had expected to see, but this was both bedroom and sitting-room. Perhaps she would call it her boudoir. I remembered something a friend had told me, a woman more educated than me, that boudoir was French for 'sulking place'. Tessa didn't seem to be sulking, didn't seem to be in any specific mood. Indeed, that was what I recalled of her in the library, neutral and indefinite. She had not, now I came to consider it, made any comment, for or against, regarding the contents of her husband's will.

This, boudoir or not, resembled a sitting-room, decorated in white and pink, and having a feminine décor as befitted a genteel lady, nothing asserted, everything placidly simple and tidy. The chair she was sitting in, though, was a practical, plumply upholstered easy chair, with wide arms and flared wings. She nested in it with her hair free of any restraint, and therefore wildly framing her face with rampant curls. I had the impression that if the curling process were discontinued it would eventually reach its natural state of a straight fall to her waist.

Again, as in the library, I had no hint of her mood from her expression. She gestured towards a similar, though less flamboyant chair, and nothing flickered on her face. It was a tired face, weary of the effort to remain young, discouraged from assuming any hint of vivacity, controlled from revealing the slightest sign that her whole life had been a disappointment. I couldn't be certain what had led me to that conclusion, but certainly I felt she had not achieved any satisfaction from marriage and motherhood. And yet her eyes were bright, a deep blue, and in them there was still a stubborn hope.

I wondered what might provoke a laugh, whether it would crack the mask. I waited for her to speak. She put an elbow on

55

the chair arm and rested her chin in her palm, so that the tenor of her voice was restricted to the bare essentials of intonation.

'I was wondering when you and your wife were intending to leave, Mr Patton.'

It would, I thought, have been considerably more simple to convey our marching orders through Miss Torrance.

I smiled, wondering why she'd gestured to a chair if she was in so much of a hurry to get rid of us. I hadn't taken the seat. 'We can get from underfoot at any time, Mrs Searle.'

'It's Lady Searle, but I would prefer the simpler Theresa – or Tessa. Please make it Tessa. And I was going to ask you to stay, you and your wife. Not to leave. You misunderstood me.' There was a small reproach there.

But she had given me, even now, no hint of her feelings on the matter. She wished us to stay, but there was no welcome in her voice.

I took the seat at last. 'We came', I said, 'simply to bring Mary for the reading of the will. That's over, and we've outstayed our welcome, I thought. But if you . . . well, I'm not sure what you're asking.'

'Have you any urgent need to hurry away?'

'None at all. The whole family's here. We include Mary in the family. And the two dogs . . .'

She flicked a little finger free from beneath her chin. In the background of her impassivity, it was a dismissive gesture. 'No difficulty there, I'm sure,' she assured me.

I shrugged. 'Then I suppose . . . we can stay as long as you . . . overnight, whatever.'

'Until it's finished,' she said. One eyebrow was raised discreetly.

'Until what is finished?'

I wasn't certain how I should handle this. I was having to extract every word from her, as though I had her in an interrogation room, and yet it was she who was doing all the leading. She needed, perhaps, just the odd comment here and there, to keep things flowing and to indicate that I knew what we were talking about. At this time, I didn't, so it was difficult.

It was clearly something she had no wish to say, and she was inviting me press her into saying it. Uneasily, I felt it to be very like a seduction. A verbal seduction.

Now she was leaning slightly forward, her chin still supported, her eyes focused on mine as though she was aiming a weapon at me. No . . . her gaze was focused, more specifically, on my right eye. My hand stole towards my pocket. I had a yearning to have something with which to occupy my fingers and an excuse to glance away from her from time to time.

'Smoke if you wish,' she said, realising the meaning of my movement. 'Rowland wouldn't smoke in here, but I've always wanted him to. Can you understand that, Mr Patton?'

'Richard,' I murmured, reaching out my pipe. I didn't need to fill it. I thumped my pockets to locate the lighter, realising that she was forcing me into doing this, into the lighting of my pipe and the smoking of it, where her husband had presumably felt himself to be too much of a gentleman to smoke in his lady's boudoir.

'And no, I'm afraid I can't understand,' I had to admit.

She sat back suddenly, as though defeated. 'And Geoffrey told me you're a policeman! Where's all that ability towards deduction? You disappoint me, Richard. Really you do.'

'You've set me too deep a problem,' I told her. 'And I'm not a policeman, now. Retired. And by Geoffrey, I assume you mean Mr Russell? Your solicitor. But in what way is it relevant that I was in the police?'

'It's just . . .' She lifted her free hand and stared at her nails. 'I hoped you would understand, without tiresome explanation, why I wished Rowland would smoke his pipe in here.'

I lit my pipe, leaned back and blew smoke at the ceiling, and tried one possibility. 'Because you like the smell?'

She shook her head, the tightly curled hair dancing. 'Because now you're relaxed. Not defensive, not offensive. Relaxed.'

Then I understood. She was telling me about her husband. 'He didn't relax?' I was very casual.

'With me . . . never.' She laid both hands on the chair arms. Her fingers curled, as though she needed to grip something, and hold it. 'Rowland was always, in here, cool, polite, distant, attentive – and I was nothing to him.' Her voice was flat, toneless. 'His wife. You must understand, it was necessary for him to have a wife, in his position. It was expected of him, because of the succession. I was chosen, like shuffling a pack and selecting a card. I could ride, I could shoot – but never have – I could dance, but at balls and never at dances. But I was chosen, and that was that. I had no choice. Put it this way – I was brood mare to produce his progeny. Two boys, one to inherit the baronetcy,

57

and a reserve boy in case of accidents. I was very lucky in that respect. Don't you think I was lucky, Richard?'

I was finding it to be annoying to be embarrassed in this way. She now knew I had been a policeman, but no longer had an official standing, and she was using the situation as a means of unloading past grievances. I was a nonentity – in the middle. Heaven knows I'd been faced by many matrimonial embarrassments, and was hardened against them, but she could know nothing about the degree of hardness. She watched my eyes bleakly for a sign of withdrawal.

'In what way', I ventured, 'have you been lucky?' I hoped that she couldn't detect how much I resented her attitude.

'It would have been so thoughtless – and wasteful – if I'd produced girls. Now – don't you find that amusing?' But her eyes were hard, the blue now an icy chill. It was clear that she'd never had anything to laugh at. 'Once he had the two boys, you'd have thought he'd have been satisfied. But no. He wanted a girl. Yearned for a girl. And his brood mare couldn't foal for him this time. Now don't you find that ironical? And so . . . Mary Pinson.'

She was quite calm about this, her emotions not, apparently, touched. It had probably taken a long while, and a considerable amount of practice, before she had been able to come to terms with her marriage. It had drained a great deal from her.

'Why are you telling me this, Tessa?' I asked, as gently as I could.

'I want you to understand.'

'I can't see that it matters whether or not I understand.'

'Yes. It does matter.' And now, at last, her voice faltered. She lowered her eyes.

'I know about Mary Pinson,' I told her quietly. 'So does my wife. I can't see that it's affected the situation – not very much, anyway.' It could well have been, I thought, that she resented the inheritance of £10,000.

She didn't react as I'd expected. Her eyes seemed now to be staring beyond me. Then, without any change in her tone, she went on, 'I'm going to marry Geoffrey Russell. As soon as the will's gone through, and he's no longer involved with me in a purely legal manner, I intend to marry him.'

'Does he know?'

Even that didn't provoke her, though it had been facetious, which was what I'd intended.

'I think he guesses. By that I mean that he guesses he doesn't have to wait very long for me to be out of mourning. Then he will ask me, and I shall say yes. Yes, yes, yes! I'll shout it from the rooftops. And I can be free of this . . . this prison, which is what it's been all these years.'

'I'm pleased to hear your intentions,' I assured her. It was quite true; I've always hated to see people unhappy. 'But I still don't quite understand why you're telling me this. Your friend Geoffrey's told you I was a policeman. That involved criminal law. I can't . . . If it's advice you're asking me for, I can't see in what way I can help. There's no criminal matter anywhere around here – nothing for me to pick up and look at.'

There was only the peculiar contradiction that Paul had been in France at the time when he was supposed to have been making distracting quarrelling sounds in his father's presence. And *that* could not be described as criminal – though the cover-up of Paul's absence might well be described as suspicious.

Then, because she had in no way responded, not even so far as the flicker of an eyelid, I added, 'Not even what seems to have been a conspiracy to hide the truth about your husband's death.' It was a random venture, just to see what would or would not shock her into reaction.

She leaned forward again, but it was the other palm beneath her chin now, and my left eye on which she focused. 'And what, exactly, do you mean by that, Richard?'

'The truth of how your husband died, and you knew very well, Tessa, what I meant. The story you must have concocted with your no doubt personal physician, something persuasive to present to the Coroner in order to explain the fall.'

'There was no inquest.'

'I know that. It was because the doctor was sufficiently persuasive to convince the Coroner that he didn't need to hold an inquest.'

'The doctor raised no difficulties,' she said with a hint of a smile, no doubt at my naïvety. 'He was quite satisfied, I can assure you.'

I shook my head solemnly. 'Not quite satisfied, I think, otherwise the story wouldn't have needed to be backed up by a poor story of Jeremy and Paul shouting in the background and creating a distraction.'

She clapped her hands together. Once. 'How splendid. At last you're being a detective. How very clever of you.'

I was determined not to be distracted. 'It's a bit thin, isn't it, that your husband – I'll call him Rowland, it's easier – that Rowland, who'd used that staircase all his life, should trip himself up because he was looking in all directions for the source of the shouting? Just a little thin. You have a good doctor, Tessa. Not on the Health scheme, I would guess.'

Just the smallest hint of a frown came and went in a second between her eyes. 'Health scheme?'

I was suddenly aware of the extent to which she had become isolated from reality, almost confined between these grey walls.

'A free availability of medical treatment to anybody,' I explained. 'But you, I assume, wouldn't avail yourself of that. Your doctor's simple check that Rowland was dead, and the certificate to cover it, must have attracted a very robust fee.'

'How would I know that?'

'If you paid it,' I said patiently.

'But I didn't. Jeremy would have attended to that.'

I couldn't reply at once. My mind was racing, computing the possibilities. Jeremy had been home. Had he been shouting at himself? Eventually, I managed to say, 'Then that seems to clear the matter. I can't understand why you felt it necessary to consult me.' Consult! My mind was still with the doctor; I still saw him there, kneeling at the foot of those stairs. And listening.

She said, 'Because it isn't finished, what happened that day – that evening. It was eight o'clock. Two minutes past eight, if you want to be precise. That time is fixed in my memory. It was eight o'clock when Rowland walked out of this room. So . . . two minutes past. It's the truth I wish to tell you, Richard. And something legal I want to ask you.'

She sat back again, and now there was a small amount of emotion expressed on her face. Perhaps that was the reason she had sat back, so that I wouldn't observe it. Suddenly, I felt an intolerable pity for this woman, an almost stifling sympathy. I saw her, for the first time, as the no doubt beautiful young woman who had come to this house – as a brood mare, as she'd expressed it herself – and had had to learn, quickly and irrevocably, that she had no feelings to express here, that feelings were of no importance, that she had no one to whom she might offer them. She was offering them to me now. How could I hesitate in extending an understanding?

60

Oh, how I wished that Amelia was with me!

I smiled. 'Please ask. I'm sure it can't be serious.'

'Isn't murder serious?' she asked, with a wry little twist to her lips.

'That surely wasn't the question you intended. I'm sorry. I distracted you. Ask your intended question, and I'll try to answer honestly.'

She said nothing for a long while. Then she gave a small sigh. 'It must be more than thirty years since I've dared to trust anyone. You'll have to forgive me if I . . . if I hesitate.'

'There's no hurry.'

She lifted her chin. 'Then tell me, Richard . . . that doctor's decision, that it was an accident. Can it be altered – overridden – by any other authority?'

It would have been a tragedy if I'd shown surprise, even glanced away from the appeal in her eyes. I had her trust; I would have rejected it with one wrong gesture, one unconsidered word.

'If any evidence conflicting with an accident got into the hands of the police,' I told her, 'it would have to be investigated.'

'But you're not now a policeman.'

'I still *feel* like an officer of the law, with duties. Unwritten, but duties.'

'And if I must tell you —'

'No, please. Let me say this. I've got no witness to what you might intend to say. No witness, therefore, to how far I choose to ignore what you tell me. As a duty, I mean. Personally, I'd feel free to speak to nobody.'

'Your wife . . .'

'I'd like to have her here.'

'Then please – will you ask her to come in?'

'Certainly.' And with relief.

I knew she had to have a few moments in which to collect herself, though she still seemed to be in complete control. It had taken a great deal of effort to reach this brittle strength. That a tiny crack in it was now visible was evidence that the strain on her was almost overpowering. The basis of it was in no way belittled by the lack of emotional expression, rather was it strengthened in that it showed signs of breaking.

Quickly I went across the corridor. Amelia was standing by the window. 'Richard . . .'

'Can you come in, love?'

'Of course.'

'No time to explain. She wants to tell me something. I may need help.'

'Then let's not leave her alone too long, Richard.'

I held the door open into Tessa's room, and Amelia preceded me. Tessa had her head back, her eyes closed. She opened them as she heard the door latch click.

'I hope he hasn't been bullying you,' said Amelia.

It provoked a smile. A tiny and tentative smile. Maybe smiling hadn't been used very often, either.

'Quite the reverse, I'm afraid,' said Tessa. 'But please take a seat. That's right, where I can see you. Richard, there's another chair over there in the corner.'

I fetched it. She was doing her hostess act. I sat. It was now Amelia whom Tessa faced.

'I wanted advice on a legal problem,' she explained. 'I don't quite understand why, but clearly your husband needed you.'

'We share confidences,' Amelia explained. 'It saves time.'

'How very lucky you are.' Tessa nodded to confirm this judgement. It was an aspect of married life she had not experienced. 'What were we saying, Richard?'

'You were about to tell me something which you weren't certain I might keep secret.'

'You, Richard?' Amelia asked. 'Of course it would be secret.'

'It was a question', said Tessa, 'of whether he would have to report a crime, if one was confided to him.'

'If he discovered one, yes, it would be his duty,' declared Amelia solemnly, looking straight into those blank blue eyes. 'If he was told, that too. If it was confided, no.'

'You're so certain.'

'I wouldn't allow him to report it.'

'Even a serious crime?'

'Even that.' Amelia didn't hesitate. I'd have kissed her, if it hadn't been quite the wrong time.

'Even murder?' It was little more than a whisper.

'That', said Amelia, 'would depend on who killed whom, and why. Don't you think, Richard?'

I nodded agreement. 'That would certainly be the criterion.'

'Very well. It was I who killed Rowland.'

Amelia bit her lip. I said, 'How did you kill him, Tessa?' I was trying to make the question sound casual.

'I pushed him down the stairs. There was no quarrel between the two boys, of course not. Paul wasn't here. I was behind Rowland at the head of the stairs, and I pushed him.'

Once again, a hesitation would have been disastrous. My mind was skating all round it, and I had to say something.

'And there was no distracting shouting?'

'There *was* shouting.'

'Jeremy?'

'Not Jeremy. He was in the gallery at the time.'

'Then who was shouting?'

She stirred uneasily in the chair, no longer able to maintain any pose of indifference. 'It's of no relevance – it was not distracting. I pushed him, and he fell.'

'If there was shouting, then somebody was near. It would've been an . . . an inappropriate time to push Rowland . . . if there was any possibility of a witness.'

'The shouting was from the kitchen area,' said Tessa, a dullness, a weariness now entering her voice. 'The door was open. It was distinct shouting.'

'You must tell me who was doing this shouting, Tessa. It's very relevant.'

She hesitated. Her eyes switched briefly to Amelia, then returned to me. 'If I tell you . . .' She left it on a query.

'You'll have to let me make up my own mind, on that.'

'On whether you'll have to rush straight round to the local police station?'

'No. On whether it can be discounted.'

She hesitated again. 'I don't think it can,' she said at last.

'Then you must certainly tell me,' I said, more firmly now.

'Very well. It was Charles Pinson. Charlie, they call him.'

Mary's brother? 'But he doesn't work here,' said Amelia, just before I could. 'We met him on our way here. He told Mary . . . wasn't it something like Corrie Lane, Richard?'

I knew she'd remembered quite clearly. She was simply trying to make the tone more chatty, lighter, to lessen the gravity of what Tessa was telling us.

'Don Martin's,' I said. 'So – Tessa – if he works for somebody else, what was he doing here, and why was he shouting?'

'He was shouting for Rowland, demanding to see him.'

'Well, then . . .' said Amelia.

Tessa leaned forward slightly. 'Rowland was terrified of him,' she confided directly to Amelia, woman to woman. 'Terrified. He didn't want to speak to this Charlie, but I knew he had to. He just stood at the head of the stairs, hesitating. So I pushed him.'

I cleared my throat. 'But you had no intention of bringing about a fall?'

'No. Of course not. Urging him.'

'You meant him no harm?'

'Most certainly not.'

I looked sideways at Amelia. She had her lower lip caught in her teeth, her eyes bright.

'Well, Tessa,' I said, 'in that case, you could go to the police station yourself and tell it all to the Superintendent there, and he'd send you packing. He'd laugh at you. It wasn't murder, it wasn't even manslaughter, because you intended to do no more than urge him. It was purely and simply a fatal accident, which was how it must have been accepted in the first place.'

She was silent, staring straight ahead with no expression on her face, then she shook her head as though freeing her mind, and I saw that two tears were running gently down her nose, slowly and undemonstratively. We waited.

In the end she gave a sudden shudder, like a shaggy dog shedding rain-water. Her voice was very quiet, though quite steady. 'I'm much obliged to you.'

I shrugged. 'For very little.'

'It has been a . . . a weight on my mind.'

'And now?'

She managed a thin smile. 'Now I can marry Geoffrey.'

'With a clear conscience?'

She made no reply to that, her thoughts reaching away into the future. Then at last she spoke, for the first time with decision. 'I shall sell this place, of course.'

Amelia knew nothing of Tessa's plans, but she used her imagination. 'Isn't it the ancestral home?' she asked chattily, as though it was of no more than minor interest.

'Ancestral?'

'The Searle home. Jeremy the seventh baronet, or something. You just can't . . .'

She laughed. She wasn't used to laughing, and the tone it produced was flat and humourless.

'Oh no – it's not like that. It's not an earldom. Rowland wasn't Lord Searle of Penhavon. No . . . the house has nothing to do with it. Jeremy will be – is – Sir Jeremy Searle. This doesn't have to be his ancestral home. He can live in a bed-sitter – as I believe they call them – and he'll still be Sir Jeremy Searle. I think you'll find the bequest, in that respect, is valid. I have the house, and what money there's left. I don't expect there'll be much.'

I couldn't imagine a comfortable future for Sir Jeremy Searle. 'And Jeremy personally? I understand he's short of ready money.'

She gave a minimal shrug, and seemed to ignore the question. 'I shall put the place on the market, as they say, though I understand the housing situation is very difficult at this time. The boys can stay here until it's sold. I suppose. Or would vacant possession be a better way of offering it? I believe so. Penhavon Park, with vacant possession. That sounds very attractive, don't you think?'

The worry had been lifted from her mind. She was now more fluent and more self-possessed. The practical woman was emerging, released after many years of living beneath domination, or that was the impression she wished to convey. But she'd had no time to think it through.

'And Jeremy?' I asked.

'Jeremy?'

'He's been virtually dispossessed. The oil paintings are worth nothing.'

'I'll look after him.'

'Virtually dispossessed on purpose.' I was trying to make it plain to her.

'Well, yes. I rather expected that. Jeremy has been a great worry. I know for a fact that Rowland helped him several times. Jeremy has proved to be a very incompetent accountant – or a very unscrupulous one.'

'But you'll help him out, nevertheless?'

'If there's anything left after estate duties and the rest – yes. But I fear there'll be very little.'

I glanced at Amelia. Tessa, though treated as an appendage by her husband, had seen and heard what had been going on. She was certainly not stupid.

'And', she added, 'after the sums of money Rowland paid to Charles Pinson.'

65

Her words lay heavily on the ensuing silence.

'Bookmakers in this district have become very rich,' she explained drily.

I cleared my throat. 'There would have to be something –'

With a note of acid in her voice she interrupted. 'When that was really a gamekeeper's lodge, there was a gamekeeper. Rowland used to invite friends, influential friends, to shoot over his land. Charles Pinson was the gamekeeper.'

Then she looked beyond me, her lips clamped together firmly, leaving me to make what I might from that statement.

6

We were back in our room, and I'd told Amelia the details of
what she'd missed from Tessa. She had asked whether we might
care to stay the night, but in a tone that suggested it would be for
her benefit rather than ours. I still wasn't at all certain what she
expected from us, unless she felt that something might be about
to happen. If so, I couldn't imagine what.

And it really wasn't convenient. We had come unprepared, expecting no more than an hour's visit. A reading of the will, that had
been the full agenda. We might now, logically, take Mary back with
us. Or Mary might wish to make a short stay of it, with Jennie. That
would be logical. Then . . . it would need only a phone call from
her, and I could easily run over to pick her up, at any time. But no
– Lady Theresa Searle had requested that we – Amelia and I, but of
course including Mary – should stay overnight.

It was now nearly five o'clock, dark outside but with the stars
clear and brittle. A frost, I thought, we're going to get a frost.
Presumably, there would be afternoon tea, though there had
been no information on that, and evening dinner at eight thirty
or nine, I had to assume.

'We could run home for a change of clothes,' said Amelia.
'Perhaps pack a bag. Oddments. You never know . . .'

'Hmm!' I gave it consideration. 'But I'd feel easier if one of us
stayed here.'

'Why? Why would you feel easier?'

'Can't you sense it?' I asked. 'The whole damned house is quiet
as a morgue – and I don't like it.'

'I'll stay, Richard,' she said quickly. 'And keep an eye on
things. If that's what you want.'

'But you'll keep out of it?'

'Oh yes. Of course. But how will you know what to bring for
me?'

I smiled at her. 'I rather thought I'd take Mary.'

'Well . . . you crafty devil, Richard. You want her to yourself – probing and questioning. It's not very pleasant, is it, spying on a friend?'

I kissed her on the cheek. 'Look at it the other way. Finding out the background – discovering any danger hanging around.'

She frowned heavily. 'Danger, Richard?'

'Embarrassment, then.'

'You've got something in mind, haven't you?' she demanded. 'I'll not have Mary worried. I'm warning you . . .'

'Now, now,' I said. 'I'm on her side. Remember? I'll just pop into the kitchen on the way out – might cadge a cup of tea – and I'll bet that's where I'll find Mary.' I went to the door and paused with my hand on the door handle. 'Oh, by the way – how old do you think she is . . . our Mary, I mean?'

'Now how can that possibly . . .' Her hand flew to her mouth. 'Richard! You're not thinking . . . oh dear.' She stopped.

'Thinking what?'

'That she could've been under sixteen when . . . oh, but that's ridiculous. Jennie can't be more than forty.'

She bit her lip to silence.

'And Mary . . . now?' I asked softly.

'I'd . . . I'd always thought of her as being at least sixty, but, but . . . Oh, damn you, Richard.'

I grinned at her. 'And if she's younger? She'll not have had an easy time of it, you know. Hence the touches of grey. And with the age of consent at sixteen, then and now, and if Mary was a little under seventeen when Jennie was born – and she *did* say something about being only seventeen, and Jennie about forty-ish, now, that would make Mary around fifty-eight. Maybe fifty-nine. Would you say I'm a little younger than Mary? Five or six years, say.'

'No, no. You mustn't even suggest it to her. Not so much as a hint. Richard . . . I think I'll come with you myself.'

I shrugged. 'If you don't think it matters . . . and you surely don't think I'd *ask*?'

'Oh damn you, Richard. You trap people. And how does it matter?'

I considered for a few moments about shrugging it off and saying something very futile about instincts and feelings. But Amelia had to know my thoughts on it.

'Tessa told me that Charlie Pinson was here, that day Rowland died. Shouting. Shouting for Rowland. She maintains that Rowland was scared of Charlie. Now why would that be, I wonder? That's what I have to ask myself. And the answer keeps coming back the same – that Charlie was the gamekeeper. It was in his cottage – or lodge as they call it – that Rowland and Mary used to meet. She hasn't said so, of course, and I only dared to make a guess at it. But that seemed to be obvious. But . . . it would have to have been done with Charlie Pinson's knowledge. Had to be. With his connivance, even. But Charlie would have known his own sister's age, to a day. He'd have known that Rowland was committing a crime, if she *was* under sixteen when it happened. Over sixteen when Jennie was born, perhaps, and Mary's said seventeen – but she might have been playing safe. But it would've been something like criminal assault, if I'm guessing right. Could Sir Rowland Searle of Penhavon Park afford such a thing to be revealed? Not on your life. Perhaps Rowland slipped him a fiver, each time they used the cottage. Later – it would have become straight blackmail.'

Amelia was staring at me, pale, her eyes huge. 'But not – surely not continuing all these years. It would be past history. Not recently, Richard.'

'I don't know. Rowland could have thought the danger was still around. And it may not be true, what Tessa told us. Charlie might not have been here at the house when Rowland died. It could all have been a pack of lies. Don't ask me why. I don't know. But I'd dearly love to find out.'

'Mary', she said softly, 'must be closer to sixty-five than sixty.'

'I'm sure she is,' I said soothingly. 'I'm sure.'

'Then don't you dare to go asking her.'

'Of course not. I'll just find her, and we'll be off. She'll want a change of clothes herself, anyway.'

But Mary, when I found her, chatting in the kitchen with Gladys, seemed well equipped with clothes. Jennie and she were much the same build, so that no end of Jennie's clothes seemed to be available to Mary. But they were a younger person's clothes. Now, in dark slacks, a white cotton shirt, and a short black jacket, Mary could indeed have been no more than sixty . . . though the brown hair, shot through with grey, was mislead-ing. But at the moment she could have been even less, though I had to take into account the fact that this exciting day had flushed away a number of years, and she was as bouncy and chirpy as her daughter.

'Richard?' she asked as I entered, half rising to her feet.

I placed a hand on her shoulder. 'I've just come to cadge a cup of tea, then I'm off home.'

'We're going back —'

'I am. A fleeting visit, Mary. Tessa's asked us to stay overnight. Amelia and I, that is. You're taken for granted – she'll obviously not expect you to rush away. But we all need a change of clothes. Who knows, it might stretch to more than one night. And I thought you might care to come along. I might not make too many mistakes in choosing things for Amelia, but I wouldn't care to rummage through your dressing table, or whatever.'

This assumed that Mary might not be happy about wearing Jennie's clothes.

'I'd think not – indeed,' said Gladys.

'Oh . . . I'll come,' Mary decided, nodding. 'I'll come, certainly. And I did want a little chat, Richard. Now? Are we going now?'

'After I've had my cup of tea.'

'And I'll take a tray up to your wife,' said Gladys.

I thanked her, found a spare chair, and sat beside Mary, not at all disappointed with the way it had gone. But I'd planned my approach carefully, on my way down the staircase, aware that walking down the centre of the treads was a minimal hazard, as they were naturally wider at the centre than at the edges. In fact, the extra width made the fall less steep. How difficult it would be to break your neck falling down there! You'd really have to try your very best.

And now . . . here I was, presented with the fact that Gladys obviously went up and down that staircase many times a day, sometimes with a tray in her hands, and with no chance of using the banister then. Yet she had survived.

Tessa's strained admission of a push – an urging push – was becoming less and less credible the more I considered it.

So – where did that leave me? Nowhere.

In cardboard boxes, padded with old and tatty blankets, the dogs were comfortably dozing. They hadn't leapt forward in welcome at my entrance, having Mary safely in sight. But when she got up to leave they were out in a flash. Both of us leaving, so they had to be in on it. I fussed them a bit, and promised to be back. But all the same, as we walked round from the kitchen, I heard one of them howl. Jake, that would be. Amelia would hear, and come down to them, possibly even take them out for a short walk. But it was dark, no moon, only the stars. It wouldn't be pleasant, with the grim, grey building looming over her.

I settled Mary in the passenger's seat, made sure her seat-belt was fastened, and then we were off.

It was an ideal evening for driving, and I knew the route now. Later, perhaps, there could be frost. I would have to consider that on the way back.

Mary was silent all the way through the lanes and villages, until we hit the open road. Then she said, 'You know very well Amelia would have come, Richard. So why me? Is it because you want to throw questions at me?'

'I thought we ought to have a quiet talk,' I admitted. 'You said the same thing.'

'Interrogate me, you people call it.'

'That's the point of the car, Mary. Interrogation is face to face. In a car it's informal. One friend to another. Hmm?'

'If you care to put it like that.' But she seemed distant and cool. 'What is it you wanted to know?'

'I'm not at all certain. How the adoption came about – what about starting there?'

I was aware that I was assuming a lot from very little evidence, but I had to take the risk.

'Came about?' she asked.

I was silent, overtaking a farm tractor along a narrow stretch of road. Then I said, 'It must have been terrible for you, Mary, parting with Jennie.'

There was no answer. I glanced sideways. She was very still, and a little withdrawn. When she eventually replied, it was so quietly that I had to strain my ears above the engine hum and the tyre whine.

She was hesitant, her voice unsteady. 'When . . . when it was obvious I was going to have a baby, the mistress – I thought of Tessa as the mistress in those days – she was all for getting rid of me as fast as possible. You can imagine. Of course, she'd guessed the truth. She'd have had to be very foolish if she hadn't. Guessed the child would be Rowland's, I mean, and this was when the doctor had told her she couldn't have any more children herself. Poor Tessa. Oh, I did feel miserable for her. But Rowland refused to dismiss me. There were the two boys, you

71

see, and we were very attached to each other. Rowland wouldn't have it. The house had room for another child, he said. All it would mean was that I'd have three to look after, instead of two. But that was Rowland, dreaming his dreams – and I do believe he thought Tessa had no idea about the father. So silly. I went away to have the baby, of course, a private place. Rowland paid for that. Just think, if I'd been living back in our old cottage by the Red Lion, that's where I'd probably have had her. But it was a proper maternity home, and I brought Jennie back from there. As though Tessa was going to let me stay at the house! It was too obvious. Too obvious.'

'Obvious?' I wondered how it could've become more obvious than it had been.

'Obvious that Jennie was Rowland's child, of course. Tessa said she had the Searle nose.'

This was quite absurd. The long, aristocratic nose of Jeremy and Paul was clearly Tessa's – in her family line – and nobody could dispute that Jeremy and Paul were her children. The Searle nose? Had she been taunting Rowland?

'A baby?' I asked. 'Surely —'

But Mary, once launched, was determined to sail ahead.

'Tessa saw what she wanted to see. She's always been like that. She wanted me and the baby out of the house. There were hysterics. Oh . . . she can be quite placid. You'd never think she *felt* anything. But it makes things worse, don't you think, Richard? Bottling it up. She'd go into sudden tantrums. "Get them out of my sight!" That sort of thing, when the boys had been too noisy for too long. And certainly, positively, I had to go.'

I noticed that now it was Mary who'd had to go. Tessa had perhaps softened her line on the baby, Jennie. Had been obliged to. But Mary was the most important one who had to go.

'I think I can understand what she felt,' I said quietly.

'But, poor Rowland!' she said. 'It left me as the bargaining issue. As though they were haggling over the price of a new dress she'd bought. No – that's backwards. Haggling over a new shotgun he'd bought. I'd become a "thing", to be argued over. And what could I say, amongst all that?'

'I don't know, Mary. What *did* you say?'

She was silent. I didn't do anything to encourage her, just left it to her decisions. Then at last she seemed to draw herself up in her seat, and sighed. I heard nothing . . . I felt it.

'I had to get a bit of peace, by myself,' she said quietly. 'The boys, they were just bewildered. As you can guess, at their age. Let me see. Jeremy would have been about five, and Paul . . . three or so. Too young to understand, though I think Jeremy was upset by all this wrangling going on. But Jennie was their little baby sister, and they were delighted with her.'

'And so . . .'

I was driving more and more slowly, prolonging the trip, and because I realised my mind wasn't completely on my driving.

'It was Rowland who suggested adoption. That sent Tessa over the edge, right over. They had to send for the doctor, but when he came she'd made a splendid recovery. Weak, but smiling bravely.' She paused. I thought I detected a quick, searching glance at me. 'I'm sorry, Richard. That was a bit bitchy – wasn't it?'

'You're doing all right. Just fine. But don't go on if you don't want to.'

'I'd better get it out into the open, I think. It clears the air. D'you believe that, Richard?'

'Sometimes it helps, certainly.'

'Hmm! But Rowland, you know, had a lot to answer for. It was *he* who wanted the adoption. And I wasn't even consulted. Not at first. It wasn't until he'd got Tessa to agree . . . oh, I don't know *what* persuasions he fed to her, what promises and threats. Though he wasn't very good at threatening, poor Rowland. Perhaps he threatened to leave her. Oh . . . I don't know. Leave her and go away with me . . . now, wouldn't *that* have been a scandal! As though he would! Ask yourself, Richard. As though he would!'

'Seems unlikely.'

'It was what I wanted to hear, of course, Richard,' she said brightly. 'Really . . . in all that worry . . . it was all I could wish for. My little girl – and Rowland. Looking back, it seems so . . . so immature. But I did love him. I did! A young woman – I knew nothing about life. Stupid, I was, perhaps. But he was everything to me, my whole world, and I had dreams . . . you know, Richard, dreams that he'd come to me and say that.'

She stopped, nodding, I could detect, to herself. I decided the best thing to do was remain silent. Then she went on, and I felt, from her tone, that she was smiling – at herself, no doubt, at her immaturity.

'I was so young, you see, Richard. That was the trouble. Young. A child myself, that's all I was.'

73

Then she was silent so long that I feared she would abandon this theme. In the end, I had to prompt.

'Not a child, Mary. Surely not.'

'I wasn't seventeen when Jennie was born. Oh . . . I know, today it's so different. So mature and self-confident, the youngsters are! But I knew nothing. Nothing at all. And then one day he came to see me, not as I'd dreamed it, but with one of those fate things.'

There was a pause while I tried to decide what she meant. Then I got it. 'A *fait accompli*, they call it. French for: it's too late to alter things now.'

'That was it, exactly. I'm so pleased you understand, Richard.'

It seemed that I understood rather more than she did, but I had no intention of explaining.

For some minutes I concentrated on my driving, wondering how far I dared to pursue it. As is often the case after long pauses, we spoke together.

'And the adoption?' I ventured.

'Jeremy would be about forty-six.'

We stopped, laughing, which at least released some of the tension I felt to be inhibiting the conversation. I said, 'You first, Mary.'

'I was only saying that Jeremy would be about forty-six, now, and Paul forty-four. But poor Jeremy looks older than that. Don't you think? It's the worry he's had . . .' She allowed it to tail off, her tone pensive. 'Still has, I suppose.'

I could make a guess that sundry hints would have been showered on Mary as to the best investment of her inheritance, and from all quarters.

'I thought he must be getting on for fifty,' I said, just to keep things moving. 'He looks it.'

'Yes. That's the worry he's had. But he keeps himself very fit, I understand. He tells me he works out, as they call it. Some gym or other. And plays something he calls squash. I don't know what that is.'

'It's a ball game, played inside a kind of room. It's supposed to be very energetic.'

'Hmm!'

She was silent. Two miles hummed away beneath the tyres. I said, 'And the adoption? You were telling me about that.'

'Oh yes.' A pause. 'Rowland came to see me – all bouncy, he was, as though he'd accomplished something grand, and he told me it was all right, because he and Tessa were going to adopt my Jennie. He stood there . . . oh, I'll never forget it . . . so pleased with himself. As though it was a great victory, and I was expected to applaud it. Sometimes men have no imagination at all. My Jennie – and what was I to do? I'll tell you what I was told to do, Richard. I was going to accept a month's notice, instead of the usual week's, with pay. Then go. Leave. Wasn't that splendid of him? And I was to receive money, extra money – out of his own pocket. A hundred pounds, to start me off, as he put it. A whole hundred pounds! I can see him now, bouncing up and down on his toes, and smiling that wretched false smile – as though I was nothing to him. And, he said, there would be some papers to sign before I left. Signing my Jennie away. And he was smiling!'

There was a catch in her voice, only her bitterness holding back the tears, I thought. Her pride, too.

But Mary didn't understand how the situation must have been for her Rowland. He would have had to put on the greatest act in his life, pretending that he was happy to send her away. Perhaps this had been necessary, so that the hurt should not have been as terrible as it might have been if he'd clung to her in passionate distress, the pain at bay behind the anger.

'He's never forgotten you, Mary,' I pointed out gently. 'He remembered you in his will, and after all these years.'

'Yes.' She nodded vigorously. 'Money covers it all, I suppose. Conscience money, they call it.'

'But you *did* sign the papers?' I asked.

'Oh yes. In the end. Somehow, I managed to persuade myself it would be the best for Jennie. I looked at all the difficulties, I suppose. Because . . . where were we to go, if I took her with me? I was *so* helpless and inexperienced.'

I didn't pursue that. She was silent for a long while. In the end, caught by a sudden realisation, I asked, 'But Mary, Jennie knew you at once. How old was she when you . . . left?'

'Six months. They brought in a nurse . . . and . . .'

'But Mary, she *knew* you. She came down those stairs and shouted out, "Nana!" So how did she know you?'

'I don't understand that. I haven't thought about it. From the boys, I suppose. They'd talk about their Nan. Perhaps they would have had photographs they could show her.'

75

She was silent. It was a thought she hadn't pursued, and the boys, of course, would have grown up knowing Mary to be Jennie's real mother.

'You ought to be flattered, Mary,' I told her.

'Should I?' She paused, then touched my arm. 'It's very flattering, yes. I suppose.' Then her tone changed, self-disgust claiming her. 'And I'm the mother who parted with her for money.'

I said nothing. Amelia had warned me not to bully her. But it was she who was pouring this out. I hadn't had to reach for it. Damn it, why do people always feel they have to confide in me? But hadn't I invited it?

'Oh!' she said. 'Is this Bridgnorth already?'

'Yes. Coming in through High Town. Five minutes and we'll be home.'

Nothing more was said, though I knew there was so much more to be revealed, hiding behind it all. How had she been persuaded to part with Jennie?

The Beeches seemed dark and unwelcoming. This was because I had always been able to turn into the drive to the sight of warm lights. If Amelia and I were out together, Mary would be there with a welcome. If I was out alone, both of them would be there. Never a silent and unwelcoming house.

'Do we get a dinner when we turn up at Penhavon again?' I asked.

'Oh yes. Nine o'clock, it's always been.'

'I hope we don't have to dress for it.'

'Oh no. Of course not, Richard.'

But I would have expected that. The assumption fitted what I'd learned about Sir Rowland Searle. In his lifetime, perhaps, it had been so.

We parted into our respective rooms. I packed what I thought would be necessary, and allowing for more than one extra day. You never know. Then Mary entered with her own case packed, and sorted out a few of Amelia's things.

'Put in some sturdy walking shoes,' I told her. 'We don't know how much walking we might have to do.'

Inside twenty minutes we were ready to leave. I was just about to slam the front door behind us when the phone began to ring. I walked through quickly into our living-room, and Mary hovered in the doorway.

76

'Oh Richard,' said Amelia, relief in her voice. 'I'm so glad I caught you.'

'You did, but only just. Trouble, is there?'

'You can probably guess. Jeremy and Paul. I'm sure that man's quite crazy.'

'Do you mean Jeremy?'

'Yes. There's been such an upset. I think Jeremy must've been drinking. It's the gallery argument again.'

'Ah yes.'

She took a breath. 'Jeremy's been talking as though it's his house now – and of course it's not. I heard them shouting, Jeremy and Paul. I was looking for something to read, in the library, and I heard Jeremy going on about getting things out of *his* house. His.'

'Things?'

'He was talking about those funny stone heads.'

'The masks?'

'Yes. They called them masks. Can you get back here quickly, Richard? But do drive carefully.'

That would present some difficulty, satisfying both conditions. 'Yes. Of course. And what happened?'

'Jeremy wanted the masks outside the house. He kept saying that. The masks. Not the watercolours. He's decided those are his, in with the oil paintings. So . . . the masks. Then he can lock the room up, all secure and safe. Something crazy like that.'

'All right, love.'

'There's been such a fight. We're waiting for the ambulance.'

'Ambulance?' I repeated numbly. It all had to happen when I wasn't there! 'Why the ambulance?'

'Paul might have to have an X-ray,' she said numbly. 'His jaw could be broken.'

'And Jeremy?'

'He's busy packing those stone things – the masks – into two suitcases. Says he's going to put them outside. Outside the house. And Richard . . .'

'Still here.'

'It's turning frosty here, so watch the roads, won't you?'

'I'll do that,' I promised. 'We're on our way.'

'Yes. 'Bye . . . for now.'

I hung up. I'd never before heard her so rattled.

As I was ushering her outside again, Mary asked, 'Trouble, is there?'

'Yes, Mary. Trouble. I'll tell you as we go.'

I took the car fast out of the drive. It was now after seven, and the commuting traffic would have eased. I restrained the car a little until we were out of Bridgnorth, then, in open country, I let her go. In the hedgerows I could see the frost sparking, but there was no feeling of it through the tyres.

I told Mary what had happened. She said, 'I knew it. I just knew it. That ridiculous will! Rowland must have been crazy. I ask you. Jeremy should surely have had the house. He'll be Sir Jeremy now. She'll be Dowager Lady Theresa. I think. I don't know. Whatever it is, she doesn't deserve it. The remainder of my estate, indeed! Foolish. Though I reckon there'll not be much money left in the kitty. Oh, do be careful, Richard. You're going too fast.'

I'd felt the back end breaking away on the last corner. I had to concentrate, but Mary chattered on.

'But – come to think of it – Jeremy's probably gone through most of the spare money, by now. Oh yes. He's made a hash of that accountancy business, if you ask me.'

'How can you know that, Mary?'

'Gladys told me. Gladys Torrance. She knows everything.'

I accelerated out of another skid. The night was crisply clear, the headlights reaching ahead.

'Even about Charlie,' said Mary. 'She knows that.'

'What about Charlie?' I was forced to ask it, before she went wandering off again into her memories.

'It was him what done it.' In her agitation, she'd slipped back to the vernacular of her childhood.

'Did what?'

'Fixed it with Rowland. About the adoption.'

Again she was silent, recalling it. A glance sideways indicated that she was leaning forward against the seat-belt, pressing forward into the past. I didn't hurry her. This promised to be important, and I wouldn't have wished to think I'd urged her into confidences she might regret.

'Between them', she said bleakly, 'they made it impossible for me. Tessa insisted that Rowley had got to dismiss me. He'd been holding back on that. Never could make a decision, that was Rowley. I'd got nowhere to go. Charlie and his wife wouldn't have me. Our parents were dead. That flu epidemic. And I thought I might be able to go back home, seeing that the cottage was empty. It was Rowley's place. He owned half the cottages in the village. Maybe Tessa does now. Anyway . . . Charlie got at him. Got another family in there, double-quick, and I reckon he got Rowley to dip into his pocket for that. I can't blame Rowley, Richard. I can't blame him. He wanted Jennie. And Charlie, he'd got something he knew about Rowley. I don't know what it was. But Rowley could always come up with a bit of spare cash for Charlie. Oh . . . I've said that. Don't drive so fast, please, Richard. You're frightening me.'

Fractionally, I eased down. The road surfaces were more treacherous now, out in the wilds, the lanes winding round tighter corners. She was silent. I was silent.

Two miles short of Penhavon, she said, 'We've been very quick, Richard.'

'Yes.'

Then, as though there was so much left to say, and she wanted to get it said, the words tumbled out.

'He did it all, Charlie did. My own brother. Everything I tried, to find somewhere, anywhere in the village, where I could live with my little girl, he'd manage to put a block on it. Somehow. Hated me, he did. Said I was a tart. Something special, he thought he was, him with his criticisms. Who was he to call me names, and Rowley paying him to go and watch the pheasants while we were at the lodge! Hypocrite! Preaching to me! Harlot! That was another name Charlie threw at me. Sanctimonious, that's the word for him. And all the time he was telling Rowley it was the only way to do it – make it impossible for me, make me sign that paper. And in the end I had to . . . and I left. Never looked back. How could I? Never. I got a place, a job, this side of Bridgnorth. Aston Eyre. They wanted a milkmaid. I'd never milked a cow in my life. But I learned. And that was where Amelia's Uncle Walter found me. Milking cows.'

She allowed herself a tiny, warm and nostalgic laugh. Then she went on.

'And there was Mr Walter – I always called him that – standing and watching me. Chuckling to himself. He was a great chuckler. He said something about me not being very good at it, and I said I was learning, and he asked what I'd done before, so I told him an under-maid at a big house, and a kind of nanny. Then he asked if I'd like to go and look after him. Be *his* nanny, he said, and he gave one of his big laughs. I said yes. It was the laugh that decided me. I've always wondered what he was doing there, at the farm. I always intended to ask him, and never got round to it. It's just how life is, I suppose. So I went to live there, at The Beeches. And I've never seen Charlie since. Not until today.'

I noticed that she'd twisted things round at the end, so that she could mention Charlie. There had to be something subconscious in that.

'Never even gave him a thought,' she murmured.

Not, I realised, until that morning. Heavens, I thought, *this* morning. I'd lost track with time. She had met Charlie then. He'd seemed pleased to see her. Seemed. And she him. Seemed.

The village was now very dark and deserted. The lights in the cottage windows were dim, and only the Red Lion showed any sign of human activity. It would be a very restricted life, living here, I thought.

I took the winding hill cautiously, and the driveway slowly. Even though I now knew its turns and its unmaintained surface, I wasn't going to take any risks, not now I'd come this far safely. Now, strangely, the lights of the house seemed to be welcoming us.

Almost, I felt, I was coming home.

7

Amelia had the front door open before I'd actually drawn to a halt. She had obviously been watching for headlights. I kissed her when she raised her lips. She seemed cold, and her eyes were dark.

'They're in the drawing-room,' she said quietly. 'Oh, Richard, you should have been here! I wish you hadn't . . .' She didn't finish that, gave a thin smile to Mary, and asked, 'Can't we go home? Just away from here. I wish we'd never come.'

'I don't think we can leave it now,' I said. 'Somebody has to be here. Somebody outside it all.'

Outside all the wrangling, I meant. Outside the hatreds and the jealousies. Rowland Searle must have been mad, making a will like that. I was surprised that Geoffrey Russell had allowed him to sign such a will, though I had to suppose that a solicitor takes instructions. Advises, but can't interfere directly in a client's wishes. In any event, Russell would have been in a difficult situation if he already knew, or intended, that Tessa would marry him when Rowland died.

But . . . be fair, I told myself. Russell could not have known the relative values of the items willed to the two brothers.

There was something malicious about that will, as though Searle had deliberately set out to cause trouble. I could see him sitting down at his desk, a thin smile on his lips, working out how best to distribute his worldly goods so as to bring about the maximum upset. I could have hated him, had he not been dead.

Perhaps, though – give him his due – he had been soured by the forced departure of Mary. Pressure had been put on him. It had bruised him permanently.

This I was thinking as Amelia led the way into their drawing-room, directly opposite the gallery, the room to which the ladies would have withdrawn, in the past, whilst the men passed around the port. In the prescribed direction, of course. But that was in the past.

It was by far the most pleasant room I'd seen so far, intended for comfort and with a modicum of grandeur thrown in. Carved ceilings and a chandelier, embrasures bearing pots of flowers around the walls, and pictures, too. There had been no mention of these in the will. Then, my attention aroused, I saw that these must be Paul's. Now professionally framed, they gained in stature. Earlier work, I guessed, as they were more representational than those in the studio. There was a definite touch of Cotman in them. No wonder he was very possessive about the watercolours in the gallery.

I was surprised to see that Paul was there. My impression had been that he would have gone for an X-ray. But there he was, in a wing-back chair beside a fire that was stacked, and burning furiously. He leaned forward towards it, as though cold. Shock perhaps. I went over to him, put a finger beneath his chin, and gently raised his face. Angrily, he thrust my hand away.

'Only looking,' I said equably. 'Nothing broken, then?'

There was a heavy bruise on one side of his chin, the lip swollen to meet it, and a cut over the other eye. Jennie helped him out, from behind me.

'The ambulance came. They had a look and said it was all right. Because he could move it. His chin. They said we ought to have sent for his doctor, not them.'

'It's often difficult to decide what's best,' I agreed, as she'd sounded a little guilty.

'I'll live,' said Paul thickly.

'More's the pity,' murmured Jeremy from behind me.

I had not realised he was in the room. All the chairs were high-backed, and as nobody seemed to want to face anybody else, they were scattered randomly. Tessa was there, too, sitting with her head back and her eyes shut, hoping it would all go away if she didn't watch it.

I advanced on Jeremy. He had caused this upset, but I couldn't feel anything but sorrow for him. He was, after all, the elder son, the eldest child, and he had been badly and unfairly treated.

'And you?' I asked, advancing on him. My training naturally gave me a touch of authority in this situation, but I was trying not to exert it. 'Let's have a look at you.'

82

He was seated with his knees spread, forearms on them, and had been staring down at his feet. His head came up challengingly. There were traces of dried blood on his upper lip, and a bruise over his right eye, which was slightly closed. His nose was red and swollen.

'Not exactly civilised behaviour, is it?' I asked. 'You *and* your brother.'

'Don't blame me,' put in Paul quickly. 'It's that bloody will. It's not fair. It's just not fair, whatever way you look at it.' This, from Paul, was quite magnanimous.

Amelia said, 'Life doesn't have to be. There's nothing in the rules about fairness.' But I caught her eye, winking. They weren't in the mood for philosophy.

'All right,' I said. 'It's not fair. But it's a legal will. You can't get round it. Contest it in court, yes. You could do that, and I think Mr Russell would confirm that. But it all takes time. Three months at least to prove the will, so how long if it's contested?'

Jeremy made an angry gesture of rejection. Paul said, 'I'm not taking it into any court, and that's that.'

'Nor me,' said Jennie, obviously thinking of her plans with Joe, who had clearly gone back to his own place.

Jeremy looked at her with raised eyebrows. 'Oh no . . . you're all right. Suits you, Jen, doesn't it?' There was a bitter tone in his voice.

She bit her lip and turned away.

'So . . .' I asked. 'What was it all about?'

'Can't you guess?' Paul asked in disgust. 'He wanted me to take the masks away.'

'Away!' put in Jeremy angrily, the basis of his complaint again being presented to him. 'I want those damned mask things out of that room. That's all.'

'Then', said Paul, 'he wants the Sotheby's rep to look at what's left in there.'

'So why not?' Jeremy's voice was rising.

Tessa straightened herself stiffly in the chair. 'I'll have no squabbling in my presence.'

I was surprised she'd used that word – squabbling.

'That's all right . . .' Jeremy was speaking pedantically now, in measured tones to lend emphasis to his claims. 'That's fine. Blame me. All I want is those damned ugly things out of that room, so when he comes he can see the rest, all together.'

'Not the –' Paul began, but Jeremy merely raised his voice and went on heavily. 'That'll all be mine. I want it like that. From now on.'

'The watercolours are mine.' Paul was trying to lever himself to his feet. Jennie went and put a hand on his arm.

'Mine!' shouted Jeremy. He darted a glance at his mother. 'Mine,' he repeated, but more quietly. Then he went on, appealing to her directly. 'It's all I want. He can keep those silly stone heads in his room.'

'I'm not goin' to hump 'em up there. Let 'em stay where they are.' Paul made an impatient gesture. He'd heard it all before. Too often.

'Out of that gallery. I don't care where. I'll take 'em up to your room for you.'

'No!' snapped Paul.

'I don't want the man to be distracted. Worthless rubbish!'

'Rubbish!' Paul looked round the room in mock wonder at this display of ignorance.

'Or take 'em up to that damned studio of yours. That'd be best.'

'It's not mine, it's Jennie's cottage now. It's in the will.'

Jennie, almost frantic to keep the peace, said quickly, 'It's not mine yet. You can use it, though, Paul. Really. I don't mind. Really.'

Paul breathed out heavily, his shoulders slumping. 'I don't want to get you involved, Jen. That's all. That idiot over there doesn't know his foot from his elbow, and if he sells my watercolours from under my nose, I'll charge him with theft. Theft.' He darted a look at me, sudden humour in his eyes. In the middle of this, he could find something amusing! 'Isn't that so? You tell him. You were a copper. Theft. It'd be a laugh.'

I ran my hand up the back of my neck. It wasn't simply that I didn't wish to become involved, it was that, by offering an opinion, I would be trespassing on Russell's preserves: civil law. But he had already expressed the basics, and I could see no harm in repeating them. All the same, I couldn't help sighing.

'It seems to me,' I said, 'from what Mr Russell told us, that nothing can be sold until the will's proved. Otherwise it would be theft from the estate of your father. Which means, Jeremy, that you can't even attempt to sell your oil paintings. As to the watercolours –'

'I'll kill him if he touches those,' said Paul flatly.

84

'Don't talk like a child.' I told him sharply. 'You're all acting like children. Let me finish. I would suppose that if Jeremy sold the watercolours, it would be theft, in any event, before or after the probate of the will. If I'm understanding it correctly. But *that's* another problem. You'll have to get another legal opinion, not simply Mr Russell's, as to the meaning of that phrase in the will, and whether it includes the watercolours with the oil paintings. Or not. But why argue about it now? Why not cool off? There's months you've got to wait.'

'But I *can't* wait!' Jeremy burst out. 'Can't.'

There was silence. We all stared at him. He gestured wildly. 'I need money. Lots of money. And soon. Or I'm in trouble, and that's that.'

'Just a second.' I held up my hand, halting him. 'Don't say another word. I don't want to know.'

There was a shocked silence in the room now. Coal moved and the flames flickered. Tessa was staring fixedly at the chandelier. I went over to Jeremy.

'I don't want to hear another word about it,' I told him quietly. 'Do you understand? Any hint of anything illegal, and it'd put me in a very difficult situation. A positive statement, and it'd be my duty to report it. Understand, Jeremy? Is that clear?'

He raised his eyes to me. I feared he was not far from breaking into tears. 'Can't you help?'

I shook my head. 'Who can? Even your mother...' Tessa looked at me, startled. She must have been thinking along these lines. 'She can't touch the estate. Only for day-to-day expenses.'

Jeremy looked at his feet. 'Then I'm sunk.'

Paul spoke quietly, his eyes on the fire. 'It's only the watercolours I want. You can have the damned masks, if it'd help.'

Jeremy's head came up. There was a wild light in his eyes for a second, then the hope faded. 'No. They're yours. I'm not arguing about that.'

'I can give 'em away, can't I?'

'You can't dispose —' I began, but Paul jumped in, and I was surprised at the anger in his voice.

'And you can just keep out of it! You an' your damned law. He can have 'em. He can raise money on them, can't he! That bloody stupid will wouldn't stop that. Wouldn't.'

I supposed this to be true, but I had no chance of expressing an opinion. Jeremy came into it again. 'I don't want 'em. They're yours.'

'I told you —'

'And probably worthless, anyway,' said Jeremy in disgust.

Paul gave a flat and almost chilling laugh. 'One of those masks went at Sotheby's last month for over £9,000.'

There was silence. Then Jeremy whispered, 'What?'

'There're nineteen of 'em, Jerry. Nineteen. That's going on for £180,000. Wouldn't *that* dig you out of it – whatever it is?'

Probably the watercolours were worth that much, too. I had no idea. Paul didn't think of them in terms of financial value. He wanted them to look at. But the masks . . . Paul clearly didn't cherish those. It was, therefore, a very generous gift of £180,000, and not to be rejected lightly. I expected Jeremy to pounce on it.

But all he said, hoarsely, was, 'No. They're yours.'

Perhaps this had been easy to state before, when Jeremy had no idea of their value. Now, to make that statement must have been agonising.

But clearly I had not understood Jeremy. My guesses as to his worthiness and honesty had been based on his possible fraudulent behaviour. But he possessed a pedantic, ingrained sense of fairness. Life wasn't fair; it threw rocks at you when you weren't looking. Therefore, Jeremy had to counter this with his own personal moral code. On fairness he was rigid. The masks were Paul's, in Jeremy's mind, the paintings his. Anything else was not fair. This he clung to with desperation.

How this reconciled with his possible fraudulent activities, I found it difficult to understand. Perhaps, once money passed into his keeping to be invested, it became a set of figures, a nebulous hypothesis. And you couldn't steal figures; you manipulated them. That, he could rationalise. If it was pointed out to him that it was theft – fraud – he wouldn't be able to understand what you were talking about.

And yet, subliminally, having as he did the basic instinct of rightness and fairness, he must have had difficulty in reconciling his actions. He had perhaps not examined these fully, but the knowledge that he was encroaching on his own deeply felt principles must have concerned him. He could have come very close to self-disgust.

Thus, to have his morality challenged in this way, to be faced with a chance to reprieve himself, but only at the cost of relinquishing his sense of personal fairness, must have torn him apart distressingly.

His reaction was violent. In a second he was on his feet, waving his arms wildly, fending off his own mental chaos.

'No. They're yours. Yours! No. I can't touch 'em.'

'No need to touch them, Jerry,' said Paul quietly. 'Leave them where they are, and somebody could come, somebody who knows. He'd advance money on them, like a shot. More than enough . . . wouldn't it be? More than enough.'

This generosity pushed Jeremy just too far, into fury. 'No! You get 'em out of there. D'you hear me? Up to your bloody room —'

'No. Don't be an idiot, Jerry.'

'Or your damned cottage. Out of my sight.'

It would have to be out of his sight, with a Sotheby's agent at his shoulder and the masks under the same roof. The temptation to show them would drive him insane.

Paul got to his feet, straightening languidly. 'And certainly not there. It's not secure. Act your age, Jerry. The offer stands.'

And Jennie, wanting to help, bursting with a desire to smooth the way but not really understanding the moral problems here, said, 'Oh . . . it's all right, Paul. The cottage is mine, or will be, and you can use it how you like. Really, Paul.' She'd tried it once; she was trying it again.

Paul gave her a weary smile. 'Thanks, Jen. Good of you. But I'm not going to have nearly £200,000 worth of antiques sitting inside a cottage you could open with a toothpick.'

'You can just get 'em out of that gallery!' Jeremy shouted.

'I'm going up for a bath and a change, ma,' said Paul, and he ambled towards the door.

I had caught sight of his face as he turned away. It was apparent from his pallor that he wasn't feeling too good. He went out, and closed the door quietly behind him.

'You get 'em out of there!' Jerry shouted after him.

'Oh dear,' said Tessa. 'What are we going to do with them? They'll be the death of me.'

Jeremy turned his head away and stared at the fire, watching his basic principles dancing through the flames. They would either melt, or emerge case-hardened and stronger. In this, he was on his own. It was his life he was staring at. Could he live with himself, sublime in his principles, if he discarded them just this once?

Jennie went across and sat on the arm of his chair, then ran her fingers through his hair. He jerked his head angrily. Women find it soothing, I believe, but men don't. Something for Jennie to learn.

'I've got a bit of money coming, Jerry,' she said softly. 'If it'll help.'

He looked up at her with his eyes angry, his lips twisted in an ugly line. 'How can it . . .' Then he caught at his anger, and his voice softened. 'Thanks, Jennie love. But it's not enough. Oh Lord, not near enough.'

She laughed it off, flicking his hair back to where it had been, and sliding off the arm at the same time.

'Never mind. If you don't want it, I know Joe can use it.'

She had a level head, Jennie had. Marriage would work for her; Joe would.

It was with this thought that I calmed my own anger, which I'd tried to keep to myself so far, though I was aware that Amelia was eyeing me with concern. Now I found myself missing my former official authority. In those days I would have tossed both the brothers into cells, far apart, and left them overnight to contemplate on life and the effort of living it.

It was at this point that Gladys Torrance put her head in and announced that she was ready to serve dinner. Tessa nodded. 'Thank you, Gladys. We'll be right in.'

It was going to be, I thought, a miserable meal.

This was not so; Tessa seemed to be a person of strong character, as she put behind the tensions she couldn't really ignore completely and acted the part of hostess. But how often must she have done that, when the county friends visited, and she had to hide the fact that her personal life was in chaos?

She chatted to me, enquiring as to the tribulations of attempting to uphold the law, and to Amelia about the strain it must be to live with a policeman as her husband. We didn't tell her that this had not been so, as we had met during what turned out to be my last case, a murder, during which she had emerged as the principal suspect.

Mary, of course, was completely immersed in Jennie. Jeremy was silent, and ate very little, I noticed. Paul did not put in an appearance, but his mother made no comment.

Afterwards, there seemed nothing to do. Tessa had assumed we would be staying the night, though Amelia, once we were alone in our room, declared that she would like to go home, and right there and then.

The tension that seemed to permeate the house was the reason for her uneasiness. But it was exactly that atmosphere that told me we ought to stay.

'It's just . . .' She waved her arm vaguely. 'We seem to be intruding in something that's entirely a family matter. I don't find that very pleasant, Richard.'

'Somebody ought to be here, love. Don't you think?'

'Somebody? But who're we to offer ourselves? Oh, I know all about your experience. But Richard, it's not fair. Not fair to take sides. They're all expecting you to take sides. And you mustn't do that.'

'I'm trying not to,' I assured her, staring out at the night. 'D'you know which is Paul's room?'

'Oh, Richard! Must you?'

'Just to check he's all right.'

'Now . . . you're not being honest with me, Richard. It's not like you.'

'Come with me, if you like.'

'May I?'

I laughed. 'Of course. Now all we've got to do is find where his room is.'

'Oh, I know that. I saw him coming out of the bathroom, with a robe on, so I know where he went from there.'

'We'll make a detective of you yet.'

So she took me along the corridor and indicated the bathroom in question. We would need to know that, anyway. Paul's room was directly opposite.

I knocked on it, and he called out, 'Come in.'

I put my head in. 'Are you decent? I've got my wife with me.'

'Oh, come in, come in. You're both welcome.'

He had put on slacks and a shirt and a roll-necked sweater. On a side table there were used plates. Gladys had brought him something to eat. He was standing by the window.

'Don't make me shout again,' he said. 'It hurts.'

'It doesn't look as bad as it did.'

'It feels a damn sight worse. Here, you have the chair, Mrs . . . I'm sorry.'

'Amelia will do,' she said.

It was a basketwork chair with one cushion. He gestured for me to sit on his bed. Which I did.

'I wanted a word with you, anyway,' I told him.

'Me first,' he said. 'Then you probably won't need to say yours.'

I smiled at him. 'Very enigmatic.'

'It's a point of law.'

I sighed. 'You know I'm ignorant of civil law.'

'This is criminal,' he said. Then to Amelia, 'D'you mind if I smoke?'

'No, no. Richard smokes a pipe.'

I felt for it. Yes, I had it. 'What's your point of criminal law?'

I was taking it lightly. I'd had enough of any kind of law for one day.

'Well . . .' He lit his cigarette, blew out smoke, then stared at its tip. 'Is it true that a convicted criminal isn't allowed to profit from his crime?'

I tried to maintain a casual attitude. 'That's so. There'd be no point in sending someone down for robbery, then handing the proceeds of it over to him to spend when he comes out.'

'That's pretty obvious,' he said flatly. 'I'm serious, Mr Patton. Don't make fun of it.'

'Sorry. But this is purely academic, surely?'

'No. Not academic. It'd mean, then, that a murderer couldn't inherit . . .'

'Now hold it right there!'

He ploughed straight on, ignoring my protest. '. . . from a murder. Couldn't benefit from —'

'Is this a joke, Paul? Are you serious?'

'Couldn't be more. I believe Jeremy killed our father.'

8

I had felt that something like this would have to be produced, but I hadn't imagined what form it would take, nor who would offer it. Certainly not Paul.

I said quietly, 'I don't see how you gain from this.'

'Gain! That's what everybody thinks about: what's in it for me!' He shook his head violently, and winced. 'I've got what I want. All I ever expected. More.'

'Then why make this accusation,' I demanded, 'if there's nothing to gain by it?'

He looked disgusted, and muttered, 'Gain! Well, all right. Just think about it. To start with, wouldn't it be peaceful for all of us if Jerry was locked away in a tidy little cell? And think about this. No more worries for him. No more problems. The Fraud Squad would be straightening out all his financial tangles, and he could sit back and read a good book. An improving book, as they used to say.'

I couldn't be sure how serious he was. He stared at me with his head cocked, his expression almost derisive. Paul was a man who would have contempt for his own motivations. At no time could I take him at face value – or rather, at word value. He tossed them at me, to field and throw back.

'I don't think he'd survive long in prison,' I said quietly. 'It wouldn't be a pleasant life. Quite a leap, it would be, from Sir Jeremy Searle, baronet, to 7392416, convict.'

'They'd ignore his title,' Paul decided. 'I mean – it wouldn't sound right, the warders having to call him Sir Jeremy, and the rest of 'em hey you!'

I glanced at Amelia for a clue as to how she was taking this, but she seemed confused, and simply shook her head. But clearly Paul was leading somewhere. He was merely, now, laying down his terms of reference. Perhaps what he wanted to put over was

91

so distressingly serious that he could deal with it only if he was thought to be facetious.

Amelia, trying to help, said, 'And if it killed him, this prison of yours, would you inherit the baronetcy, Paul? Would it be like that?'

'I don't know. Possibly it'd relapse, die, cease to exist.'

'But you wouldn't want it, anyway?' she suggested, smiling at him and challenging his serious intent.

'Not really. Think of it. Me – submitting paintings to the RA under the signature: Sir Paul Searle. It'd sound funny.'

'They wouldn't take you seriously?' I suggested.

'I shouldn't think so.'

'Nor do I, right now. Jeremy killed his father, indeed! There's not one atom of evidence to support it.'

'Isn't there?'

He asked this gently, then he waited for me to take it on. I said nothing. In the end he was forced into pursuing it, and he chose to start with motive.

'Sir Jeremy Searle! Now doesn't that sound impressive? I expect, for Jerry in his line of business, it'd be a big asset. He could edge his way on to boards. It'd look good on the company letterheads – Company Accountant: Sir Jeremy Searle, Bart. Lovely. It breeds confidence, that sort of thing. They wouldn't even guess he was a conniving, fraudulent bastard.'

'You're pushing it too far,' I told him sharply.

It must have taken a very cynical appraisement of the situation to produce this from Paul, who had seemed to be wanting to help his brother.

'Yeah, yeah. I suppose I am. But I get so damned tired of it. Anything I try to do for him, he throws it back in my face. What's his is his, and he won't budge an inch. What's mine is mine – and he won't touch it. He's just a damned fool, and he'll go down waving his righteous flag.'

'But not, surely,' I said, 'fool enough to kill his father for a title.'

Paul touched his chin. It was still painful. 'It's making it hurt, talking.'

'Then stop talking,' I advised. 'Particularly this nonsense.'

He was silent for a few moments. I thought perhaps that I'd got through to him. We waited. Eventually he lifted his head.

'You don't know him, that's what the trouble is. All pernickety when it comes to procedure, that's Jerry. All the rules have to be obeyed. It'll drive him mad till he gets his own personal legal opinion on that one phrase in the will – does it include the watercolours? It'll go right up to the Lord Chief Justice, before he'll accept it. And d'you know why it's driving him mad? No? Then I'll tell you. It's because he went so far as to kill his own father, and it's got him nothing.'

'Now Paul . . . be sensible,' I said, because I was tired of this proposition.

'They hated each other, you know,' he went on. 'Damn it all, I've seen it going on for years. Oh . . . I know it all came from dad – he started it. He always treated poor old Jerry with contempt, because Jerry hated shooting and fox-hunting. Is it surprising that Jerry picked it up and threw it right back?'

There was silence, apart from my own breathing and the rustle as Amelia moved uneasily in the basketwork chair. Finally, I cleared my throat.

'You probably don't know that your mother blames herself for your father's death. She's told us what happened. It sounded . . .' I hesitated, too long, I feared. 'It carried a certain amount of conviction.'

'Oh, it would. She'd fall over herself to protect him. Jerry's always been her favourite. He never could go wrong, could Jerry. Never.'

And Jennie, I guessed, had been the father's favourite. After all, he'd forced through the adoption, and paid for it. And she was his. Had *he* called her Jennie, I wondered. Probably not. Janine, more likely, if only to separate her more concisely in his mind, Jerry and Jennie sounding so alike. And Paul, therefore, had been left in the middle, nobody's favourite. That would have explained the bitter tone in his voice.

I had to force my mind back to the subject under discussion, the circumstances which I wanted to impress on Paul.

'Your mother's given us a very graphic description of how your father's death occurred.'

'I'll bet she has. And what load of rubbish did she heap on you?'

'She told us she pushed him, from the head of the stairs.'

'Hah!' It was a choked laugh of disgust, which twisted his mouth with pain. 'D'you really think that'd break his neck? Of course it wouldn't. A few bruises, and he'd be on his feet again. And . . . hey, have you thought of *this*? He'd know he'd been

93

pushed. Know it. How would she face him then, if it didn't do any more than bruise him? How would she explain it? To his face.'

'You're doing too much talking,' I told him, 'considering it gives you pain. Try listening for a minute. Your mother told us it was an accident. She said that Charlie Pinson was at the house – downstairs – and he was shouting. Your father, she said, didn't want to see him, didn't want to face him. So she did no more than urge him. He'd got to face Pinson, she said.'

'Urged him a bit too hard?' He tried to sneer, but his swollen lip made a mockery of it. 'And you believed that?'

'I had to. She seemed sincere.'

'If Charlie Pinson was shouting from the kitchen, Gladys would've known.'

'I realise that.'

'Have you asked her?'

'I haven't dared to.'

I was finding it a novel experience to be at the wrong end of an interrogation. But strangely, it seemed the only way to handle it. Amelia touched my arm. It was a signal that she didn't want to hear any more, but I knew there had to be more, and that it mattered. Paul hadn't previously expressed this theory, I gathered. That this outburst followed on from a dramatic and violent incident seemed to add veracity to Paul's claim. He had been driven to it.

He allowed the silence to build up. He stared out of the window at nothing. Then he said, 'Have you asked Charlie?'

It hadn't occurred to me. 'No.'

'Then perhaps you ought to. I reckon he wasn't here that day. I reckon the whole story was faked between them.'

'Your mother, Jeremy and Gladys Torrance?'

'The time it happened, I've reckoned, Gladys would've been out doing the shopping. So there's no point in asking her.' Yet earlier he'd suggested I should.

But I couldn't get past him. He watched me, patiently, calmly and confidently.

'I suppose you know that Jerry works out at a gym?' he asked at last.

'I've heard something about that.'

'But not the sort of gym it is, I bet.'

'No.'

94

'It's martial arts. He's getting fairly well advanced now. Reckons he could snap your neck like a stick of rock.' He smiled thinly.

'He didn't use it on you,' I pointed out.

'Oh no.' Again that painful smile. 'It wouldn't, you see, be fair.'

'But you're suggesting he thought it was fair to use it on your father?'

He shrugged. 'He hated father. He doesn't hate me. He tries to, but it doesn't work.'

Damn him, it was the calm way he rolled it out, like a great run of carpet.

'I shall have to give it some thought,' I told him, giving Amelia the tip. She eased herself to her feet. I didn't see that, just heard the creak of the chair.

'You do that.' Paul had his hand to his lip, supporting what had to be a grin. 'But you've just got to listen to this last bit. It's the best. You'll laugh.'

I doubted it, being so far from laughter. Nevertheless, I nodded.

'The will says: art collection. Right?' He waited for my agreement. 'Well . . . what you don't know is that father considered the library to be part of his art collection. He said the word "art" included writing. But that's not what I wanted to tell you. I reckon you're just the same as everybody else – you don't *see* things. Rows and rows, shelves and shelves of books, and all you see is books. But there're spaces between the bookcases. Look for yourself. Narrowish vertical spaces, just to break up the rows. Gaps of about ten inches. It was most likely my grandpa set it up like that.'

'Is this leading somewhere?'

'Oh yes. Yes, it is. In those gaps – if you use your eyes – you'll see pictures. Little ones. Mention paintings to people and they think of something three feet by two, or even up to seven by four, like Reynolds and Gainsborough. So they ignore the small stuff. But every one of those little paintings in the library is the work of one of the Impressionists. Oh yes, they painted small, when they had to. They were usually scratching around for the odd franc or two, just for the price of a meal. They'd paint on anything, bits of plywood or cardboard. You name it. If it'd got a flat surface, they bunged something down on it. And every one of those pictures in the library has got its own history and provenance, as they call it. There's a folder of documents in the drawer at the end of the table. And most of them are oils. Check for yourself. So . . . if we keep to the correct legal phrasing, then those are Jerry's – and there's a fortune in it for him.'

I wasn't liking the sound of this. 'So why haven't you told him?'

'Two reasons. One: he's never even noticed they exist, the ignorant moron. And two: this.' He touched his jaw. 'And because of his whole ridiculous attitude to everything he comes across that doesn't suit him. And don't tell me – I know that's three reasons. But the point is: are you going to tell him? Are you?'

I tried looking him in the eyes, but he didn't flinch. If there was anything in what he said regarding the small paintings, then Jeremy had to be told. And Paul knew that, so this aspect of it wasn't in question. The real reason he had wanted to see me was in order to put across his theory as to his father's death.

It was perhaps a theory that had grown from wishful thinking.

I paused in the doorway, looking back. He pursed his lips and pulled his left ear-lobe.

'Of course I've got to tell him,' I said. 'Anyway – why doesn't he know? If your father called the library part of his art collection, then Jeremy must have known that.'

He shrugged. 'Why don't you ask him?'

Then, his good manners deserting him, he turned his back on us and stared out of the window into the dark night.

Quietly, I closed the door behind us. Amelia was waiting to see what I wanted to do next.

'Richard?'

'The library, my love, surely.'

'Yes. And perhaps I can find something to read. They don't seem to have heard of television here.'

I grunted. It went towards support for the feeling I had, that here I was living in the past.

The Brontë sisters, I was sure, would have loved this house, particularly when it was pouring with rain and the wind cutting like a knife down the valley. Jane Austen would have filled it with happily unmarried daughters and worried mothers. Trollope would have peopled it with receptions, and politics dustily resounding from the walls. And P. G. Wodehouse would have gone into ecstasies over the staircase, and thrown butlers and secretaries down it with an unsurpassed glee, and with not one broken neck between them.

Fortunately, the library door was unlocked. I held it open for Amelia as I put on the light, and she pounced on the bookshelves. Just to check, I went and tried the gallery door. It was locked. From inside Jeremy, hearing the latch, raised his voice.

'Who is it? Go away.'

'It's Richard Patton.'

'I'm busy.'

'I might have something to say —'

'I said, bugger off.'

I decided not to say my little bit, not now, not later perhaps. He was not in the mood. I wondered whether he'd already contacted Sotheby's, and was preparing to welcome their agent.

Amelia turned as I entered the library, her eyes shining, excited, and already with her hands dirty.

'Nobody's dusted for years,' she said. 'But it's just as Paul said. The pictures are here. Look.'

I stood, slowly turning, and for the first time concentrated on my surroundings in there. Oh yes, I'd spotted that they were a random and unorganised collection, but now I was being more critical. Of course, Paul would have had something to back up his claims, but there was a certain aura of permanency in this room, a stolid sense of waiting for eternity. It seemed that nothing had ever disturbed either the books or the furniture. The place stank of discarded years, each one having inflicted no movement apart from the gentle drift of dust.

The paintings, if they existed, could have hung there – huddled there, it seemed – for another eternity, without discovery.

But Paul was an artist. Their presence would not have eluded him. And – by heaven – there they were.

There were five spaces between six blocks of shelving. I could not think of them as bookcases, because there was nothing protecting the books, no glassed doors. There were therefore five spaces between, each about ten inches wide, and recessed by a foot. In these spaces there were dimly visible fifteen small rectangles, three per space, mounted one above the other. The light was not good, and it was not surprising that they would have escaped notice because, whatever dusting the room itself might have received, this had not been extended into the alcoves. No feather duster had reached in to tickle their surfaces to life.

Each one had a tiny plaque beside it, bearing no more than a number, these dimly detectable, one to fifteen in sequence, moving in a clockwise direction from the door.

I peered closely. Amelia was doing the same thing, the other side of the room. It was almost impossible to detect any variation in the dusty, grimy surfaces, nothing in any way suggesting a picture. Each one was framed, matching frames in plain, black narrow wood. And they were behind glass, I realised.

This, to me, seemed at first to disqualify them as oils, which are not usually framed behind glass. But the framing might have arisen, I realised later, from the necessity to support the material used by the artist. It wasn't until I stiffened my nerve sufficiently to try a duster on them that I discovered the glass.

This duster I'd found in the drawer at the end of the table. I was searching, in fact, for the folder Paul had mentioned, containing what he'd called the provenances. Carefully, I tried the duster, and glass was revealed on No. 1. It also revealed that it was supported by a simple ring hooked on to a simple nail in the wall. I therefore lifted it off and placed it on the table, where I could see to clean it properly and inspect it on the open surface. Even now the light was poor, from a single central globe. One would have expected better light in a library, but clearly it had never been intended as a room in which to read.

This was No. 1. The glass in this event was at once justified, as I found I was looking at a pastel painting, a simple sketch of a solitary young woman on her points, as I believe the ballet enthusiasts say. Surely . . . a Degas?

My heart began to move a little more quickly. I had never imagined that I might find myself holding a Degas. There was nothing resembling a signature, and no sign of a date. It seemed to have been done on cardboard.

'The folder,' whispered Amelia, barely able to contain her excitement.

There it was, a simple octavo folder wallet. Inside there were fifteen separate packets, or large envelopes, as they could have been. In each one – and they were sequential – there was a letter, folded and with no envelope of its own, and a separate slim envelope. I drew out the packet marked No. 1.

It was the letter I read first. I opened this cautiously. Letters are personal to the recipient, but I saw at once that this recipient would be long dead. It was dated: Paris, May 14th, 1872.

The ink had been black, but was now a faded brown. The script indicated an educated hand. It was headed: 'My darling Emily.' It read:

How I wish you were here with me! If I had realised that my business could have become protracted, I would certainly have insisted that you should accompany me. The French, though, are so delightfully casual about business. It seems to consist here of keeping one eye on the weather, as to discuss business with the sun outside in May in Paris appears to be unthinkable to them.

This therefore means that I shall not be home as soon as I had expected, and also (infuriatingly) that you might conveniently have travelled with me without having to sit around in hotel rooms alone, and becoming bored,

To alleviate your disappointment, I enclose a little sketch I picked up on the west bank of the Seine yesterday (Sunday). I think this to be quite professional, and he did it for me as I watched. Chalks, he seemed to be using, so you have to be careful you do not smudge it. This is the reason for the quite complicated packing I have had to do in order to protect the surface.

I do hope you like it. As soon as I can I will search for further little treasures.

With my deepest love, my darling,

Stephen.

P.S. The man claimed he had exhibited his works several times. One cannot accept these claims, of course, but it is possible. It is not signed (How could he have signed with a stick of chalk?) but he said his name is Edgar Degas.

Amelia gave a tiny squeak of excitement. She clutched the painting to her, held it away, clutched it again. 'I swear I could steal it away,' she said. 'She's floating. Like a feather.'

'There are more,' I reminded her.

In the separate, smaller envelope there was a statement or certificate dated July 27th, 1923, and signed: Prof. Aloysius Pelly, FBA, PhD, MA. It was an affirmation that 'Girl on Points' had been examined, and that he was satisfied the work was that of Edgar Degas, 1834–1917.

No. 10 (I had impatiently jumped forward in sequence). My hands shook a little as I unhooked it. A quick polish with the duster revealed a framed glassed picture, eight inches by ten, this time certainly in oils. But I am not sufficiently expert to offer opinions on styles. We found the letter in package No. 10. The result was:

Paris, Feb 23rd 1873.

My darling Emily,

I know, I know. This is becoming stupid beyond belief. That I should have to return to Paris to finalise the matter was expected. That it should once again become protracted is stretching my patience too far.

You will not believe it, but Paris in February is in no way like Shropshire in February. They stroll the banks, and in sunshine, though the temperature demands furs. And yet, they are still there, my artists. I now consider them to be friends. They make no attempt to cheat me, I feel. You must by now have nine or ten of their little offerings.

I am becoming more and more fond of these small ones, almost miniatures, you might say. There are larger ones available, but so many of these painters, they themselves claim, are becoming known for their strange movement called Impressionism, that they now charge the most outrageous prices for anything larger than a cigar box. And this one, I believe, is actually painted on the lid of a cigar box. I find this quite amusing. At least, it is easy to post to you, when a larger one I would surely find much more difficult to despatch safely. And no, my sweet, it is not that I am mean. I paid all of ten francs for the enclosed.

Yes, I enjoyed the opera, and no, I was not accompanied by M. Courbet's daughter. Most certainly not.

I was forgetting to tell you. This artist's name is Claude Monet. He claims that he, like all the others, has exhibited several times. I doubt this, as his style appears to me to be hurried and offhand. But I do hope you like it.

Your adoring husband, Stephen.

P.S. I think it represents a railway station. S.

Again there was a confident identification of the artist, but by a different professor.

It no longer seemed necessary to investigate all fifteen of the paintings, but we couldn't leave without dusting each off, lifting it from the wall, and looking at it beneath the light. Looking at it – just looking. It was a strange and somewhat moving experience to handle these sketches by painters now famous, and to realise that they had been a link between a bygone baronet Stephen Searle and his wife, Emily. Perhaps these paintings had saved a marriage which, if not breaking up, at least had shown tiny cracks here and there.

There was a small notebook in the folder. It listed the paintings, one to fifteen. There were two by Degas, both pastels, but the rest were all oils. Two by Sisley, a Boudin, an early Van Gogh, two Manets, the Monet we had seen, two by Berthe Morisot, a Renoir, two Seurats, and a Redon.

I put the folders away. The obvious next move was to find Jeremy and show him. It might at least assure us a quiet night. But when I knocked on the gallery door it brought no response this time. I shrugged. To hell with him. He was either sulking in there, I thought, or sulking in his own room. As it was now quite late, and I didn't know which was Jeremy's room, I decided to leave it all until the following morning.

Nobody can go through life without making mistakes.

9

A few lights had been left on, and I had to assume that the last to retire was supposed to turn them off. We were clearly the last, so we did that.

Our room seemed cold. They had central heating, though with ugly old radiators. When I put my hand on ours I could barely detect any warmth.

'Bed?' asked Amelia. She had brought up a book to read.

At that time, at home, we would have been drinking hot cocoa and nibbling a biscuit or two. Some part of our life seemed to be missing.

'What about the dogs?' I asked, suddenly realising.

'Heavens, I was forgetting.'

'I'd better go and see, and I'll bring a hot drink back. That do, will it? D'you think?'

'Yes, Richard. You do that.'

Outside, the moon had risen. There was a soft silvery light spread across the landscape. It was a decent evening for taking out the dogs, I thought. I went down once again, being as quiet as I could, putting on lights as I went.

The kitchen was in darkness. There had been no scramble of the animals as I walked in. I snapped the lights on. They were well settled into their respective boxes. They opened a weary eye each; they flicked a bored ear. Clearly, they'd had enough of the outside for one day. Perhaps Mary had taken them for a last outing, more likely Gladys Torrance. She knew dogs. Unless I was very much mistaken, she knew a lot of other things, too, probably more than any other single one of the occupants.

I made a pot of tea, found a tray, put out cups and saucers, sugar and milk, perched half a dozen thin arrowroots on a saucer, and returned upstairs quietly, lights going off again behind me.

Amelia was well settled in with a pillow behind her against the bed-head, and reading the book she'd found downstairs. It was one of three, I saw, the other two lying on the bedside table.

'Found something, then?' I asked.

'*Pride and Prejudice*. I can read it over and over.'

'Then why the other two?'

'They all go together. Volumes one, two and three. I doubt I'll even get through volume one, though. I just thought they ought to be kept together.' She clearly envisaged our staying yet another night.

Idly, I picked up one of the other two. The binding was of soft calf, but when I opened it the stitching seemed a bit rough. But of course, this was probably how it had been done in those days, stabbing through, way back in . . . when was it? I opened it to check. The title page read:

PRIDE AND PREJUDICE
A novel in three volumes
by the author of "Sense and Sensibility."
Vol. II
London: PRINTED BY T. EGERTON, Military Library, Whitehall.
1813.

This I recognised, because there was a similar facsimile printed in Amelia's copy at home, which was in one volume, and in that the facsimile was numbered: Vol. I.

What I had here, therefore, was not a facsimile at all, but the second volume of an original. This – the three volumes – was a first edition of *Pride and Prejudice*.

I offered it to Amelia, not priming her, giving no hints as to why I wanted her to consider it. She got it at once, and her eyes, wild and excited, turned up to me.

'I wonder', she whispered, 'if there are any more . . . any more first editions.'

We stared at each other for all of thirty seconds.

'I'll have to go and check,' I decided at last, clearing my throat.

'It's long after eleven, Richard.' But it wasn't a protest.

'Will either of us be able to rest unless I've made sure?' I tried to tack a smile on the end of that, but I was exhausted through and through and it probably looked like a grimace.

She returned the smile, but hers was almost sad. 'Then hurry, love.'

'Just a quick look round . . .' I promised this vaguely. I meant a look round until I *did* find something more.

So it was a trek along that corridor once again, the carpet silencing my feet, putting lights on as I went, down the staircase with my hand to the banister because the corridor light left the treads shaded. Even so, I would have had difficulty in tripping myself up, I thought, my mind refusing an outright rejection of Paul's claim.

Dimly, the direction not easy to locate, I heard a sound, not a slam, not a thump. A sound. I stopped, half-way down the stairs. The sound need not have signified anything unusual; perhaps someone visiting one of the bathrooms. It was not repeated.

I continued, and slipped silently into the library, closing the door gently behind me, and putting on the light.

There was absolutely no order to the books on the shelves – no author's name sequence, no segregation of fiction from non-fiction, no discrimination as to age and importance, trash elbowing treasures.

But the treasures were there, scattered around. In the minute or two I allowed myself, my fingers lifted out a first edition of *Wuthering Heights* (Ellis Bell – 1847), a battered but nevertheless genuine first edition of Tobias Smollett's *Roderick Random*, printed in 1748. And Ouida! Would she be a collector's author? If so, I was holding a first edition of *Under Two Flags*.

I spared myself no more time. If, in two minutes, I had located these, how many more first editions of great value might there not be?

I put off the lights and gently closed the door behind me. From somewhere in the house, like an echo (though there could have been no echo of the minimal sound I'd made) I thought I heard another door close. My nerves, I told myself, were becoming stretched.

'Well?' asked Amelia, the moment I had our door firmly but silently closed behind me. 'What did you find?'

I told her quickly, emphasising that I'd had only a very quick look around. She was fascinated, watching my mouth saying it. By that time, I was sitting on the edge of the bed, so that our voices wouldn't disturb anybody, drinking warm tea.

'You didn't bring them to show me,' she said, disappointed.

'Sorry, love, but they *were* rather dirty. I expect you had to dust the Jane Austens you brought along.' She nodded. 'But I left them together so that I could put my hands on them again.'

'I'll see them in the morning, then.'

'Yes. It's fascinating, though, isn't it. I bet that nobody's really looked at that library for heaven knows how many years. But . . . bring in an expert, and I reckon he'd find dozens of them, and all first editions. D'you know what I think?'

'Not unless you tell me, Richard.'

I went on, not pausing. 'I wouldn't be at all surprised if the writer of those letters, probably a baronet himself – Paul's grandfather or great grandfather – Sir Stephen Searle . . . I wouldn't be surprised if the collecting bug got hold of him after those paintings, and he switched to books. First editions. Amelia, my sweet, there could well be two fortunes in that library, the books and the paintings.'

She seemed to have gone pale at the thought. 'And Paul . . .' she whispered. The corners of her mouth twitched.

'Yes. It's very amusing, really. I can't wait to tell him in the morning. There he was, calling his brother an ignorant moron for seeing only the books and not the paintings, and he himself had seen only the paintings and not the books. Oh . . . isn't it lovely!'

She eyed me with her head on one side, smiling gently. 'Come to bed, Richard. You're tired. But you'd better go and wash your hands first. Those dusty books . . .'

'True. But d'you see how that —'

She interrupted. 'Get undressed and come to bed, Richard.'

I recognised the light in her eyes, and did exactly as I was told.

But not to sleep. I lay awake long after Amelia had turned over and buried her head in the pillow. As far as I could see, this would sort things out very neatly. It needed only Tessa's agreement that in her late husband's mind the words 'art collection' had included the library. Then the two brothers would be able to split the contents, paintings to Jeremy (the thirteen that were oils), the first editions to Paul, and the financial balance would be restored. Reasonably well, anyway. Then peace would enfold us.

On this thought, I slept.

It was Amelia who woke me. The dawn always jerks her into life. Our bedroom window faced south-east, so that the rising sun warmed the room with light, we not having drawn the curtains. She had been standing at the window, running her fingers through her hair, lifting it from her neck. But now she was very still.

'Richard . . .' she said, in a tense whisper.

I was at her side in a second. She pointed.

Jeremy was walking with heavy, ponderous and determined strides away from the house. He was heading for the wooden bridge, then pounding across it, and without hesitation he swung to his right. It was obvious where he was heading: for the path up through the trees to the gamekeeper's lodge. For a second he stopped, his arms fully extended by the weight of the two large suitcases he had been carrying. He put them down and straightened his back, turning to look up to the windows of the house, and clearly checking whether he'd been observed. He must have seen us, or somebody else at another window, because he put up his arm and made an obscene gesture with two fingers, I thought to me. Then he bent to the two cases, hefted them once more, and plodded on, taking the path towards the sunken garden. Twenty or so yards short of the four steps he disappeared behind the hedgerow.

'The damned fool!' I said in disgust.

It was particularly annoying that he should have made this move when I was in a position to clear Jeremy's worried mind of his financial problems. Paul, I guessed, would not do so until the last moment before the thunder-clouds burst over Jeremy's head. Otherwise, he'd have done so before now.

Cursing him, cursing both of them, I grabbed for my trousers. There was no time to make myself respectable, and I dragged them on over my pyjamas. My jacket on quickly . . . a check that I had the car keys . . .

'What're you doing, Richard?'

'He'll ruin everything. Don't you see? He's taking those blasted stone masks up to Jennie's cottage. Just to defy Paul. And just think what'll happen —'

'You don't need to get involved,' she protested.

I paused. There was really no desperate rush, I realised. It would take him all of twenty minutes to slog up that hill, carrying (I made a quick, vague calculation) about 120 pounds of stone masks. And I could do it in two minutes in the car.

'Does it really matter?' she asked worriedly.

'I think so. Can't you imagine the row there'll be . . . And I could just about be waiting for him in the car – and bring him back. Oh . . . I don't know. I can try to do something, anything.'

But when I got out into the corridor I realised I wasn't going to be able to avert anything, because Paul was ahead of me, and running down the stairs.

'Wait!' I called out.

He took no notice. I caught him on the drive outside, caught him by the arm and swung him round to face me. His face was white with fury. I could feel that he was shaking.

'Take your hands off me,' he said, his voice distorted.

'My car's easiest to get out,' I told him. 'There's really no rush. How long d'you think it'll take him? He'll have to stop to get his breath, get a rest. If he doesn't give himself a heart attack, that is. We can be there waiting for him – talk a bit of sense into him.'

'Talk! Y' don't think I'm going to *talk* about it? He'll just have to bring the bloody things back, that's what he's going to do. I'll see to that, and to hell with his bloody obsessions.'

'It's not all that terribly important, after all.'

He poked a finger at my chest, and stared at me as though I was mad. 'I am not . . . *not* having him dump those masks in the cottage. Do you understand that? And all for his damned stupid principles!'

I thought that there could be more to it than that. Jeremy had a strangely distorted personality, I already knew, and I'd attempted to reconcile his now undeniable fraudulent activities with his frantic belief in the sanctity of fairness. It could only be that his mind separated the two fields of his convictions, but subconsciously he felt he had to flaunt his code of fairness in order to balance his flouting of professional rectitude.

It was clearly, at that time, useless to present such a theory to Paul.

'Come on . . . come on!' he said wildly.

I was scraping the frost from the car windows. 'There's no hurry, you know. If we're too late, and he's unloaded the things into the cottage, we can simply bring them back in the boot.'

'It wouldn't,' he said, his teeth clenched, 'be the bloody same. He's got to be stopped. God knows what he'll think up next.'

I said no more about it. We got in the car, and the glass began steaming immediately. I glanced at my watch. It was eight minutes since I'd watched Jeremy disappear behind that hedgerow. He would need at least another seven or eight minutes, even if he managed to do it without collapsing.

As I turned the car, I caught sight of Jennie, wildly waving from the front door. She, too, had thrown on something quickly, and a padded anorak on top.

'Don't waste time with her,' said Paul tersely.

Calmly, I halted the car, and reached back to unlatch the rear door. She clambered in.

'What on earth's he up to?' she asked, leaning forward.

'Nothing to do with you, Jen,' said Paul shortly. 'What d'you want to come along for?'

She was angry with him. 'It's my place, isn't it? Or it's going to be. And that's where he's heading. The lodge. And with those two heavy suitcases. You don't have to tell me – he's got those stone faces in them. Hasn't he?'

She reminded me that I hadn't taken the time to check that. I turned to Paul. 'Did you check? In the gallery – did you put your head inside, and make sure?'

'I looked in,' he said flatly. 'Can't we get moving?'

'Take it easy, Paul.' I wasn't going to be hurried, if only with the objective of making the whole expedition less tense. 'And they'd gone? The masks?'

'Stripped out. Every one of 'em. What else could it be . . . we've got to stop him, stop him!'

I detected the movement as Jennie slid along the seat to be behind Paul. She put a hand on his shoulder. 'I don't mind if they're left there, Paul,' she said quietly. 'Let him do it. Let him have his bit of victory. It can't hurt. I'll phone Joe, and he'll drive over and take them away. Somewhere safe.'

Paul laughed. We were now on the move, but all the same, for him to laugh at that time, even in a flat and derisive tone, and to say what he then said, raised him several notches in my estimation.

'And he'd put 'em in an empty kennel and leave his dogs to guard 'em!'

'Can you', she asked quietly, 'think of anywhere more safe?'

And in that she was quite correct, I had to admit to myself, though the thought of around £180,000 worth of masks sitting out in an open kennel – dogs or not – was a little disconcerting. Even ludicrous.

I saw no reason for taking it fast, in spite of Paul's insistent, 'Come on! Come on!' I drifted the car along until we were opposite the rear of the cottage, and drew to a halt. They both scrambled out, leaving the doors swinging, then they raced each

108

other for the gap in the hedge, Jennie winning by a yard as she hadn't had to run round the car.

'Take it easy!' I shouted after them. 'There's barbed wire all over the place.'

But Jennie was already leaping over tangles of it, Paul nearly abreast of her now. I took it more steadily, having a good idea what I would find, and strolled round the cottage to what had been designated the front.

And there he was, though it was not as I'd expected.

Jeremy was sitting on one of the suitcases, the other standing beside him. His head was hanging wearily, and he was still gasping in air. He was wearing only trainers and jeans and a T-shirt, in spite of the frost, no doubt having anticipated the difficulty of the task he had presented to himself. And it seemed to have drained him completely. His face was red, perspiration streaming down it, the T-shirt clinging to him. His elbows were on his knees, and I noticed that his hands were shaking. The other two simply stood and stared at him, their anticipations not having conjured up this exact picture.

'It's locked,' Jeremy managed to say numbly, as though this possibility had not occurred to him. 'The bloody door's locked.'

'There's a spare key under the flowerpot,' Jennie reminded him severely. That he should have succeeded in the immense task of bringing up the two suitcases, to Jennie a virtual impossibility, but had finally failed through such a minor issue as the key . . . this seemed to annoy her. She was disappointed in him. Jennie spread her affections far and wide, and, to her, Jeremy deserved a share. And he had fallen short of her expectations. 'Oh really, Jerry!'

I reached down and lifted the flowerpot, just as Jeremy spoke in a dull tone of utter defeat. 'It's not there.'

There was no key under the pot.

'You could've borrowed mine,' Paul assured him, his voice cold. 'Seeing you were making off with my Olmecs, you might as well have done it without all this fuss. I'd have helped you, if it means that much.' And there was quite a sour note in his voice when he rounded off that sentence. 'We must all bow to your stupid obsessions.'

'But he's quite right, you know,' I said to the group. 'The spare key's not here.'

'What?' Paul was suddenly alert. His mind had been lagging. 'What d'you mean? I've got valuable stuff in there. Valuable to me. Is the door open? Have you tried . . .'

'D'you think I didn't?' asked Jeremy wearily.

I was beginning to feel uneasy about this situation. For the first time I gave the rather flimsy front door my undivided attention. I concentrated.

There was no handle to that door, and it naturally opened inwards. This meant that, on leaving, you would have to use the key, in the lock and half-turned, in order to draw it shut. Then you would turn the key to lock it, withdraw the key, and replace it where it had come from. Your pocket, or in this case, under the flowerpot. Then you would leave.

Yet it wasn't there. So – where was it?

I turned and faced them. 'Who's got a spare key to this door?'

'I told you – me,' said Paul. 'I come up here to paint.'

'Jennie?'

'Oh yes. I've got a key, of course.'

I couldn't see why it should be 'of course'. She read my expression. 'I come up to tidy it a bit for Paul. Sometimes.'

'So it's you . . .' Paul burst out. 'No wonder I can never find anything.'

I shook my head, silencing him. 'Something you need to know before you get married,' I said, smiling at Jennie. 'Never tidy for a man. We don't like it.'

I was trying merely to lighten the combined tension I could read in their eyes, no doubt generated by my attitude to the situation. But there was something strange – out of place – and in those circumstances I can't prevent myself from becoming concerned.

'You, Jeremy?' I asked.

He shrugged. 'Never needed one. I've got one somewhere, I think.'

'But you came all the way up here, with that weight . . .'

'I knew there'd be one under the pot.'

'But there wasn't?'

'No!' He seemed infuriated that he should have been defeated by such a minor obstacle. By now he'd had time to recover. The flush had left his cheeks and he was breathing more normally again.

I looked consideringly at their array of faces. They all three seemed uneasy, but that was because they couldn't understand what was worrying me. I turned away, and considered the window beside the door. It was the only window into the room, but nevertheless it was small. I went to it and attempted to see inside, but my bulk shaded it, and it was fogged with rain-cast dirt. When I drew back a little the bright sky behind me was reflected in the glass. I saw nothing.

'What the hell's all this?' Jeremy demanded.

'You might as well know, then perhaps you'll have something to suggest. The key was there, under the flowerpot, yesterday. I saw it myself. If it's been used since then, to open the door, and it hasn't been put back, which would've been the natural thing to do, then there's only one explanation.' I looked at their blank faces. 'It's not definite, I suppose, but the odds are it means the person who used it is still inside.'

For a few moments they were baffled, then they understood. The blood ran from Jennie's face. Jeremy got to his feet, stumbled, and recovered, then demanded, 'Who the hell could be inside, damn it? And why would he be lying low – when we're here? Why?'

'I don't know that.'

'Then what do we do?' The pitch of Jeremy's voice had risen. He was clearly exhausted, and was trembling on the edge of panic – or possibly from the chill of the sweat, now cooling rapidly.

I smiled to calm him. 'What we do is try to confirm it, one way or the other. I want all three of you to come round to the other side – the back. All right?'

They nodded. Jennie's eyes were huge. 'Me too?' she asked, waving her arm, trying to dismiss the situation. Her imagination was leaping round all over the place.

'All three,' I said. 'Come on. And you can leave the cases there, Jerry.'

This was another attempt at lightening the atmosphere, but he took me seriously, shrugging his shoulders. Paul grimaced.

I led the way to the other side of the building. Here was the flimsy door to the tiny kitchen. The other three were silent, a tight group. I said, 'There's not necessarily anything to worry about. Now . . . this is the kitchen door, Jennie?'

'Of course.'

'And I suppose you remember how flimsy the bolts are? You'll remember, you couldn't shift them for rust?'

'Yes. Yes, if you like,' she muttered. She stared at her feet.

'And it's fastened now?' I put a shoulder to it. It moved a fraction, but that was only the slack in the hinges. 'Paul – come and put your shoulder against it.'

111

'Why should I . . .' He was impatient.

'Just to confirm it *is* fastened. But don't go too heavy at it.'

Giving Jennie a shrug, and Jeremy a lift of the eyebrows, Paul did as I'd asked. 'So what?' he asked.

'Just to confirm it *is* fastened. Jennie, do you mind if I break it open?'

'Mind? Me? Why me?'

'You're the closest to being the owner. I need permission, otherwise it'd be breaking and entering enclosed premises. And I want all three of you to remember exactly what I do.'

'Why?' demanded Jennie. 'Why this daft pantomime?'

'So that you'll all three be able to confirm my actions, and why I'm taking them.' Playing safe, really. Just in case.

They stared at me, only now understanding that I was suspecting something strange, if not serious.

'Gerron with it,' said Paul. He was frowning. At least, he of all of us had something inside there that he considered important – his paintings – and he wasn't too happy at the thought of somebody having trespassed on the property.

So I leaned more heavily on the door. Nothing splintered. Simply, the bolts came away from the hasps, or rather, the hasps came out of the frame and tinkled on to the red quarry floor.

I turned. 'Stay where you are.'

By this time, my seriousness had impressed itself. They nodded wanly.

The kitchen showed no indication of having changed since I'd seen it last. The tap still dripped mournfully. The door into the sitting-room opened away from me, there being not the space for it to have opened into the kitchen. A touch of my shoulder creaked it open.

Now I could see much more easily than I'd been able to from outside. The floor space had been completely bare when I'd last seen it, so that there was no difficulty in detecting that the bulk of a large man was spread out in the centre. He was lying face down, but with his head twisted sideways, arms and legs spread. There was a dark patch, presumably blood, but colours were difficult to detect in the poor light. It spread sideways from the head, though not extensively. Head wounds do not bleed much.

I knelt beside him. My eyes were now becoming accustomed to the gloom, and I could detect that the side of his head, just above his left ear, was smashed in. Moving round, lowering my head as far as I could without having to support myself with my hands, I tried to examine his face. It was difficult. But, considering the bulk and the general shape, the bandy legs, the near-baldness, I was quite convinced that this was Charlie Pinson.

The ex-gamekeeper had come home to die.

I got to my feet and stood there, casting my eyes around and trying to impress the setting on my memory. I knew I wouldn't get the chance again. But there was very little to see. The floor, other than for the body, was completely bare. No ... there was one other item. Beside his right hand, an inch or two from his reaching fingers, there was lying a chunk of rock, still, I could just detect, with earth and bits of grass clinging to it.

Then I had to accept grimly that I was in the presence of violent death. It had been all very well to fling my imagination around and indulge in strings of fanciful theories involving the will and its multiple effects on people's lives. But now, abruptly, the situation had changed. This had to take precedence over paltry matters such as inheritance.

I didn't know how long I had been standing there, perhaps only seconds. There was still one more thing to be done. I crouched down and touched the back of Pinson's outstretched hand.

It was cold. Even, it seemed, colder than the air in the room, though that was impossible. But it meant to me that he'd been lying there all night.

I straightened, and walked out to the others. They were standing in an awkward, tight group. They must have been aware, from my extended absence, that I'd found something ... well ... unspeakable. Yet the question was stark on each of the three faces.

'It's Charlie Pinson,' I said flatly. 'He's dead, and it looks like violence.'

Jeremy looked about, as though desperate for a suitcase to sit on. But they were round at the front.

10

I wanted a word with the two brothers, so the answer to one question was obvious. It was Jennie who had to return to the house.

'Jennie,' I asked, 'do you drive?'

'Oh yes.' She seemed dazed. I didn't know whether I could trust her to remember what I had to ask.

'Then take the car – I left the keys in – and drive down to the house and call the police. Just say there's a dead man in the cottage here. That'll set the wheels rolling. Tell my wife, if you see her, that I'm stuck here, and why. She'll understand. If you see your mother, Tessa, tell her, if she's at all interested, that Pinson's dead, and that it'll be a police matter. If you see Mary —'

'D'you think I'm a silly kid?' she demanded, though her voice wasn't steady. 'I know what to do and what to say.'

'Yes. I'm sure you do. Now get along with you. Oh . . . and bring something back for Jeremy, or he'll get pneumonia.'

She stripped off the anorak and tossed it to him. 'It's his, anyway. I just grabbed the first thing.' Then she turned and ran to the Granada.

I said nothing to the other two until I'd watched her get away. The drive was too narrow for her to turn the car, so she had to take it into the lane and back it round. She did it smoothly and neatly, then she was away.

There was silence. The two others were waiting for something from me, not looking at each other but at their feet. I led the way round to the front of the cottage, aware that Jeremy had to have something to sit on. He headed straight for the suitcases, and sat heavily. There were two of them. Paul didn't avail himself of the other, but plodded around, backwards and forwards. I waited. My years in the police force had been good training in the use of patience. I wondered who would speak first.

It was Paul. 'Now what do we do?' His voice was toneless. He was lost in a situation he couldn't handle.

'We do nothing. Just wait here for the police to turn up.'

Jeremy lifted his head. 'Why can't we wait down at the house? It's stupid, just hanging around here.'

'Yes,' I agreed. I lit my pipe. The smoke barely drifted in the still air, and my breath was condensing with it. 'Very nearly as stupid as bringing a hundredweight of stone masks all the way up here, and well nigh giving yourself a heart attack from the look of you.'

'Tcha!' he said in disgust. 'I keep myself fit.'

'I'm certain you do. Physically, you're probably A1. It's mentally I'm doubtful about.'

He simply scowled. We were talking to avoid discussion on the death of Charles Pinson. Nobody wanted to talk about that. But Jeremy had to justify himself.

'I wanted the damned things out of the gallery. That's all. So's not to distract the man when he comes.'

'Comes?' I asked blankly. Playing it stupid, it's called, a useful interrogation procedure. I was surprised to find that this was what I was doing. Not directly. Not firing off questions. Just nudging things out into the open.

'When the agent can manage to get here,' said Jeremy, not willing to specify Sotheby's because that had originally been Paul's suggestion, and he was unwilling to concede anything, even a thought, to Paul.

Paul was moving around restlessly, turning his back on us, staring into the woodland as though we might have provoked movement from a hidden stag. He jerked a few angry words over his shoulder. 'We don't have to argue about that. They'll be here . . .' He shrugged, and was silent. He, at least, was using his common sense.

'Give them time,' I said.

'Why can't we go back to the house?' demanded Jeremy.

'You've already covered that,' I reminded him.

'And you dodged round it. Why not?'

'They'll want to see you – you in particular, Jeremy – about why you had to come up here, and this early in the morning, with two heavy suitcases.' I made a gesture. He interpreted it as: get on your feet. This was what I'd intended. He stood, and at a further gesture, moved away a yard or two.

115

I went over and stood between the two cases, bent, seized a handle in each hand, and picked them up. As I'd guessed – I reckoned I had half a hundredweight in each hand. I would have bet I was stronger than Jeremy, though perhaps not so fit. I'd not have wished to carry them far, and certainly not up a slope, one that had had me breathing heavily with no weight at all to carry about but my own.

I put them down again. 'That', I said, 'is why we've got to wait here. We can't take these cases away from here. Get it? They're evidence of why we're here at all, this time in the morning.'

I stared Jeremy in the eyes until he looked away, almost in shame. Oh yes, he could well be ashamed of himself now, sobered by the chill fact of a sudden death.

'I don't see that it's got anything to do with . . .' He made a gesture. 'With what's happened here.'

'Jerry,' I said, 'you've got to realise how things stand. This isn't just a case of Pinson getting in the cottage here, and dying a nasty and sudden death. I didn't want to say so, with Jennie here, but Pinson was murdered.'

'What!' snapped Paul.

'His head's bashed in. He didn't do that by slipping and falling. So you'd better get to terms with it pretty damned quickly, and realise that from now on *everything's* got to do with the police. And they'll be very interested to know why you, Jerry, did such a damn-fool trick as carrying these two cases up here. And try . . . try, Jerry, to make it sound convincing.'

'I wanted 'em out of the house!' Jeremy burst out, though only after a slight hesitation for thought. 'Out of that gallery.'

'Then, they will ask, why not simply into the hall? That would be out of the gallery. Why not in another room? Why not in your own bedroom upstairs? That would've been less of a physical strain than this.' I gestured, embracing the cases and the slope up which he'd brought them.

'Why're you asking all these questions?' demanded Jeremy heatedly. 'You're not a copper. Might've been, but you're not now.'

'I'm not asking questions, Jerry. All I'm doing is rehearsing you. It's a favour. You ought to be thanking me. Now you'll know what to expect.'

'I wanted 'em outa there!' shouted Jeremy wildly, and something heavy did stir, somewhere amongst the trees.

'But why here? They'll ask you that. Why here? And why now? There was no hurry, surely.'

'It's sorta Paul's place.'

'Unconvincing,' I said. 'D'you know what they'll think? They may not say it, but they'll think it.'

Jeremy eyed me suspiciously. 'What's that?'

I flung a wild idea at him, an unprepared possibility that I hadn't had time to consider. But it was necessary to jerk him into the realisation that the police weren't going to look at Pinson's body, ask a question or two, and conveniently disappear. They would dissect every scrap of information, relevant or not, from everybody even marginally involved, until something came together with a click. I shrugged.

'They could say you'd arranged to meet Charlie here, with that load, and hand 'em over for him to hide . . .'

'What the bloody hell . . .' Jeremy began, and Paul whirled round and stared at me blankly.

'And then you'd be able to claim that you'd left 'em here and they'd been stolen,' I went on firmly, giving them a taste of what they might have to face from officialdom. 'You knew this place wasn't secure —'

'You can keep your bloody mouth shut!' Jeremy shouted.

I smiled at him, but this did little more than make his face even redder. 'I am only preparing you for every possibility, however wild. And that's no more wild than the reality.'

Jeremy was silent, turning away and almost choking with rage.

Paul said, 'And what d'you know about it?'

I shrugged. I'd been here – I knew as much as they did. But Paul took it up. I'd given him ideas.

'I know you, Jerry. You've convinced yourself the watercolours are yours as well as the oils. You wanted the masks out of the way, 'cause you know they're mine, and there's no argument about that. Then you could get your man in – wave your hand around – and say: everything in this room. And you'd borrow money on what he'd see, including my watercolours. Then . . . could anybody say you'd sold what was mine? Oh no. You're deep, Jerry. Too deep. One of these days you won't be able to climb out. You'd raise money on what's not yours, and wouldn't bat an eyelid. But it'd be fraud. Isn't that so, Mr Patton?'

I nodded. 'It would be fraud.'

117

But why had I seen a sudden flash of satisfaction in Jeremy's eyes, and why did he turn away so that I wouldn't see it pleased him?

Paul laughed aloud, throwing his head back. 'So now where've you got to, Jerry? Explain why you brought this stuff up here, with the truth, and you'll be admitting to a planned fraud.'

Jeremy took a step forward, throwing his head back. Paul mockingly held up his palms in defence, still laughing. I said, 'Behave yourselves. They're here.'

At once, they were very still. Reality was now to the fore.

A police patrol car had pulled in from the lane. I walked round the cottage and went to welcome them, making a gesture that told Paul and Jeremy to remain where they were. There were two men in the car, the driver and a sergeant, both in uniform. The sergeant got out as I pushed through the gap in the hedge.

'What's this then?' he asked. 'A dead man, I'm told. Why send for us?' His eyes were running over the cottage beyond me. It was plain that he'd expected a natural death, an old lady or a man living on their own, perhaps.

'It's not at all straightforward,' I told him. 'This is an empty cottage, and there's a dead man inside. His head's been smashed in. Come and see.' His eyes ran over me. I went on, 'I touched the back of his hand. Stone cold. I touched nothing else.'

'Hmm! Yes.' He eyed me with his head on one side. 'Ex-police?'

'Yes. My name's Patton. Ex-Detective Inspector.'

'Just as well, perhaps. Show me.'

I gestured. 'This is what you'd call the back. I forced the door open. You'll realise, I did it with witnesses.'

'These witnesses – where are they now?'

'Two of them, waiting around the other side of the cottage. You'll see. And a third person. I sent her back to the house to phone. Ah . . . here she is now.' I nodded towards the Granada, which came to a halt facing their car.

'That woman getting out now?'

'Yes. We're all from the house down there.' I gestured. 'Penhavon Park.'

'I know what's down there.'

For a moment he stood and watched as Jennie got out of the car. I called out, 'Go round and wait with the others, Jennie.'

'You're personal friends?' asked the sergeant, having noted my use of her Christian name.

118

'We're staying here at the moment. My wife and myself.'

'This her now?'

Amelia was just getting out of the Granada. 'Yes. My wife, Amelia.'

'And you say you're staying here?'

'Yes. We came over for the day, yesterday, but we've been detained.'

He gestured towards the cottage. 'Show me.' He didn't waste one word.

Amelia was standing by the car. I indicated that the rest were round at the front, and she nodded. Then I led the sergeant to the door.

'I had to break in. There were suspicious circumstances. I have three witnesses to the fact that this back door was fastened.'

'What suspicious circumstances?'

I thought that this was too complicated to go into at the moment, so I said, 'I thought somebody had locked themselves inside, possibly illegally, and I could detect no movement.'

We stepped into the kitchen cautiously, not even disturbing the two rusty hasps lying on the floor. 'Through here.' He followed me, and I stood back, well clear.

'Is the electricity connected?' he asked.

'I don't know. I touched nothing. You can see well enough without.'

He didn't answer, but went down on one knee, examined the head without touching it, put a finger on the hand, as I had, and noted the chunk of rock lying there. Then he stood up. 'Let's get out of here.'

Outside, he said, 'I'll just call the station. If you'll go and wait with the others, please.'

He didn't call me sir, because I was not exactly a civilian. Strange, that. With my former rank, I'd have been sir, as a civilian I'd have been sir. But he couldn't decide what that made me now, so he'd compromised with: please. I was a nonentity, suspended between official procedures and civilian exclusion.

While he went back to his car, I walked round to the front. They were silent, in an awkward group, there being nothing to say. Amelia had her arm round Jennie's shoulders. Jennie had found a padded anorak of her own. She seemed lost and frightened.

'Richard,' said Amelia. It was a gentle reprimand for my having involved myself with sudden death.

'Does Mary know?' I asked.

'Yes. She was there in the hall.'

'What did she say?'

Amelia shrugged. 'Nothing. Just shook her head. It's hard to say what she was thinking. I expect it'll take her a while to decide her attitude on it.'

'And Tessa?'

'She fainted right off. We left Gladys trying to bring her round. All Gladys said was "Good riddance." She'd had dealings with Charlie Pinson, I'd guess.'

Jennie slipped herself free from Amelia's arm, and went to whisper with her brothers. I had felt she'd not wished to meet my eyes.

Then the sergeant came round the cottage, and stood still while he counted us. A squirrel, which had come lolloping along, quickly scooted up a tree, no doubt at the sight of a uniform.

'There's a team on the way,' he told our small group, his gaze running across us and back, but impersonally. 'I'll just take a few details while we wait,' he decided. 'Perhaps you'd help me with this, Mr Patton.'

It wasn't really a question, though he raised one hairy eyebrow. He'd decided on my title, I noticed.

I gave him a list of names, addresses, reasons for being at the house, though not, fortunately, reasons for being at the lodge. That could come later.

'Pinson?' he asked, when I mentioned Mary. 'Any relation to . . .' He jerked his head towards the cottage.

'Sister,' I told him. 'Mary Pinson. We drove her here.'

'You live . . .'

'Forty miles away.'

I had given him our address. He should have known its location, if he knew his county. I saw him write in Bridgnorth, and put brackets round it.

Then there was an awkward silence. He dared not trespass with any more questions into territory his superior would want to explore himself. We dared not speak amongst ourselves, and in any event nothing but banalities would present themselves, when we were all bursting to express wildly exciting and improbable theories.

In the end, I said, 'It's cold here. We've all dashed out without dressing properly, and, if the others are anything like me, they'll be thinking about a cup of tea and some breakfast.'

120

He stared at me blankly.

'I was suggesting', I explained, 'that there's no point in us staying here.'

He gnawed over this proposition. Then: 'The Chief'll want to see you.'

'I'll stay,' I told him.

Amelia made a gesture, but I shook my head. Whatever the others did, I would have to stay.

He frowned heavily over that. Then at last he nodded. 'All right. But you'll all have to hold yourselves prepared —'

'Nobody's going anywhere,' I cut in sharply, annoyed with his lack of initiative.

'I suppose not. Very well. But the Chief'll want to see you.'

He stood aside, though there was space for a regiment to stream past him.

I nodded. Paul and Jennie made a move towards the Granada, but Jeremy was hesitant, eyeing the suitcases.

'Leave them,' I said. 'It's all evidence.' I didn't say what they were evidence about, but I knew the senior officer would want to see it all.

Then I had a quick word with Amelia. 'There'll be a senior officer in charge, love, and I could get held up here. Try to keep them all from arguing.'

'You've had nothing to eat since . . .' She shook her head worriedly.

'I'll be all right.'

She glanced at her watch. 'If you don't turn up in half an hour, I'll be back with a flask of coffee.'

I kissed her on the forehead. 'Do that, love, and thanks. But I'll be back before then, anyway. Sure to be.'

She pouted, then followed the other three to the car. They were very subdued now, because officialdom had descended like a damp fog all around them. Jeremy led with a stride intended to convey confidence; Paul and Jennie whispered together, their heads close.

I stood and watched them leave, the patrol car having to reverse into the lane to allow the Granada to back round. Amelia waved, and I signalled back. Then there was silence, the sergeant not venturing a word, me not feeling like talking.

Then the car we'd been expecting arrived, a plain dark Toyota. Two men got out, one taller than the other. The shorter one was stocky, broad-shouldered, and walked with his head forward as though intending to demolish a barrier with it. I knew him – recalled him, rather, a constable in my days, now presumably a detective sergeant. Graham Tate. But his tall and lanky companion I had never met.

I saw the recognition in Tate's attitude. His head came up. He said something to his superior, who nodded. They came and stood in front of me, ignoring the uniformed sergeant.

'I'm told you're an ex-officer of police . . .' said the tall one.

'Detective Inspector,' I said.

'Right. Well. You'll be mister to me, you realise. Chief Inspector Phillips.' He didn't offer a hand. 'We've never met – I transferred in from Nottingham. I hope we'll have no trouble, Mr Patton. I do hope so.'

Trouble? I thought. Did he mean opposition from me – that I was so firmly placed as a civilian that I was not to be trusted?

'I shouldn't think so,' I said equably.

'Then tell me, in as few words as you can – the background to this.'

His expression had been unchanged from the moment I'd set eyes on him. Bleak. His voice had been hoarse, a tense whisper, as though he was forever containing his impatience, and with difficulty. And . . . gaunt, that would be the word for him. Three inches taller than me, but not much more than two-thirds of my weight, I guessed. His neck reared from between bony shoulders, like a fluted column supporting a choice example of sculpturing, which had turned out as a haggard bust, though during the carving of this the chisel had repeatedly slipped, chipping out a hawk-like nose above thin lips, and beside it declivities where cheeks might usually be found. His forehead was wide and craggy, his hair wild, and his ears might have been tacked on as an afterthought.

And white as marble, his face appeared, contributing to the imagery, a drawn white. I wondered whether he was well. He gave the appearance of being drained, his body held erect only with the greatest of effort. And yet, throughout the time I knew him, he seemed to be burning energy every concentrated second of intense activity. Mental, not physical. Certainly not physical; this seemed to be against his principles.

I told him, gesturing first towards the two suitcases. 'The elder son, Jeremy, brought those up here, almost as soon as it was

122

light, with the intention of locking them away inside this cottage. There'd been some family dissension about that.'

He brightened slightly at that. 'I'd like to hear what —'

'Let me tell you, first. D'you see that flowerpot, by the door? There was a key under that. I saw it there yesterday. It wasn't there when he got here . . . Jeremy, that is . . . so he couldn't get inside. I, we, three of us got here, perhaps a minute or two after he managed it. He was sitting exhausted on one of the suitcases.'

'Exhausted?'

'He'd carried them up from the house.'

His eyes were intent on my face. He didn't question the reference to exhaustion.

I went on, 'Because the key wasn't there, and the door was locked, I thought it might mean that somebody had used it to get in, and that they hadn't left. There was no sound from the cottage – which, by the way, is not lived in, though the younger son, Paul, uses an upstairs room as a studio. He's an artist.'

He nodded. Said nothing.

'So I broke in by way of the back door, round the other side. Three people witnessed that. I went inside and found a dead man with his head bashed in. I believe, though I've only seen him once, that his name's Charles Pinson. I touched nothing, but left the house and sent someone to phone.'

He waited. I had nothing to add.

'And that's it?'

'Yes. The basics.'

'And what's so special about the suitcases?'

'They're full of stone Olmec masks.'

He stared at me as though I was mad. 'Of what?'

I didn't answer. Let him see for himself. He walked over and stared at the cases. Then, deciding that touching them in no way destroyed any evidence, he reached out to pick one up. It didn't move.

'What the hell . . .'

He took a more purposeful stance, and heaved again. It lifted. He tried the other. It was just as heavy. He shrugged, and glanced at me.

'And he carried these up from the house? You did say up?'

'Yes. It's a steady slope. You could walk it from there, briskly, in under a quarter of an hour.'

'What the hell is he, an all-in wrestler?'

He'd offered me a tiny chink in the severity of his attitude. I didn't take it, but went on quietly. 'He's an accountant. Due to the recent death of his father, he's now Sir Jeremy Searle.'

He didn't react to that, but lowered one of the cases on to its side and tried the catches. It wasn't locked. The lid came up. He stared. 'What did you call the things?'

'They're called masks. I suppose they're death masks. About 1000 BC. Mexican or something.'

'Valuable?' He looked back over his shoulder.

'I'm told – the one you've got in your hand could be worth eight to nine thousand pounds. Give or take. And there're nineteen altogether.'

He got to his feet and stood staring down at them. 'And he was going to shut them in there?' He jerked a thumb at the cottage.

'So it seems.' I wasn't going to commit myself as to any of Jeremy's intentions or motivations.

'There's no security. You got in . . .'

'I just leaned against the back door.'

'Well, then.' He allowed a pause to develop, then ran his hand through his hair, a coiled, jumbled mass of blond curls. I wondered whether he usually wore a hat; but it probably wouldn't stay on.

'They all crazy around here?' he asked without interest.

'We've been here only a day,' I said. 'My wife and myself. Yes, they're certainly crazy.' I was trying to encourage him.

His mouth twisted and the haggard cheeks drew aside to permit a distorted smile. 'We'll see. We'll see. Get down there, yourself. You'll be walking?'

I had no alternative. 'Yes.'

'I'll just have a quick look, and I'll be down. The Scene of Crimes team'll take over up here.'

'I expect they will.'

And when that happened, nobody – and that included Chief Inspector Phillips himself – would be able to enter the cottage until they'd drained it of every scrap of evidence.

'And don't imagine', he added, turning back, 'that I'll give you much time to rehearse their statements.' He nodded bleakly.

I headed for the path down through the trees.

124

11

I try to persuade myself that I think better when walking. This is not so, however, because I always find myself involved in what is around me. That morning there was far too much to distract me down the woodland path. I naturally used this route, as a short-cut. Jeremy, no doubt, coming up in the other direction, had been completely absorbed in the simple process of putting one foot in front of the other. But I could afford to cast my eyes around.

The low sun had now cut through a thin mist that had been clinging to the ground, and was sparkling through the wet trees, glinting in the grass where the frost had not quite melted. The surface shimmered as the light breeze moved the branches. They had an uncertainty, a tentative new life, in which they danced in the sun.

I stopped, and looked back up the slope behind me. Long shadows chased around my feet. All about me was a gentle rustle as the trees shook the frost away. I walked on, the shadows chasing me, and as I at last came in sight of the house it seemed that I had arrived at a wrong destination, that I had walked into a different setting.

The grim grey stone house now presented a warm, brown and placid face, bathed by the early sun, even a welcoming face. With the wild, sunken garden ahead of me, and the four stone steps rising beyond it, the effect of placid dignity was superb. If I'd only brought my camera! But one doesn't expect photographic opportunities to arise during the reading of a will. It was a pity about the non-photogenic motor vehicles on the drive, especially the yellow and black Citroën 2CV.

So Joe had arrived.

I plodded on, my mind now dwelling on a pint of tea and a breakfast consisting hopefully of half a dozen rashers of bacon and two fried eggs. At the four stone steps, I paused. There, pounded through the thin ice layer and into the mud beneath were Jeremy's footprints, at top and bottom. His trainers, with the cleated soles. If DCI Phillips treasured any idea that the feat could not have been accomplished on foot by Jeremy – and that he'd brought the cases up in a car – there was the proof. Right footprint at the top, left one heavily in the mud at the bottom. I therefore carefully walked round them, plodded on, and as I emerged from the tall hedgerow and in sight of the house I was very nearly thrown on my back by Jake and Sheba, their leads flying behind them.

Amelia, laughing, was running behind them.

'How do they do it?' she cried, as she approached. 'I didn't see you coming, not till the very last second. But they knew. They were off, and took the leads right out of my hands.'

'They no doubt heard my stomach rumbling,' I told her, looking up from my crouch.

She was suddenly very serious. 'But we've got nothing to laugh at,' she said gloomily. 'Trouble seems to follow you around.'

I grimaced, took the two leads, and we headed round to the side of the house, hungrily to the kitchen door and the breakfast I'd promised myself.

The kitchen was crowded. Nobody had had any breakfast, and they were all demanding tea, at the very least. This, Gladys was providing, but she insisted that they all should go and clean up a little, and appear tidily in the dining-room like ordinary civilised people, where she would serve breakfast as usual.

Joe declared he had eaten, and required no more than a large mug of tea. He kissed Jennie delicately, slapped her bottom, and said he would see her later. He ushered her out of the door, waited until the rest had left, then stood with his back to the door and his eyes on me.

I said, 'Why did you send them all away, Joe?'

He winked at me. 'Wanted to have a quiet word with you.'

'Then sit yourself down. That all right, Gladys?' I asked, this being her kitchen.

She nodded, her eyes on Joe, as though measuring him to see if he deserved Jennie. She gave no evidence of her thoughts on this. Mary, I saw, had left with the others.

Joe sat beside me. It appeared that he wished to talk, confidentially.

'Some difficulty?' I asked him.

'I don't know.' He cradled the mug in his hands. 'I'm here,' he said at last. 'Jennie phoned me – I'm only ten minutes away. So I ran over in the car. That's why I'm here.'

'That's your Citroën?'

'Yes. That's mine.'

'Not much room in there for half a dozen Dobermanns,' I commented.

'It's held up so far.' He cocked his head. 'Might manage something bigger, later on.'

'You'll need every penny of Jennie's money to make that cottage habitable. I hope you realise that.'

'Don't fish, Mr Patton, please. I know what I can do and can't. The cottage will be lived in, and by us.'

'If she still wants to live there.'

'Why wouldn't she?' He raised his eyebrows.

'There's been a violent death in the place,' I said flatly.

'I don't think that'd put her off,' he said with confidence. 'If I know my Jennie. And there'll have been lots of deaths in those two cottages over the years. The odds are that some of 'em could've been violent. That worry you, does it?'

'Not a bit.'

'Then what's getting at you, Mr Patton?'

I shrugged. 'Your plans. How they might be affected. You know. It's none of my business, anyway.'

'You're too right there.'

'But you wanted to ask me something,' I reminded him.

He eyed me cautiously, as though wondering whether to trust me. He put on a casual tone. 'I was just wondering if that copper who's come here'll want to ask me any questions. 'Cause if so, I'd like to get it over and done with, then I can get back to my dogs.'

'Now why would he want to ask you anything, Joe? You don't come into it, surely.'

He put down his empty mug, ran his fingers through his hair, and grimaced at me. 'Oh yes, I do,' he said gloomily.

Gladys put a plate of sausage and two eggs in front of me. 'You too, Joe?' she asked.

'Thanks, but I've had some breakfast.'

'Thought you might fancy another.' She shrugged, pursing her lips.

127

They all knew each other around there. I felt Amelia leaning against my shoulder. She had no intention of missing one word. I dug into my breakfast.

'How do you come into it, Joe?' I asked, as placidly as I could make it sound. But I didn't like the sound of it.

'I was up there, last night. Up by the lodge, you know.'

I turned to stare at him. 'What time?'

'Around eleven, I'd guess.'

'Why?'

'Came to see if Jennie was around.'

'Why did you do that?'

'To kiss her goodnight.'

I watched as Gladys produced another breakfast for Amelia, as it was clear she wasn't going to miss a word of this. I chewed for a few moments, waved my fork. 'And you expected her . . .'

'We did that, most nights. Or sometimes she'd come to my place, and stay over. We hadn't set up anything for last night, though, but I drove over just in case she turned up.'

'But . . . hold on a sec . . . why there, of all places? Why not down at the house?'

He shrugged, then jutted his lower lip. 'Her mother . . . her Tessa-mother, she objected to us kissing and canoodling, as she put it, under her window.'

'Then why not go indoors?'

'She said I smelt of dogs. D'you think I smell of dogs?' he asked Amelia.

'How would I know? Richard probably does.'

'Hmm!' I said. 'And did Jennie turn up?'

He stared at the wall opposite to him. 'No.'

'So you went away?'

'Not straight away. Waited a bit.'

I thought about it, then said, 'Why're you telling me this?'

'I saw somebody,' he said, after a slight hesitation. 'I saw somebody, and I wondered if I'd gotta tell that policeman.'

I contemplated half a sausage on my fork. 'You saw somebody . . . where?'

Joe hesitated again. Then he went on, committed.

'I'd parked a bit of the way down the drive, sort of out of the way, and walked back. Usually, I'd walk round to the other side of the cottage and wait for Jennie there. But I thought I saw a sort of light, inside the place. Sort of like a torch, only it wasn't moving. You know. Not like somebody walking about.'

I nodded. He went on, 'Well, it wasn't like that. Didn't move at all. I reckoned it had to be a torch, right enough, but lying on the floor. You know.'

'You were . . . where were you at that time?'

'Gone round to the other side. The front.'

'You didn't say that.'

'That's what I'd done.'

It occurred to me that Joe, if he told it like this to DCI Phillips, would find himself tied in knots. But Joe was a dog-breeder, not a talker. I nodded.

'You didn't make that clear.'

'Well, I had. *Then* I saw the light.'

'You saw it through the window?'

'I didn't walk up to it. I was way back, at the top of the pathway, where Jennie would come. If she came. Which she didn't.'

'And you saw the light?'

'I didn't see it come on, if that's what you mean. It *was* on, only I hadn't realised. The moon, you see. Thought it was kind of a reflection.'

'I understand.' I was trying to treat him gently. Phillips wouldn't waste any patience on him. 'What happened then?'

For the first time, he hesitated. He stared down at the empty mug on the table. 'I looked back, down the track, and there was still no sign of Jen – so I kind of strolled up to the window to have a look.'

'You thought it might be Jennie?' So he *had* gone to the window.

'No. Never occurred to me.'

'Looking over the place that was going to be hers, perhaps?'

'No.' This denial was softer, gentler. He smiled. 'Would you expect her to? On her own, like? Nah! If that was what she wanted to do . . . well, ask yourself . . . she could've made a good guess I'd be there. If I wasn't, she'd have waited for me – outside.'

Amelia shuddered beside me. 'You wouldn't have got me up there, not at night.'

'Especially inside,' said Joe, a note of triumph in his voice at Amelia's support.

I hesitated to go on. This was the kind of thing that Phillips would want to hear, and he wouldn't be happy if he heard that Joe had tried it on me, first. I wasn't sure I wanted to make him happy.

'So you went to have a look through the window,' I suggested.

'Looked back down the path first,' he repeated, keeping it strictly in sequence in his mind. 'No sign of anybody . . . so I went and had a look.'

'And?'

He lifted his shoulders and allowed them to slump back. 'That's the point. That's it. After all – I couldn't see who it was or what was going on. As I'd guessed, that torch was lyin' on the floor. All I could see was feet. Moving about. That was all. So I reckoned it was nothing to do with me, and I cleared off.'

'You drove off home?'

'Well . . . not straight away.'

'Oh? What, then?'

He shook his head. 'Did I say – my car was a bit down the driveway? Yeah. I said that. Well . . . I got to it, and I was opening the door, and you know the way you sort of turn. Well, that's what I did, and I saw somebody walking in from the lane. Rollin' a bit, you know, like he'd just come from the Red Lion in the village. It'd be about the right time for it. An' I knew who it was. Not much light, but I knew. That louse, Charlie Pinson, that's who it was. On his way home.'

He stared inwards at the memory.

'Home?' I murmured, more to myself than anything. Then I realised. 'So *that's* Corrie Lane!'

'Yeah. He lives up there.' He looked startled. 'Lived.'

I stared at my hands on the table, turned them over and considered them again. Then I asked, 'Did you get the impression he was heading for a meeting – an appointment he'd made at the cottage?'

'How would I manage to guess that?'

'The way he walked in from the lane. Confidently, or paused and thought about it? Hesitated . . . hell, Joe, you know what I mean.' He didn't reply. I tried to be more specific. 'Did he turn directly in? Up from the village and into the drive without hesitation . . .'

'You don't have to flog it to death.'

'You didn't seem —'

130

'I was tryin' to remember. I'm doing my best to get it right, Mr Patton. An' he wasn't coming up from the village, he turned in from the other way, from up the lane.' He turned and stared directly at me. 'Not from down it, Mr Patton. From up it.'

It was a small reproof for my implication as to his intelligence. I stared at him. 'All right. Point taken. Go on, Joe.'

He said, 'As though he'd seen a light in the cottage and decided to have a look-see.'

'But he wouldn't be able to see the light, from the end of the drive.'

'*That*', said Joe tersely, 'is what I'm tryin' to say, if you'll let me get a word in. The lane bends higher up, an' there's an old gate. He could've seen that living-room window from up there. If he'd come up from the pub and stopped for a quick . . . stopped to lean on the gate.'

'It is now', I assured him, 'a very clear picture. Then what?'

'He pushed through the hedge an' went round the other side of the cottage – and I heard a door open and close.'

He sat back. It seemed he had finished.

I sighed. 'Then what did you do?'

'I started the car and drove off.'

'They'd have heard it – inside.'

'So what if they did? One finished up dead, and the other isn't going to say anything.'

I was silent, knowing what he wanted me to say, but trying to force him into asking it direct. Amelia nudged me, observing Joe's embarrassment. I reached over and touched her arm, and she sat back.

'So I want to know, Mr Patton,' said Joe at last, 'if I've got to tell this to that police chap who's running the show.'

I had my answer ready, but I looked up first at Gladys. It would be better, I thought, if she didn't hear this. She was very quick. 'I'll just pop up and see if the mistress wants anything. Help yourselves if you fancy anything else.' Then she was out of the door, and I heard her pattering along the hallway.

I got up, and went round the other side of the table, so that I could sit facing Joe. I sat, and Amelia got up to see whether there was any more tea in the pot.

'You're wondering who you might be implicating?' I suggested.

'Not really. I didn't see enough.'

'So – what's the difficulty?'

He looked down at his empty mug, staring at his fingers as he twisted it around. 'I don't want to get involved.'

'Naturally. But you wouldn't —'

He cut me short. 'The whole village knows that I'd have killed him myself, and happily.'

'And why is that?'

His head shot up, his eyes abruptly fixed on mine. 'Because I hated his guts. That place I've got . . . it's a bit of a cottage – like the one up by the gate, only on its own and better kept up. I rent it, and a bit of land, from Don Martin. Pinson works . . . worked for Don, and *he* wanted it for his second girl, who's pregnant again. He was on at his boss all the time to chuck me out. It's a month's notice, either way. An' I had a fight with him at the Red Lion.' He was silent, looking down at his clenched fist.

'Over that?'

'No. But it put a bit extra into it.' He gazed reminiscently at his knuckles, which I now saw were grazed.

I waited, but he was stubbornly silent. 'Well?' I demanded.

'He called Jennie a little bastard.'

I tried to sound casually dismissive. 'He'd be the one to know.' I knew, though, that Joe wasn't going to worry unduly about details like that. It was an outmoded word.

He glared at me. 'He said it'd suit me fine, getting in with the quality, as he called it. Jen being Sir Rowland's by-blow. That was when I hit him.'

'Thereby', I said gently, 'lending authenticity to the accusation.'

'Now you just listen here, Patton —'

'No, Joe. *You* listen. You're building up your own motive.'

'I'm not having anybody —'

'Will you listen, damn you! Chief Inspector Phillips, if he doesn't manage to keep it all confined to this house, and these people, is going to have to search further, and dig out motives. And from what I hear, he'll have a field-day of it. There'll be dozens of people who positively loathed Charlie Pinson.'

'What you gettin' at?'

'You've got no evidence to give him. You saw nothing but feet, and a torch. You saw Pinson, but we *know* he went in there. There's nothing you can say that would help the DCI. But if it came to the point of him asking you – then you'd be advised to tell the truth, as you've told me.'

132

He brightened, then frowned heavily. 'D'you think he'd believe me?'

'Well, now . . . that's a different thing. There was one bit of it . . .'

'What? Such as what?' he challenged.

'You being in the habit of driving over here at night, and Jennie walking up that pathway through the wood . . . and *that* for a goodnight kiss! I ask you!'

'It wouldn't be just one.'

'Of course not, Richard,' said Amelia.

'However many,' I assured him. 'Phillips wouldn't understand that. Laddie, by the time a policeman gets to Chief Inspector, he's had all the romance knocked out of him. He'd laugh in your face.'

He couldn't decide whether I was being serious or flippant. His expression hovered between humour and rejection.

'*You* understand,' he said at last, though whether statement or query I couldn't decide.

'I didn't make it to Chief Inspector,' I explained.

'Then I . . .'

'You sit tight at your little cottage, and if you've got any talking to do, you do it to the dogs.'

He scrambled to his feet. 'I'll just have a word with Jen . . .'

'No, you will not. Don't be a fool. Keep out of it. I'll have a word with Jennie later.'

'Yes . . . well . . . thanks.'

'Oh . . . and Joe . . .'

He stopped, peering over his shoulder. 'What now?'

'Yesterday, when we went up to the cottage, you looked at it as though you'd never seen it before. But if you'd been meeting Jennie . . .' I left it as a question.

He grinned. 'With Jen there, I wasn't going to be looking at a blasted cottage, now was I?'

'I reckon not, Joe. I reckon not.'

Then he was out of the door and heading for his car. I got to my feet to go and watch him drive away, praying that Jennie would not be waiting for him. But it wasn't Jennie, it was Detective Sergeant Tate, leaning against the Citroën and smoking a cigarette. I saw them speaking together, then Tate made a gesture with his hand, and they went together to the front door. Sensibly, Joe seemed to raise no objection.

It was clear that Chief Inspector Phillips was in complete control of the situation.

133

There being nothing to detain us in the kitchen, we went through to the hall to find out what was going on.

It was safe to assume that Tessa would be up in her room, and that Joe would probably, at that time, be telling his story to Phillips, so I had a fair guess as to where the others would be. A policeman, a DC, was standing placidly at the drawing-room door, the implication being that this was the room that had been lent to Phillips to use for his initial interviews. The DC, seeing my hesitation, asked, 'Would you be Mr Patton, sir?'

I said I would.

'Ah. Then, the DCI was asking for you, and somebody said you were in the kitchen, getting some breakfast. But here you are now, and he asked if you'll make yourself available.'

'I'm available any time.'

'He's got somebody in with him right now. But the rest are in that room there – I think they call it the library. He's seen them. If you wouldn't mind waiting in there, I'll give you a shout . . .'

'Don't shout too loud, then,' I said. 'There're already a lot of shattered nerves around here.' Just to lighten the mood.

'Is that so, sir?' he asked blandly.

I realised that I'd been indiscreet. This was no rooky constable. He would repeat anything he heard to his officer-in-charge.

Nodding to him, I turned away, and ushered Amelia ahead of me into the library.

Apart from Tessa, they were all there, Mary and the three youngsters. I couldn't prevent myself from thinking of them in that way, as really, apart from Jennie, neither of the other two had matured to adulthood. Jennie was possibly the most stable, this having settled on her from the time her wedding had suddenly become feasible, and not far in the future. Jeremy, I thought, would never mature, and Paul, though more responsible than Jeremy, could be very tricky. But the unstable facets of his personality appeared only when Jeremy entered into his life, and affected the way he wished it to go.

They were at the table, playing cards.

Paul lifted his head. 'They've been asking for you.'

'Yes, I know.' I was trying to decide what game they were playing. It was probably something they had adapted, over the years, from another card game. Mary had possibly invented it, when they were very young.

I wandered over to the window. Nothing was happening outside. Not much inside, either.

'Has he seen you all?' I asked.

Jeremy glanced up. 'Oh sure. There's nothing we can tell 'em, is there?'

'I don't know.'

'Well – stands to reason,' Paul said, shrugging. 'It's nothing to do with us – it was up at the lodge.'

There was a window seat. I sat on it, but it was low, and my knees stuck up.

'It could still involve the family,' I told him. Told them.

Jeremy's head came up. They were all still, now. Mary had put down her cards. They'd been playing only to keep their minds from it.

Paul had spoken casually, obviously attempting to cool Jeremy's aggression, which was becoming habitual. I could understand that Jeremy, now the head of the house, might have been practising the exercise of his new authority, and told DCI Phillips one or two things about the sanctity of the individual and the rights of privacy. If so, I could imagine that it had had absolutely no effect.

'This crime', I said, not wishing to use the word murder, 'was committed in the grounds. Not far in, but nevertheless on Penhavon property. It's only natural that the Chief Inspector would want to clear the field of the obvious suspects before he spreads his nets further afield.'

'What does *that* mean?' demanded Jeremy. 'Obvious suspects! What've any of us got to do with that Pinson creature?'

'Nothing, I should hope,' I replied equably, smoothing the emotional creases.

'It all seems obvious to me,' said Paul. 'He was probably stewed to the eyeballs, staggering up the lane from the Red Lion, staggering home.'

'You know where he lived, then?' I asked.

'Corrie Lane,' put in Mary quickly. 'You remember, Richard. He said that.'

'Yes,' I agreed. She was protecting her brood impartially.

'And that's Corrie Lane,' Jeremy told me. 'The one at the top of the drive. And why the hell we've got to talk about *him*, I don't know. It's obvious to anybody who's got eyes to see. Obvious to everybody. I bet he had a fight in the Red Lion, and somebody

135

followed him up the lane, and he went into the lodge . . . why the devil do we have to talk about him?'

It was he who was doing most of the talking. I eased things along.

'If there was a fight, the police will find out. There'll be a post-mortem examination, and the pathologist'll be able to say how much alcohol Pinson had got in him, and find any signs of a fight. It's all standard procedure.'

'Do we *have* to talk about this?' Amelia asked. 'It's not very pleasant.'

'And we were playing cards,' said Paul. 'Until you came in.' It was as though I'd ruined the day for them.

Jeremy threw his cards face up on the table. 'What's it matter what we do? Why don't they go away and leave us in peace?'

It was at this point that the door opened and the constable from outside said to me, 'Mr Patton . . . the DCI would like to see you now, please.'

In the hall, behind him, was standing Joe. He made a gesture, and Jennie ran forward, beating me to the door. The constable said, 'If you'd just wait inside the library for a moment . . .' Raising his eyebrows to Joe.

The DCI had been wisely waiting until he had all the statements presented to him, before he allowed anyone to go away. He would by that time know whether he had any contradictions requiring reconciliation, or untied ends hanging around loose.

I was next. I would be the last.

I rubbed my chin, which was bristly. Hopefully, after this interview, I might get time for a bath and shave, then I'd feel a bit more human. Now, I walked inside with what confidence I could muster.

12

Phillips had made himself at home. He was lounging back in one of the bigger chairs, legs spread out in front of him, and smoking a cigarette. There was a low table to one side of him, on its surface an ashtray and a used cup and saucer. On his other side was a larger table, scattered with the reports that had already come down from the lodge. And there was a tape recorder.

Beyond the table, and occupying a prime position on the glorious rug in front of a barely red fire, were the two suitcases. They had not been opened, or if they had – just to check – they had been closed again.

'Sit down, will you, Mr Patton.'

I took the seat opposite to him. He gestured towards the tape recorder. 'We move on, Mr Patton. Things will have changed since your time, no doubt. Technology triumphs. A few more years and I'll be redundant, and electronic probes will search your brain in order to sort the truths from the lies and evasions. Aren't you glad you're out of it?'

'It'd save manpower,' I agreed. 'And leave you chaps free to concentrate on motorists.'

'For an ex-copper, you're a bit anti-police.' He frowned. 'Or so it seems to me.'

I stared at my pipe, turning it in my fingers. 'More violent deaths on the roads than off it,' I commented. I didn't know why we were talking about this. 'Everybody driving about in their own lethal weapon these days. Lots of scope there for you.'

He twisted his lips sourly, but his cool grey eyes were intent. He was simply playing himself in, deciding how best to tackle me, wondering where my sympathies leaned. His face was tracked with lines of fatigue. It was quite possible that he'd been on duty for twelve hours already, and once settled into this new case he knew he'd have to see it through. You can't pass on impressions to a relief officer; you can't explain feelings. It's not very often that a senior officer finds himself faced by simple facts. Nothing is ever simple, nothing obvious, in a murder case.

'You'll have noticed the tape recorder isn't switched on,' he said flatly. From his tone, I could tell he wasn't happy about using it at all. 'They're going mad on taping, now. Future evidence, that sort of thing. How tough we might have been – how suggestive. I tell you, I don't like it.'

He left that hanging, perhaps for my observations on the subject. I said, 'There's nothing like the odd note scribbled on a shirt cuff. And anyway, the recorder doesn't record your thoughts. Unless', I suggested, 'you confide your inner thoughts to it.'

Nothing entered his face that might be described as an expression. I'd intended it as a pleasantry.

'So you can see my difficulty.' This was not a question. 'Once I switch it on, that's an interview. It goes on paper, later on, for those of us who can still read. That's why we're here, chatting and wasting time. You can help me. Short-cut things for me. I don't want to make it formal, that's the point. Okay with you?'

He was quite casual about it, looking away as he pressed the end of his cigarette to extinction in the ashtray. Then he looked back at me sharply. 'You've been here – how long?'

'Yesterday. We arrived here, Miss Pinson, my wife and myself, just about midday. Have you spoken to them?'

'I haven't had the time. I doubt it'll be necessary. Visitors. Go on. You came for the reading of the will, I understand? Wills!' he said with disgust. 'Trouble follows on their tails. But I can't see how this thing connects with the will. Anyway, you carry on.'

'The will', I said, 'of the late Rowland Searle. Sir Rowland Mansfield Searle, Baronet.'

'I know. And the whole thing sounds crazy to me. This to one, that to the other, and no logic to it. And now this character called Joe . . .' He snapped his fingers. 'Can't remember his other name. You get my point about written notes?'

'I can't help you. I don't remember hearing his surname.'

'Anyway . . . this Joe comes to me with some fantastic tale about hanging around for Jennie – after eleven at night – for a goodnight kiss, heaven help us. And the rest . . . the stories they tell! It's all *got* to be true. It's too stupid to be otherwise. Everything's chaotic, random, disorganised. It's got to be the truth, and it leaves me nowhere.'

He was silent, morose.

'Aren't you going to switch it on?' I asked.

'What? Oh – the recorder. No. Not yet. What'd be the point? You've already rehearsed this Joe person on what he should say, and you've probably warned the rest.'

'Joe asked for my advice.'

'Which was?'

'If you asked, to tell you.'

'And where did that get me?'

'I don't know what you asked him.'

'All right. I'll tell you, Patton. I'm convinced that what he told me is true. He couldn't have invented it. So he saw someone with a torch at the cottage. Right. I believe it. And that person with the light, the one who was there first, he was the one who killed Pinson, when he arrived later. Nothing could be more straight-forward.'

'Why don't you switch it on?' I asked again.

'Because you've got nothing to tell me, nothing that I don't already know, and you've had time to get yourself acquainted with these people, and you probably know all about Charles Pinson's place in their various lives, and you wouldn't want one of them – any single one of them – to be charged with the murder of Charles Pinson, and . . .' He took a breath. 'And you'd lie to me with the experience your police service has given you in lying, and I'd get nothing anyway. Nothing.'

'And you certainly wouldn't dream of asking for my advice?' I suggested.

'Certainly not.' He hesitated. 'Not on tape, anyway.'

'Off it, though?'

My experience, since I'd retired, had been that serving police officers tended to treat me with suspicion, and resented sugges-tions. They took it as a criticism of their abilities, and I can't say I blame them. But this man was different, or he used a different version of crafty technique. With all the known facts already before him, he would know that I dared not deviate from the truth, anyway. Yet he sincerely recognised that I had a lead on him, and this could be his method of digging out my thoughts.

His offhand attitude was a complete sham. He was baiting a trap.

Then he said, quite sincerely, 'I don't want your advice. I want . . . will you listen . . . can you visualise that scene last night, as the Joe person told it? The light in the cottage, the torch probably lying on the floor, Pinson walking in on it – whatever it was. Can you *see* it, Patton?'

'Very clearly,' I assured him.

He sighed. Then he burst out, 'Facts, facts, evidence, statements! Christ, I get nothing else. And nobody tries to *imagine* anything. It's not real enough for them. D'you think I'm in the wrong job, Patton? I'm beginning to wonder about that. And here I am now, waiting for a fact. One fact. Then I think I'll have a clear picture. There's something wrong, Patton. Wrong. And I can't visualise the situation clearly enough to spot it.'

'It's no good telling me.'

'I suppose not.' He paused. Stared at the ceiling. 'Nice carving,' he observed. Then he lowered his eyes and stared at me. 'Inspector Thomas is on leave,' he told me. 'Works with me, usually. *He* sees things.'

'He gets hallucinations?' I asked blandly, wondering about Phillips's own mental stability. But he didn't react.

'He can imagine things – how things were. But he's not here.'

'And I am?'

'Precisely. And Tate's useless at this. I was just wondering if you get the same picture as I do. Because mine doesn't make any sense. Ah . . .' He twisted his head at a tap on the door, and nodded as Sergeant Tate entered. Not glancing at me, Tate handed a sheet of paper to the Chief Inspector.

'That what you wanted, sir?'

Phillips glanced at it. 'Seems like it. Thank you, Sergeant.'

Tate at last looked at me. I was not supposed to seem so relaxed. I flicked him a smile, a twist of the lips, but he failed to respond.

'That's all, Sergeant, thanks.'

Tate went out. Phillips waited until the door was shut, then he said, 'This is what I've been waiting for.'

'So we can have the tape on?' I asked.

'By no means.'

'You wouldn't want to record the two of us doing this visualising act?'

'*Would* it record it? A mental image? Nah! Leave the thing switched off. Now . . .'

I waited quietly as he read the report carefully, then he looked up, grinning. It changed his face completely. It came alive. The tiny, sunken cheeks crept out and climbed towards his eyes, pouching them, and they flushed. The eyes gleamed at me from their reluctant slits.

'Got it!' he said, with obvious relief.

I wondered whether he was going to share it with me, whatever it was.

'A note from Potter,' he said. 'He's our forensic man, up at the cottage. That piece of rock, lying by Pinson's right hand – it wasn't what killed him. There's no trace of soil or bits of grass in the head wound, and the rock's covered with 'em. And it's a jagged bit of rock, but the wound isn't. It wasn't the weapon that killed him, Patton. It fits! It fits!'

'What does it fit?'

'The scene I've been imagining, that's what.'

'Which is?'

I expected him to answer that, as he'd spent a while telling me all about this visualising of his. But he didn't answer my question, and headed off in a different direction altogether.

'The key's missing,' he said morosely. 'The spare key from under the flowerpot. Missing. I mean, it must've been the one used to get in. It was there yesterday.'

'I saw it myself.'

'There you are, then. So whoever it was who got in the cottage first, the one with the torch lying on the floor, then that was the person who used the key. The spare key.'

'Seems obvious.'

'All right – so where is it?' He glared at me, as though I had it hidden somewhere. 'The spare key. They call it the spare, but I don't reckon it's been disturbed for years.' He shook his head violently, his hair flying about. 'Why would it be? They've *all* got their own key to the blasted door. Mrs Searle . . .'

'I expect she's Lady Searle. Dowager Lady Searle now.'

'Whatever.' He waved a hand in the air. 'She's got one, that Jeremy's got one, though he says he's hardly ever used it, and doesn't know where it is now. Paul's got one – he works up there. Paintings or something. So he'd need one. And that Janine's got one.'

'They call her Jennie.' I recalled he'd already used that name.

'What's in a name? Somebody said that. She's got one, anyway. She says she goes up there every now and then, and tidies for Paul. And Mary Pinson's got one.'

I stirred uncomfortably.

'But not with her,' he went on. 'It's at home in a drawer. Says she's kept it for sentimental reasons – whatever that means.'

'I can't imagine.'

He grunted, and eyed me with suspicion. 'In any event, there doesn't seem to have been much call for the one under the flowerpot.' He raised his eyebrows, his eyes becoming round and bright with inspiration. 'But there was a call for it last night. Now it's missing – and so it was the one used to open the door.'

'That seemed to be the case, right from the beginning.'

Phillips ignored that. 'Seemed' was a word he would rarely use. 'So . . .' He seemed excited, like a child with a rattle. In fact, he produced his own key-ring and rattled it in my face, presumably to ensure that I realised he was talking about keys.

'I think I have the picture,' I assured him gravely.

'Right.' He uncrossed his legs and crossed them again the other way. 'Assuming that Joe – what the *hell* is his other name? – anyway, assuming he told the truth, then we must accept he saw a light in the cottage before Pinson arrived.'

'I see it,' I assured him, before he asked. 'I see it.'

'So Pinson, also spotting it, but from further up the lane, he came back to see what was going on. Maybe from natural nosiness, maybe because he still thought of it as his cottage. It doesn't matter. He went round the front to see who was doing what.'

'Picking up a chunk of rock on his way, just in case he might need it?' I said helpfully.

'If you like.'

'I do like.'

He waved a hand, allowing me the point. 'All right. Carrying a piece of rock. Round to the front – the front! *Round* to it. Even the blasted cottages were built backwards. Now . . . somebody's inside, so they'd already used a key. Their own, or the one from under the flowerpot – it doesn't matter which, for now. The fact that the spare's missing suggests it was that one. Now . . . would that first visitor go inside the place and close and lock the door behind him? Or her?'

'A woman? Could it have been done by a woman?'

Phillips shrugged. 'Everything these days seems to be capable of being done by a woman. But it was a heavy blow with a heavy object. The odds are it was a man.'

'Heavy object?' I asked.

142

'You're not concentrating on the mental picture,' he accused me, leaning forward and pointing a finger. 'Anything *but* that bit of rock.'

'The torch, perhaps?'

'No. Probably not heavy enough. His skull was caved in. Anyway, there'd have been splinters of glass, and there weren't any. The glass would've broken. Sure to have done.'

'All right,' I agreed. 'A heavy blow.'

He lit another cigarette, blew smoke in my direction, and sighed. 'You're not keeping your mind on what I want you to visualise.'

'Say it. Say it, then.'

'The first person there . . . would he – or she, I'll allow you – would he have locked the door after him as he went in?'

I didn't waste much thought on that. 'Surely there'd have been no point. He wouldn't have expected to be interrupted.'

'And the key, then?'

On this, I used a little more thought. 'It would be left in the lock,' I decided. 'There's no handle to use on the outside of that door, for pulling the door shut after you leave. So it would be natural to leave the key in, half-turned, for when you left.'

He made a strange grimace, as though he'd started it as a grin and changed his mind half-way. 'But . . .' He wagged that finger again. 'But it had to be somebody who was confident there wouldn't be any interruption.'

'As I said,' I reminded him, 'there'd have been some considerable confidence in that.'

'Why?' he demanded. 'Why d'you say that? Is it because you know it had to be someone from this house, and you know they'd all turned in before all this happened?'

'No. It isn't. Everybody in this area must know about this empty cottage. Everybody. And each one could be confident of no interruption.'

He seemed to concede the point, as he inclined his head. 'Very well. We can now visualise someone using the spare key and going in there with a torch. And there's a logical picture of Charles Pinson quietly entering the cottage, because he's spotted a light. With a chunk of rock in his hand. What then? A row. Whatever it was. And the first visitor lashed out —'

'With something heavy?' I asked.

'Yes. That. With something heavy that wasn't the chunk of rock . . . then purely and simply he ran off in a panic.'

143

'Yet . . . in this picture we're guessing at . . . with all this panic, pausing to lock the door behind him?' I said this with scorn.

'And *that's* what I'm getting at.' He slapped his knee. 'I get that far, and the picture goes all blurred. If this character was in a panic, wouldn't he have simply legged it away as fast as possible? And left the door open, swinging open, with the key still in the lock, and disappeared into the night? Why not? It wouldn't have made any difference to the fact that a man had been left behind, dead, door open or not.'

'But in the morning, the door was locked. I had to break in at the kitchen door.'

'Exactly.'

'And the key wasn't in the lock and it wasn't under the flower-pot.'

'Exactly.'

'So . . .' I paused. Now I was with him. 'So this *wasn't* a person who was in a panic? Is that what you're saying?'

He banged both palms down hard on the chair arms. Little puffs of dust arose. Tessa wouldn't have been pleased to observe it. Then he positively beamed. It was not an engaging sight and seemed to give him pain. 'That's exactly what I'm trying to get across. Somebody who could afford to stop and think. To give it time. What's best to do? He's standing there, thinking it out. Can you see him, Patton? This is somebody who doesn't expect to be observed, standing there, thinking it through.'

'Who didn't', I put in quickly, 'therefore know anything about Jennie and Joe's habit of meeting up there?'

He waved a dismissive palm. 'If he'd known, he certainly wouldn't have gone there at that time. Oh no. He took his time, and asked himself, "What am I doing? What's the best thing to do?" And the answer came back: to lock up again.'

'And he didn't panic, you say?'

Again he pointed a finger at me, as though it was my fault. 'And *that's* what I'm getting at. The door was locked, and the key taken away or thrown away. Not, you'll notice, returned to its rightful place under the flowerpot. But that would have been the natural thing to do. To round it off. To leave the cottage looking normal. So why? Why take the key away?'

'And you ask me to visualise the scene?' I asked gently. 'And come up with an answer?'

He was staring at me, nodding, nodding in encouragement.

144

'I'm sorry – I haven't got an answer.'

He said nothing, just stared. I had to go on, feeling a ridiculous and imperative urge to release him from his trials and concerns. 'All I can do is agree,' I admitted. 'Why throw away, or take away, the key? Yes, I get your point there.'

'But . . . can you see an answer? There must have been a reason. It's the only point where the logical reconstruction falls flat on its face. Can you see an answer?'

'No,' I admitted. 'To have left the door open and cleared off, that would have been logical. To shut and lock it would've been logical. But to take the key away seems quite illogical. It would've been simple enough to bend down and pop the key back under the flowerpot.'

He eyed me steadily for long moments, slightly frowning. Then he said quietly, 'I think you might know the answer. Or guess it.'

'No,' I assured him. 'It's a mystery to me. First catch your man, and then ask him.'

He sighed. 'Never mind. You tried. And when we arrest him, he'll probably say something ridiculous like: I just didn't think about it.'

'Yes, that's how things go.'

'But I've got an idea that he did think, Patton. That's the trouble. I believe he had a damned good reason.'

I stirred in the chair. 'D'you want me any more, Mr Phillips?'

'No. I don't think so. Not at the moment. But . . . if you hear something?' He raised an eyebrow. I've never mastered that.

'That'll depend rather on what I hear,' I told him. 'They're not suspects to me, they're friends.'

He nodded. He hadn't expected anything different. I paused at the door.

'You didn't take a statement from me after all,' I reminded him.

'True, true. I'll ask you things when the questions arise. All right?'

'Any time.' I said this casually, as though the choice would be mine.

The DC was still standing outside the door. He seemed not to notice my presence. He could well have gone into a trance. I could hear the rest of them chattering in the library. Voices were again being raised, and it didn't seem to be anything to do with a card game.

Paul was shouting, 'You had no bloody right. I bet you just chucked 'em into the cases, any old how. I tell you . . . if you've chipped one of them —'

I opened the door. There was an abrupt silence. All eyes swung round to fasten on me avidly. Amelia came quickly to me, taking my arm.

'You've been such a long while, Richard.'

It hadn't seemed so to me. I shook my head.

'Yeah,' said Jeremy, looking sullen, like a disappointed child. 'He'll have had to tell that lanky character every damn little thing he knows about all of us.'

'Well, now . . .' I wandered into the room, pushing past Jeremy, who'd tried to stand challengingly in front of me. 'I wasn't asked, you know. It seems he already knows all he needs to. Detective Chief Inspector Phillips, I'm talking about.' I looked round from face to face. I was their connection with officialdom. There was suspicion and reservation, concern and eagerness. 'Well . . . as it happens we didn't discuss anybody, not any specific person. Joe was there, in the discussion, but only because he saw Charlie Pinson arrive on the scene.'

I looked round for Mary. She wasn't there. From what she had told me, I didn't suppose she would be prostrate with distress over the death of her brother.

'Where's Mary?' I asked.

'I think she went to sit with Tessa,' said Amelia.

Surely Tessa would have had no interest in Pinson's death, I thought. 'What's wrong with Tessa?'

Amelia shook her head. I didn't know whether it was a refusal or an answer. Her lips were tightly clamped, but nevertheless they twitched. I looked to Jeremy for an answer. He was, as the eldest, the responsible adult of the family.

He shrugged. 'I had to go and see her. I mean, police all over the place. I had to explain. My mother's always refused to listen to anything that might upset her, so I was a bit . . . you know . . . chary about it.'

'But she'd have to be told,' I said. 'You can't wrap her in cotton wool. You told her, then, that Charlie Pinson is dead, and the police are here to investigate?'

'Yes. I told her.'

146

'And?'

'She had hysterics.' Jeremy shrugged. 'You'd need to know my mother. She's always been highly strung. I mean . . . you never had to take problems to her. Well . . . the very thought of police all over the house – and I had to warn her they'd want to speak to her – that really set her off. I went to get some brandy, and to look for Gladys. No nonsense about Gladys, you know. But I couldn't find her, so Mary . . .' Even now, he was hesitant about using her name. She was still Nanna to him. 'Mary went to her.'

My eyes switched to Amelia. She pouted at me. 'Tessa's drunk,' she said. 'Jeremy left the brandy decanter with her.' Her eyes were huge. 'When I saw her, she was singing to herself.'

It was unlikely that Phillips would need to trouble Tessa, as it was too difficult to imagine Tessa's involvement in Pinson's death. So I couldn't feel concerned that Tessa might be drunk. But I *was* concerned about the possibility that she might be celebrating.

13

There now seemed to be a hiatus. A long time stretched ahead of us before lunch would break the monotony, and I had the feeling that although instructions might not have been given, Phillips would prefer the main group of us to remain together. I had a ridiculous and almost impossible to suppress inclination to go up to the cottage to see what was happening. But I would undoubtedly have been sent away – a depressing and humiliating thought. I wondered whether I had time for a quick shave.

But . . . while we were all together . . . 'Where's Joe?' I asked Jennie.

'He had to get back to his dogs,' she said. 'It's all right. They said he could go, because they'd know where to find him.'

'Yes,' I said.

'But they won't want to see him again, will they?' She frowned worriedly.

'They probably will,' I told her, explaining so that she wouldn't worry if they did. 'He was up there, you know, at the cottage.'

'I know,' she whispered. 'He's told me about it.'

'They may want to check his story.'

'Oh . . .'

'Have they asked you to confirm it?' I asked.

'What? Confirm what? How can I confirm anything?' She seemed agitated. 'I wasn't there last night.'

I grinned at her in encouragement. 'Only to confirm that you'd done it before, Jennie. Going there . . . and expecting to meet . . .' I left it at that.

She blushed frantically. 'But Joe would . . .' She stopped.

'Because he'd done it before?' I knew he had. That they had. But I wanted to hear it from Jennie.

'Yes,' she whispered.

'Then that's all right.' But I pursued the subject. 'Have you told everybody?' I looked round at Paul. He and Jeremy were staring at Jennie.

'Told everybody what?' Paul asked.

Jennie quickly glanced at both of them, then stared down at the floor. She spoke almost in a whisper. 'I used to go up there, late-ish. And if Joe was there . . . well, you know, we'd say goodnight.'

'There, you see.' I looked round, smiling. 'I knew it would be all right.'

'Richard, you're talking riddles.' Amelia was frowning at me, thinking I was trying to pressure Jennie into something that could be disturbing. 'What's all right?'

I looked round our little group. 'You mean Joe hasn't said anything?'

'He hasn't said anything to me,' Jennie said, swallowing.

'Oh well. Never mind. I'll tell you. He was up there – eleven-ish – at the cottage last night.'

'You've said that, Richard.' Amelia seemed impatient with me.

'But has Joe told the others?' I looked round, meeting only blank stares. 'Has he told everybody that he saw a light in the cottage? Did he say he saw Pinson arrive, and go into the cottage? To any of you?'

Jeremy said, 'He didn't tell me.'

'You, Paul?'

Paul had been staring out of the window. He turned. 'What? No. Joe hasn't said anything about it to me.' He looked slightly belligerent, slightly worried. 'Why?'

'It's just . . .' I ran my hands over my hair. 'He'd had a set-to with Pinson in the Red Lion. It could be argued that he might not have told the truth. I mean – about having seen another man at the cottage. A torch in there, and moving feet, anyway. Could have been a woman, perhaps. But that's unlikely.'

'Man?' said Jeremy. 'What man?'

'He didn't see any more than the light from a torch lying on the floor. That was Joe's story. But the police'll be scouring the village by now, searching for any little scraps of information. And the first place they always go to is the local pub. So . . . by now they'll know Joe had a motive for killing Pinson. I'm not saying you ought to be worried about it, Jen, because Joe's so obviously honest that they'll realise it. I'm just laying on the possibilities, so that you'll be prepared.'

149

Worried? Already her eyes were full of it, her lips working. But I thought it would be better like this, coming from me. Better for her. And I was reaching for anything . . .

'You see,' I explained gently, 'Charlie Pinson could well have seen a light in the cottage, but the DCI would suggest the light was in fact Joe's. No . . . let me say it. You can't argue that such a thing wouldn't be logical, because it sounds so damned likely. Joe having a look round on his own, working out what had to be done to the cottage, and what was feasible – and maybe wondering what to do about that staircase. So . . . Pinson seeing the light, puts his nose in . . . and before you know where you are, they're finishing off the row that started in the pub.'

'No!' cried Jennie.

'Richard!' said Amelia, a warning note in her voice.

'But Amelia love, isn't it better to come from me, rather than from Phillips?'

'I'll have to go to Joe!' cried Jennie frantically.

'Now, Jennie . . . ask yourself. Would that help?' I asked. As though that mattered to her! 'Quite frankly, you'd help more by staying right here.'

'How?' demanded Amelia.

Jennie flapped her arms on her thighs. 'How can I do *anything* for him, when I'm stuck here?'

'You'd help him by telling all you know to Phillips.'

'I don't want to speak to that man.' More flapping.

'Listen!' I waited until she was silent and more composed. 'Had Joe ever been inside that cottage before yesterday?'

This was more practical. She was slightly more calm. 'No. Not with me, anyway.'

'And when we went up to there, the group of us, you were using Paul's key. Remember?'

'Oh yes. Yes.'

'Good. Then Joe wouldn't even have known there was a spare key under the flowerpot?'

She stared at me blankly for a moment, then her eyes opened wide and bright. 'Oh . . . yes!' she cried. 'Of *course*. I see now.'

'You told *me* there was a spare under the flowerpot . . . remember?'

'Yes . . . yes.'

'But at that time Joe was walking around looking for boundaries, or something.'

'Yes. I remember that. I showed it to you.'

'There you are, then. If he didn't know about the spare key, how could he have been inside when Charlie Pinson came nosing around? All right. So there's another possibility, but that's not valid, either. If Pinson was the first one there – and Joe told a bit of a lie about that – and they had a fight, then why did Joe lock up afterwards, or why didn't he simply leave the door open, or lock it and leave the key in? Why would he take it away – or throw it away?'

There was silence. Then: 'Throw it away?' asked Paul. 'The key?'

'Well, it's disappeared.'

'It certainly wasn't there when I got up to the cottage this morning,' put in Jeremy, showing no shame at all for having done so.

'Exactly,' I agreed.

'Exactly what?' asked Amelia. She was now rather suspicious of my intentions.

I shrugged. 'It all goes to show that Joe couldn't have done it. And if Jennie was to go and explain it to the DCI . . . that's the chap lounging in the drawing-room, Jen . . . if you go and tell him that Joe *had* got a reason for being around there, and for not wasting time looking round the cottage, because he was waiting for you – hopefully, and had a reason for expecting you to come along there . . .'

She flushed. Her hand went to her mouth. 'It's too . . . too silly.'

'It's what Joe told them,' I explained. 'His explanation of why he was there. Frankly, I think Mr Phillips accepted it. He said it was too ridiculous to be anything but the truth.'

'Ridiculous?' asked Jennie, offended.

'Well . . . if you don't mind my saying so . . . you're neither of you sloppy teenagers. And to walk all the way up through those trees at night . . . I'm afraid Phillips can't remember when he was young and sexy. So if you told him, Jen, then it might persuade him that Joe had a personal reason for being there.' I looked at her with my head tilted. 'I can believe it myself. Frankly, if I was in Joe's shoes, I'd have waited every evening, rain or snow or fog . . .'

'Richard!'

'It's all right, love. Just making a point.'

'And you think I ought to tell him?' asked Jennie, biting her lip, her resolution crumbling.

'To help Joe, yes,' I said.

Without another word, she turned, walked out, and we heard her talking to the DC in the hall. A door opened. It closed.

'Well . . . Richard!'

'There's a reason, love,' I said quietly. 'Phillips skated round it.'

'Round what?' Amelia was suspicious.

'The fact that Joe really needs an explanation for his presence there. A peaceful reason, something non-aggressive. I'm not sure Phillips was pleased with what I told him. Maybe – from Jennie – it'll sound feasible.'

'I'm sure of one thing,' said my wife.

'What's that?

'You never cease to surprise me, Richard.'

I hoped she meant this as a compliment. 'Just trying to help. And, talking about that, isn't there something else?' I turned to look at the other two. 'Have you told him, Paul?' I asked, nodding towards his brother.

'What's this?' demanded Jeremy suspiciously, so Paul clearly hadn't.

It seemed as good a time as any to settle the business of the pictures and the books. And it would take their minds from the murder for a few minutes.

'Have you mentioned it to your mother?' I asked Paul.

'What *is* this?' demanded Jeremy.

I shrugged. 'It's just a minor issue.' Oh, but it wasn't! 'It's simply that Paul said your father always considered this library here to be part of his art collection. Did you know that, Jeremy?'

'I don't know. I suppose so. He was always pontificating. Thought he was a patron of the arts or something, did dad. "One of these days," he used to say, "I'm going to donate this library to the British Museum." Or some nonsense like that.' He gave a harsh little laugh.

'I trust that he didn't.'

'No. Not him. He was a show-off. Anybody here for the evening – and in those days there'd be dinner parties – he'd bring 'em in here and say he was giving all this to the nation. As though they'd want to put one finger on anything in here!'

'Perhaps he knew what he'd got,' I suggested.

Jeremy looked puzzled. I explained. 'The point at issue is that your mother inherits the balance of the estate after all the other bequests have been dealt with. Does she, in other words, inherit this library and its contents, or is it included in the phrase, art collection?'

'Dad always thought so,' put in Paul. 'He'd show people round. "Let me show you my art collection," he'd say. And he'd bring 'em in here as well as into the gallery next door.'

'Puffed-up idiot!' said Jeremy.

There had certainly been no affection crackling between Jeremy and his father.

'And what's it matter?' Jeremy added.

'I'm getting to that. If it's so, as you say, then the contents of this room would be legally distributed between you and Paul, the oil paintings to you, and the remainder to Paul.'

Jeremy shrugged. 'So what? There aren't any oil paintings.'

Paul laughed.

'Show him, Paul,' I said.

Then Amelia and I stood and watched with amusement while Paul demonstrated the truth of the paintings. He unhooked them from their supports and spread them out, nicely cleaned by me, on the table. Then he produced the folder I'd already explored.

Jeremy stared blankly at the small pictures. 'They're mine?'

'Subject', I said warningly, because I didn't want any misunderstandings, 'to being able to establish that this room, within the meaning of your father's will, is included in the description: art collection.'

'They don't seem much to me,' said Jeremy, pouting.

Paul slapped him on the back. 'They're previously unknown paintings, sketches if you like, by some of the French Impressionists. Jerry, they're worth a fortune.'

'Gerraway.'

'It's right.'

'I don't believe it. They've been done by some kid, a learner. Done 'em all.'

'You'd better try to believe it,' I told him. 'Everything to prove their genuineness is in that folder. They'll go mad over the things at the auction rooms. Put 'em all in as one lot, including the letters, and Jerry, you'll be rolling in the stuff you're so short of at this time.'

'All but two,' Paul warned. 'They're pastels. That makes those mine. But I'm not going to sell those. Oh no.'

'You're not?' Jeremy wasn't actually burning with delight. So far, the reality had not been assimilated. He merely smouldered gently. He was even suspicious. 'Why not?'

'I'll want 'em to look at. Sell them to a collector, and nobody ever sees them again. Locked away. An investment. No – I'll have 'em on my walls. Wherever my walls turn out to be.'

'Weren't you going to have the watercolours on your wall?' I asked.

'Well, sure. The Degas pastels – I'll have those with them. Lovely.'

'None of your own?'

'What? I wouldn't dare. Not those and mine in the same room! I'd be ashamed. Anyway, mine are for selling.'

'Sold many?'

He gave me a distorted grin. 'Not yet. I haven't really tried.'

'There's one up there in the cottage I'd like to buy from you,' I told him.

'You what? Oh no. Not on your life. You can take what you like, Mr Patton, when you . . .' He looked suddenly puzzled. He had forgotten the present overriding situation. 'When you leave.'

'Well . . . thank you,' I said. I smiled at Amelia. 'Isn't that generous, love?'

She nodded, lips pursed, eyes aglow. But we didn't know when we *would* be able to get away, and there was no point in considering it while the police had full occupation of the cottage.

The two brothers seemed temporarily to have forgotten about this. Their respective financial situations were now becoming more clear, and more satisfying. They stared at each other, then they grabbed at each other's arms and thumped shoulders, dancing around, as though there had been no anger between them, no bubbling antagonism and fury.

'We'll sell the Olmec masks,' gasped Paul, out of breath. 'Split between us. Then we don't have to keep arguing about where they are, and where they ought to be.'

'Yeah, yeah.' Jeremy punched his shoulder, his principles suddenly awry.

Amelia tugged at my arm. I looked round. She was smiling her delight. All was blessed harmony.

Then, as they cooled a little, as they stood panting and grinning, I said, 'That's not the end of it, is it?'

They were instantly still, suspicious.

'Now what?' demanded Paul, his head lowered, staring at me from beneath his brows.

'You, Paul – so clever, claiming that Jerry saw only the books and not the pictures! But what about you, eh? What did *you* see? Only the pictures and not the books.'

'The books? What books?'

'First editions, Paul, that's what I'm talking about. Last night, my wife borrowed something to read from here, and she found herself looking at a first edition of *Pride and Prejudice*. Now think about that. Would you consider that to be valuable?'

'You're having me on.'

'No. Not a bit of it. You're here, and the stuff's all round you. Why don't you look for yourself?'

'I wouldn't know what to look for. I know nothing about books.' Paul's face was set, his mouth firm, as though I might have laid him a trap. 'First editions, you say? Are *they* valuable? Oh well, I suppose they could be. But I can't imagine . . .' He waved vaguely around at the dusty and unorganised miscellany around him.

The previous night I had restored the ones I'd looked at to their rightful home – the shelves – but in one batch, so that I could readily find them again. I now went round and lifted them out, one at a time for maximum effect, and placed them on the table surface.

'*Roderick Random*,' I said, 'by Tobias Smollett – 1748. Surely that's worth a packet to somebody. And here's Ouida's *Under Two Flags*, first edition, 1867.'

'Hey!' said Jeremy. 'I've read that. When I was . . . oh, a teenager. All right, I thought. A bit old-fashioned, though.'

'This particular copy?' I asked.

'Oh sure. I used to grub through these shelves for anything readable.'

'And you never realised they were valuable in themselves?'

'Why would I?' Jeremy shrugged. 'I was after something worth reading.'

'*Wuthering Heights*?' I asked, placing it beside Ouida. 'Ellis Bell, 1847. Did you read that?'

Jeremy frowned. 'Couldn't get on with that. Too heavy for me.'

'Ellis Bell?' asked Paul. 'Never heard of him.'

'It's not a man. It's Emily Brontë. Her pen name.'

'Oh.' He thought. 'I suppose somebody might like to have it.'
I nodded. Somebody most certainly would.

'That's just from a quick look around,' I told them. 'Imagine
how many more valuable first editions there must be. Have a
search through the shelves. Go on, why don't you find out what
you've been living with all your lives?'

Then Amelia and I stood around and watched the other two
get on with making themselves filthy and nearly choking themselves with dust. From time to time there would be shouts of:
'What about this, Mr Patton?'

But I couldn't really help unless it was an author I recognised.
Amelia wasn't saying anything, just watching with a vague
smile of pleasure.

They discovered some Dickens, clearly old – *Pickwick Papers*. I
didn't really know about that. Weren't they published in magazine form first? Did it matter? The same with Conan Doyle. *The
White Company*. I was reasonably certain that it had been published in one volume. If so, there it was. It was going to need an
expert to assess all this stuff. But – *The Adventures of Sherlock
Holmes* . . . I was certain those had appeared first in the *Strand
Magazine*.

But, although Amelia exclaimed at each recognition of an
author's name, there was no way any of us could estimate values
and rarities. At their end of the table, beneath the window, the
promising stacks of volumes grew. Paul became increasingly
excited.

'Hey! Look at this.' And: 'What d'you say to this, then?'

By this time their hands were black. They had smudges on
cheeks and forehead, Paul on the end of his nose.

'I think that'll do,' I said, at last. 'It was only so that you'd both
see what your father meant. You'll have to get an expert in here,
Jeremy. Somebody who knows what they're worth. You might
as well leave things as they are for now. And you'd both better
go and get cleaned up.'

'Hey!' said Paul, staring at the book in his hand. 'Look at this.
Lady Chatterley's Lover. I never did get to read this. Think it's a
first . . .' He turned to the title page. 'No! It's in French. Paris,
1929, it says. And . . . hello, that's strange. It's in English.'

Jeremy snatched it out of his hand. He'd gone very pale, grey-
white against his smudged cheeks. He stared at it, and flipped it
open, then he slammed it shut. His eyes were suddenly wild.

'Yargh!' he shouted, a choked sound of revulsion, then he threw it away from him.

I assumed this to be the action of a rather prudish person, distressed by the language he thought to be unprintable. Yet it *had* been printed. Paris 1929 meant that we had here a copy of the first print, the very first unexpurgated version in English. It was probably priceless, as it had been illegal, at that time, even to bring it into this country. And Jeremy saw fit to consider it only for its contents!

I watched it sliding the length of the table, when a fall to the floor might split the spine, and thus detract considerably from its value to a genuine collector – who would probably never dream of reading one word of it. I think I shouted out. I could not have reached the far end of the table in time.

The door opened, and Mary stood there. As usually happens in the split second of realisation, she reacted, put her hands forward, and caught it.

'Oh . . . well fielded!' I cried, aware that this revealed my tension.

Mary stood still, shocked at this sudden assault by a flying book. For a moment she smiled in pleasure, that she had accomplished such a feat. Then, still smiling, she looked down at what she had in her hands, and became very still. She opened it, flipped over a page here and there, put it down firmly on the surface, and clutched at the table, it seemed to support herself.

'Mary?' whispered Amelia.

I thought Mary was about to faint. The blood had run from her face, and she swayed. Then she turned, fumbled open the door, and ran into the hall. She didn't pause to close the door behind her. I could clearly hear her stumbling feet on the parquet, then abrupt silence as she took the carpeted stairs.

Amelia caught my eye. She was startled, and was herself pale. 'I'll go to her,' she said. 'Richard . . . what is it?'

I shook my head. I didn't know. The reactions of both Mary and Jeremy had been far too extreme, and I couldn't understand the reason.

'I'll go to her,' she repeated.

'Yes, love. You do that. Where do I find you?' I meant that I didn't know where Mary's room was.

'She's two doors past us.' Then, after one quick, worried look around, she hurried after Mary.

The book was beneath my right hand, but it was Jeremy and Paul whom I was considering. They were standing so still and stiff that I felt they would never move.

I said casually, 'What was all that about, then?'

Paul shook his head. His face was completely blank of any expression. 'God knows.'

'Jeremy?' I asked.

He also shook his head, and looked away.

'Well?' I demanded, more forcefully.

'I thought it'd been destroyed,' Jeremy said, his voice low. His right fist was quietly, gently, thumping the table surface.

'That would have been a terrible thing —'

'It's vile!' he interrupted, his voice suddenly too loud. 'Revolting.'

'All right,' I said. 'All right. But it's only a book. Black marks on paper. It doesn't become anything until you read it. The whole thing's a miracle, you know. Little black marks. Your eyes scan them, and your brain turns it all into images. They're your own images, Jeremy. Inside *your* brain. It's not the book. It doesn't shout the words at you —'

'I don't want a bloody lecture!' he shouted. 'I thought it'd been destroyed. It *had* to be . . . oh Lord . . .'

He put his hands over his face. I glanced at Paul, who was looking completely confused, even embarrassed. Those two, brothers, with not too many years between them, had probably thrown at each other all the words Lawrence had used – and which had been expurgated from the first edition in England – and had probably discussed and argued over the same sensual and erotic aspects that Lawrence had exploited. So why, now, this attitude from Jeremy? Paul's shock – and he *was* shocked, I saw – was at Jeremy's response. Jeremy's shock, still possessing him, seemed to have disorganised him altogether.

His eyes were wild when he at last looked directly at me. He shot out a hand. 'Give it to me. Hand it over.'

'No, Jeremy. Sit down. Relax. It's only a book.'

'It's mine —'

'No. If anybody's, it's Paul's.'

'I've got to get rid of it.' Jeremy said, one arm flying out wildly.

'Control yourself, Jeremy, for God's sake.'

'Give it to me!' he shouted, his voice breaking, and close to a scream.

158

Paul raised his eyebrows, glancing worriedly at his brother. I said, 'And have you tear it apart? I'd as soon hand you a fistful of tenners to tear up. Stop acting like a fool, Jerry.'

I tucked it firmly under one arm. He stared at me with murder in his eyes. If I'd dropped down in a fit, he'd have gone first for the book. But I was too big for him to tackle – even he with his martial arts – because they would have taught him that every move, every blow, had to be calmly calculated. Not in anger. His face crumpled. I didn't want to see a man his age weeping. I'd seen such a thing, several times before, and I'd never got used to it.

I turned away. I said, 'I'll take care of it. When you're feeling calmer, Jerry, we'll discuss what to do with it.' Then I turned and walked out. At that point, it would've taken a regiment to tear it from me, because I knew it had to be important, for some reason or another.

The DC was still at his post. If he'd heard anything of what had been going on, he gave no indication of it.

I took *Lady Chatterley* up to my room. There had to be something to be understood involving it. I wanted time to think . . . and Mary? Maybe I'd get time to have a look at it before I went and spoke to her.

I sat on the edge of our bed and opened the book across my knees. It creaked a little, and I was having to be very careful with it. At once, I was in some difficulty, because I had persuaded myself that there had to be something special, something different about this copy, other than the fact that it was less dusty than the other books had been. But I wasn't in a position to assess anything. I had never read it, in any version. I'd only heard of it.

It wasn't at once obvious. I dipped into it at random, not being selective in any way. A phrase here, I read, a phrase there. And I came across nothing that would shock any reader of a modern best-seller. But then I spotted something: an annotation. Then more, as I flipped through, now knowing what to look for.

They were in pencil, one with a hard lead, very tiny and delicately in the margins. It was as though brief comments had been made with the expectation that they could be eventually erased. But they hadn't been. They were short, mostly monosyllabic. 'Absurd' and 'Yes, yes', 'Fool, fool!' And 'Now – oh, please . . .' 'No!'

I closed the book on my lap, and sat, thinking about it. I couldn't remember having seen Mary's writing. Little notes, she had left for us, yes. I had read those, but not attentively. And in any event, these furtive little comments had been entered so minutely that all trace of normal script would have been extinguished. But Mary . . . if the notes had been hers . . . well, I knew her. No notes. Simply, she'd have laughed it off, on catching the book. 'Well, fancy that. This old thing!' Yet I had difficulty imagining Mary defacing a book.

But that hadn't been her reaction. I decided that there was no alternative but to face her with it, not the fact of the annotations, but the fact of her obvious distress.

Yes, I decided, that was what it had been. Distress.

14

At last I heaved myself to my feet. I felt stiff and tired, and very worried. I took the book in my hand, quietly went out into the corridor, then strolled along to the door two past ours. I tapped on it.

'Is that you, Richard?' Amelia's voice.

'Yes.'

'Then come along in.'

I did so, leaning back against the door until the latch clicked. Mary was sitting on the edge of her bed, with Amelia facing her, seated in another of those basketry chairs, which seemed to have been bought as job lots. Mary had her fingers linked in her lap, and was staring at them. She looked up, and twisted her lips at me with a smile that didn't quite get there.

'It seems to be all peaceful now,' I told them. 'They're going through the books like a tornado, now, hunting for more treasures.'

In fact, they had been standing there as though suddenly frozen.

'I expect they'll find a great many,' said Mary, not registering any enthusiasm either way.

'But not . . .' I allowed myself a small smile. 'Not one that'll get the same reception, perhaps.'

There was no response to that. I put the book down gently on to her bedside table, its fate in the balance.

'And I don't suppose there'll be any more with little notes in the margins,' I went on, trying to remain casual.

'Notes?' asked Amelia.

'Annotations,' I told her. 'In pencil. Comments or reactions – I don't know.'

'Then Mary couldn't have had anything to do with those.' Amelia smiled at me, but there was concern in her eyes. I smiled back, dismissing with a flick of my hand the likelihood that Mary could have been involved. But Mary knew something. I went to look out of the window, standing at it and seeing nothing.

'But you did recognise the book, Mary,' I said gently. 'At a glance, and it'd come flying at you.'

'Mary's explained that,' Amelia told me, the hint being that she would fill me in afterwards. But I had to ignore that. Amelia might not have known the correct questions to ask.

'Mary,' I asked softly, 'where had you seen it before?'

'I thought it had been destroyed,' Mary answered quietly.

'But where had you seen it before?'

I turned to face her. She had not been weeping, but now the tears were there for the shedding. I hated to think I'd provoked them. She didn't answer, tucking her lower lip between her teeth to prevent it from betraying her.

'Mary?' I persisted gently – I hoped gently.

Amelia was severe. 'Richard, I won't have you bullying Mary.'

'As though I would! But I've got to know, love.'

'Then I can tell you all you need to hear.'

I wasn't sure exactly what I would need to hear. Mary, observing my dilemma, put in, 'But it's all right, Amelia. Truly. Richard and I are friends.'

'That's true,' I said.

'And I don't mind him knowing. After all . . .' There was a bleak attempt at a smile. 'After all, I was only young. Sixteen or so at the time. Naturally, I'd want to dip into it. I'd heard about it, you see, that book. I was naturally curious about it – and the first words my eyes fell on – oh, it was shocking! I can remember now. I went hot all over. So I put it back quickly, and got on with my work.'

'Your work?' I prompted.

'Well . . . you know . . . I was a kind of a maid at that time, but I remember . . . I'd started taking on the looking-after of the boys. Jeremy would've been only about four, and Paul only a toddler.'

I was listening carefully, but not with my eyes set on her, in case she found my attention embarrassing. It was nervousness loosening her tongue.

Amelia prompted, 'I'm sure they were delightful children.'

'Oh yes. 'They were a bit of a handful.'

She stopped. I had to ease her back into it.

'And where did you find the book, Mary?' I asked.

'I thought I'd told you that, Richard. Oh, men never listen. Don't you find that, Amelia?'

'Richard's a terrible listener,' Amelia agreed, not risking a glance at me.

But I made up for it with patience. 'No, Mary, you didn't say. But you did mention you were still doing your maid's duties. That, I take it, involved dusting, tidying up, making beds?'

'Yes. Yes, all those, and more.'

'And – I suppose – you came across the book during your tidying?

'Yes.'

'Where . . . exactly?'

'In the bedside table drawer.'

In illustration, she drew open the drawer just below the surface of her own bedside table. These tables, as were the basketry chairs, seemed to be standard throughout the bedrooms.

'In there?'

'Not *this* one – I didn't mean.' She looked at me sternly, disappointed in me.

Avoiding the direct question, I asked, 'Did your duties include dusting inside drawers?'

Mary still had a reserve of composure. 'Not really. But I peeked.'

'Ah. Maids are notorious for that. Just peeked?'

'The first time, yes. That's when I saw what it was. The book. Then I slammed the drawer shut.'

'Ashamed to be looking at it?'

'Ashamed to be caught looking at it,' said Mary, giving Amelia a conspiratorial glance.

'You see, Richard,' said Amelia.

I didn't know what that meant. I smiled at Mary, and went on, 'But I suppose you went back to it, at a more . . .' I snapped my fingers. 'More auspicious time.'

'Yes. I just couldn't help myself. I *had* to.'

'And how did those occasions arise?'

'Oh . . . in those days we had stables and horses and foxhounds.'

'Gladys mentioned that.'

163

'So the master and the mistress used to go out riding together. Most days when the weather was fine. Sometimes when it was terrible. Then I had the . . . the time.'

'You pounced on it?'

'It was not exactly like that, Richard,' said Mary reprovingly. 'Not pounced.'

'No. Of course not,' I agreed. 'Shall we say – you took the opportunity?'

'Yes. That's right. If Mrs Hughes was out of the way.'

'Mrs Hughes?'

'The housekeeper. We had six maids at that time, and a chauffeur. For the Rolls Royce Rowley used to have.'

'And you then had time to read it?' I asked.

'Oh, Richard – I was so innocent then. I knew nothing. I was shocked, frightened. Frightened of the . . . of the emotions he was writing about.'

Amelia smiled at me. It was almost a sad smile – a reminiscent sad smile. I said nothing on that subject. What did I know about a woman's emotions?

'And it was then', I suggested, 'that you made the pencil notes in the margins?' This I said without any tone in my voice, although I knew that Mary wouldn't have dreamed of doing such a thing.

'Of course not!' Amelia burst out. 'What *are* these notes you keep talking about?'

Mary reached across and put a hand on Amelia's. It was all right. Men had to be excused for being so brash and so lacking in understanding.

'Now, you know I didn't, Richard,' Mary said. 'Those were already there. I didn't understand them, really I didn't.'

'You didn't understand what they meant – or what they implied?'

Mary's eyes were now huge. 'I don't know what you mean.'

'No, Richard. Explain yourself.'

'The meaning of the actual pencilled words – or the meaning of what the writing of them implied.'

That got me two frowns. One from each one of them. I sighed, not knowing how better to put it. But I reached over for the book, opened it at random, found I'd fallen lucky, and indicated a pencil note in the margin. Amelia took the book from me.

'Well, never mind,' I said to Mary. 'It doesn't matter. Did you ever get to finish it?'

164

'Oh no. Barely a quarter of it. A tenth.'

'Why was that?'

'One day it wasn't in the drawer any more. I simply assumed it had been destroyed. That's all it was fit for.'

'Hmm!' I went again to look out of the window. Now, at least, I was seeing and focusing. But nothing was happening out there. It was all happening inside this room, and I couldn't crack its shell.

'But later, Mary . . .' I turned back. They had been whispering together. I waited until the heads turned. 'Later, surely, you understood?'

Mary didn't answer.

'Understood what it all meant, Mary,' I said patiently. 'Why the notes were made.'

'I see what you mean,' said Amelia, looking up, startled by the realisation.

Mary shook her head at me. But I could see I was expecting too much of her. Then I caught her eye. She was frowning at me, and there was appeal in her expression. Don't make me say it, Richard, please. So she *did* understand.

I smiled at her. 'No. I suppose you didn't.'

If my thoughts on the matter were in any way marginally accurate, I could see now that I would cause her further distress by pursuing it. If she had never understood, then I would be doing her a disservice by revealing it to her. If she had understood, she didn't want to admit it.

'And this bedside drawer where you found the book – I suppose that was in Sir Rowland's room?'

'Oh no. Of *course* not. It was in Lady Searle's.' She used that title now because she was mentally again a teenager. 'Tessa's,' she amplified, dragging herself into the present.

'Ah yes,' I said, trying not to look surprised.

Amelia's eyes were worriedly on me, but from her there was no surprise. She had guessed.

'I'll need to have a word with her,' I decided.

'Oh . . . no!' cried Mary.

'Not, of course, mentioning you, Mary.'

'Must you, Richard?' asked Amelia, her brow furrowed.

'I think we must.'

'We?' She grimaced.

'I don't think I'd like to tackle this alone.'

165

If the thought crossed my mind that I ought to bring this to the attention of DCI Phillips, I allowed it to pass on its way. It seemed to have nothing to do with his murder, and it would take an hour to get over to him the meaning of all the undertones, and I'd find myself thrusting a virtual stranger on to Tessa, when at least I was more a friend than an enemy.

'But how will you —' began Mary, agitated.

'I shall merely say I've come across this book in the library, and I'm trying to find out who'd entered the notes.'

And failed to rub them out again, was the thought that I had to consider. For, after all, the very gentle way the pencil had been used indicated that erasure had been in mind.

'Must it be now?' asked Amelia.

I hunched my shoulders at her. 'The less wholesome tasks should be tackled at once.' Oh – how often had I told myself this! And ignored it.

'See how strong and masterful he is, Mary,' said my wife. 'Full of upright principles.'

Mary managed a minimal smile. 'I hadn't been aware of it,' she admitted. 'But I suppose he's quite correct. Do it now. Yes.'

'Then perhaps', I suggested, 'you wouldn't mind going to her to ask if she's prepared to have a word with us.'

'Richard!' Amelia was annoyed. 'Mary's not a servant now.'

'No. But she's closer than we are to Tessa. And if it takes longer to do it than we'd expect, then that only means she's used the time to slip in a little warning.'

'As though she would.'

'As though I'd dare,' said Mary, rising to her feet. 'Frankly, she's still the mistress to me.'

'I can't believe that.'

'But all the same, I'll go and ask her,' she agreed.

Then Amelia and I were alone. We weren't looking at each other. In the end, she said, 'I do hope you know what you're doing, Richard.'

'Me too.'

'You're not to upset her.'

'Of course not. But you must have realised what it's all about.'

She didn't answer for some moments. Then: 'I'm hoping . . . praying that it's not what I think.'

'Me too,' I said with feeling.

'I wish we'd never come here.'

'It's certainly been an experience.'

'This house,' she said, a little passion entering her voice. 'It looked grim when we first set eyes on it. And just look at what's coming out. And what might have to come out still.'

'Yes, love.'

But houses were like people – you could never guess from the exterior what was going on inside. Oh yes, you can be sure that the residents stamp their personality on their houses. I've seen avenues of bright and coloured exteriors; rows of terraces with dirty, drab faces to warn away the world. But what went on behind those walls, not betrayed by the faces? I've seen as much violence behind smart frontages as drab ones. This very house . . . this grey and uninspiring front . . . yet it was proving to contain, in a material sense, bright and unexplored riches. As with people. And hidden inside these walls had also been displayed a hideous tangle of emotions. As with people.

I told myself I would have to stop this futile fantasising, but if I was going to I had to start by not seeing Tessa, and by isolating myself entirely from the ongoing investigation.

And before I could make any decision on this, Mary entered and said, 'She'd be very pleased to see both of you.'

'Yes,' I said. 'Thank you, Mary.'

I casually picked up the *Lady Chatterley*.

'And you'll let me know, Richard, please,' said Mary. She was tense, poised as though for flight.

'Know?'

'What . . . what happens.'

I hadn't intended to, if my guess happened to turn out correct. 'Well, of course, Mary.'

We went across the corridor to Tessa's door. I tapped on it, and she called out, 'Come in, please.'

This time she was sitting, fully clothed, on the bed. She had kicked off her shoes and was leaning back against the bedhead with a pillow behind her, as Amelia likes to do when sitting reading. It's strange how, simply by the removal of shoes, a certain informality is established. Perhaps Tessa realised this.

'I do hope', she said, 'that you've come to tell me those police persons have gone.'

'I'm afraid not. There're so many things to be answered before they'll decide to leave.'

And when they did, they would do so with someone accompanying them, under arrest.

'Have the boys been up to tell you?' I asked.

She gave me a rueful smile. 'It's a long while since they've come to confide their secrets to me.'

'Yes . . . well . . . I'd have thought they would come and tell you their news. Their good news.'

'But you must sit down, please. Amelia . . . is that correct? Amelia, you'll find that chair very comfortable, and Richard . . .'

But I was already sitting on the edge of the bed. I could have reached over and tickled the soles of her feet. But by now she must have realised that I was carrying a book. She ought, really, to have recognised it. But there had not been the slightest reaction. It could have been any old book.

'I was going to tell you about the treasures we've been finding,' I went on. 'This is in the library I'm talking about. The library! There's been a certain amount of discussion about that – about calling it the library. The will, you see. There was that phrase in Sir Rowland's will: the oil paintings in my art collection. Now . . . the boys say that your husband always included the library in his definition of art collection. Do you go along with that, Tessa?'

'Oh yes. I see what you mean. Yes, he meant the library, too. There were some paintings in there. I don't know if they're still there.'

'Certainly. They're still there. They happen to be sketches by some of the Impressionists, and probably very valuable. Thirteen of them would come under the definition of oil paintings, which would include them in Jeremy's inheritance.'

She picked idly at the bedspread. I wasn't sure she'd noticed the book in my hand. If so, she hadn't reacted. 'I'm very pleased about it,' she said gravely.

'You wouldn't dispute that – the definition of art treasures, even though they're in the library?'

She stared at me blankly. Her fingers were now still. 'But why would I dispute it?'

'If you did – successfully – they might legally be considered to be yours,' I explained.

She was not responding. It seemed very difficult to spark any emotional response from Lady Theresa Searle.

'I don't want them.' She flipped a hand.

'They're very valuable.'

She shrugged. 'To what use would I put the money?'

It was very difficult not to glance at Amelia. This woman was difficult to understand. She never seemed to react like a normal person.

'You mentioned an intention to marry Geoffrey Russell,' I reminded her.

'It's the man's prerogative to support his wife.' She raised elegant eyebrows at me, challenging me to dispute it. 'Geoffrey is quite capable of that. And I would not like to feel that he would ask me to marry him, if he was at the same time bearing in mind that I would have money to bring to the marriage.'

I smiled. It had been most elegantly stated.

'And who would know better than your husband's solicitor the size of his estate, and what will remain as yours?'

'That is exactly as I see it,' she told me. She was an innocent, that was it. 'But surely, this isn't why you came to speak with me. No . . . make no mistake . . . I'm pleased to see you both. Someone to talk to. I do have a tendency to feel lonely.'

If so, it was entirely her own choice. She was mobile, and nobody made any attempt to restrain her.

'But . . . the will.' I had to be persistent. 'Does Geoffrey realise, I wonder, what treasures we've uncovered in the library, and what large amounts of money might drift into your bank account, if the interpretation of the will was carefully manipulated?'

She laughed. It was the first time I'd heard her laugh. It was a a tinkle, a young girl's laughter. 'You should have been a solicitor yourself, Richard. No – I don't think you can accuse Geoffrey of unprofessional behaviour.'

'It was the last thing —'

'It sounded very like it. And I assure you, Geoffrey doesn't care about my money. It's me he wants. Little old me! You don't know what that means to a woman, Richard. He just doesn't understand, Amelia. Men are all loin and muscles.'

I was surprised to hear her express it like that.

Amelia murmured, 'Richard's very strong, certainly.'

I glanced at her, hoping to catch her playful smile, but her gaze was fixed steadily on Tessa's face.

'Whatever happens,' said Tessa complacently, 'I shall inherit the house. It's the address Geoffrey wants. The address. So splendid on his letterheads. I believe he's ordered the printing already. Geoffrey Russell, Solicitor, Penhavon Park, Shropshire.'

'I think he would prefer it as Salop.'

'You're quite right. That's what he said, now I come to think of it.'

'Hmm!' I murmured, some vague memory troubling me. Then I had it. 'But didn't you tell me you intend to sell it? This place. To sell it.'

'Well . . . yes.'

'Then he wouldn't be able to use his precious letterhead.'

She laughed. It was a child's mischievous laugh this time. 'Oh, but he would. I'd sell it to *him*.'

Amelia moved nervously. I said, 'Penhavon Park . . . and you.'

'No please. Me and Penhavon Park.' She smiled. A real smile, this was. It lit her face. 'I know him. It's me he wants. The house and the grounds are a bonus.'

'Isn't that splendid!' said Amelia.

'But', I suggested, 'he hasn't yet heard about the valuable contents of the library here. And when he does, it might be that he can find a perfectly legal manoeuvre that excludes its contents from the phrase: my art collection. He might engage a barrister on this, for an opinion. An expensive barrister, one who realises the value of its contents. A whole . . .' I snapped my fingers. 'What would be the collective noun? Ah yes. A whole haggle of barristers to prove the point.'

'Richard!' Amelia said, but gently, warningly. Yet I can't help it when I see deception being practised, especially the deception of this woman, so obviously naïve, and especially by an officer of the court. I become angrily facetious. I had to take a grip on myself.

'Do you wish to tell me something?' asked Tessa, suddenly looking angelic.

I sighed. 'Only that the contents of that library are very valuable. Paintings by the Impressionists and heaven knows how many first editions amongst the books.'

'It's a dusty load of rubbish,' said Tessa forcefully.

'I think not. I brought one at random to show you.' I held it up before her eyes. At random! 'Not only a first edition, but printed in Paris because it was banned in this country. Smuggled in. It must be fantastically valuable.'

'Oh, I wouldn't think so.' She hadn't yet realised what I was showing her.

'Banned', I said, 'because it was too erotic for consumption in England in the twenties. Lawrence himself claimed he was exploring the sensual aspects of human relationships, but —'

'What did you say?'

All the animation had run from her face. It was stiff, the skin dry, the blood running from it, but flushing her neck.

'Lawrence. D.H. Lawrence. This is a first English edition of *Lady Chatterley's Lover*, Tessa. Printed in Paris.'

I held it closer to her. She tried to recoil more deeply into the pillow. 'I don't wish to see it,' she whispered.

'But it's very interesting,' I insisted, pressing on with it in spite of Amelia's expression. 'There're notes. In the margins. Can you explain that, Tessa?'

'Richard!' It was a soft but urgent warning from Amelia.

But if Tessa had reacted differently, I would have responded to her mood. If she'd smiled and waved the subject aside lightly, and perhaps said, 'Oh that! I thought it rather amusing, frankly,' I would have retreated to impersonalities. But she simply didn't wish to give it any consideration. Not even look at it. Out of sight, out of mind. But now it was within sight, and tightly locked inside the mind I was so anxious to explore. She had made no answer to my question, so I repeated it.

'Can you give any explanation for the pencil notes, Tessa?'

'No!' It was an abrupt withdrawal.

'They're written in your hand.' But this was only a guess.

'Of course they're not. How dare you say —'

I dared because I could no longer retreat, and because I now knew I was correct. There had been panic in her eyes.

'Perhaps you still have the pencil. Something like a 2H, I'd say.' It was a ridiculous suggestion, but it kept things moving.

'I don't wish to discuss it. Please go away.'

'This matters, Tessa.'

'How can it matter now? A silly old book. And it was . . . was obnoxious.'

'So you *have* read it?'

She moved her head, seeking escape.

'Have you?' I insisted, but gently.

'I admit to having read a little,' she said quietly, her voice uncertain.

'The notes run all through it.'

'I've already told you —'

171

'A man is dead, Tessa.'

'What? What's that got to do with it?'

'I think Lawrence might solve the mystery.'

'You're talking nonsense. Are you quite sane?' Now it was offended dignity she offered.

I wondered that myself. Did I have to shout it in her face, before she would admit to recognising its importance?

Amelia's hand was locked on my kneecap. The fingers closed, tighter and tighter. Nevertheless, I had to go on.

'The person who made those notes, Tessa, was a woman who must have been strongly affected by the text. Not simply that – a person who was involved emotionally. Lady Chatterley was living your life, or you hers, there on the page, and you felt yourself swept along with it. Isn't that so? The writer of these pencil notes was captured by it, shared it, even luxuriated in it.'

I waited for her interruption, which really should have come sooner. But she stared at me with a set, white face, and said nothing.

'The heroine is Lady Chatterley,' I explained, in case she'd forgotten. 'She was the gamekeeper's lover. What I believe – what I'd give my right hand not to believe – is that Lady Chatterley was born again under a different guise. As Lady Searle. But which came first, Tessa? That's the point. Lady Chatterley's lover or Lady Searle's? And which was the imitation of which? Of course, Lady Chatterley was earlier in time, but she couldn't have existed for you until you read the words. Then she became alive. Did you live her life from then – or were you already living a similar life?'

Amelia kicked my ankle. If she thought I was enjoying this, then she had me all wrong. I was hating it.

Tessa was staring at me blankly, the life draining from her face, the flesh sagging, and the years poured over her as I watched, until she clasped her hands to her face, and her whole body vibrated with her weeping, the bed with it.

I stared at her, helpless. Amelia said quite sharply, 'How dared you, Richard? I'll never forgive you.'

I had dared because I'd had to. The story was dead; Lady Searle's gamekeeper was dead. But she had been living a fantasy, lost in it. Now I had forced her into admitting, to herself, that it had been real, and her mind had tracked back to the reality. I had lost her. What might have been a distortion of

172

disgust on her face, might just as well have been a distorted smile, a reminiscent smile. And in her eyes there was nothing.

Amelia whispered, 'Please . . .'

I levered myself from the bed. Almost possessively, I took the book in my hands and turned away. We left the room, closing the door quietly behind us. I had no way of knowing whether I had left behind a tangle of misery or a gradually unwinding release from the past.

15

Mary turned from the window as I closed her door behind us. 'Well?'

It was a demand, quite out of character for our mild and undemonstrative Mary. I shrugged.

'I think we've unearthed some of the truth. Perhaps not all of it.'

Then she was herself again. 'Can't we go home, Richard? Amelia, I hate it here.'

Amelia went to her. 'Oh, surely not. Jennie's here. You don't want to leave, not yet, anyway.'

'The memories . . .' She made a gesture that embraced them, and gave a grimace rejecting them.

'And I find I've still got to trespass amongst them,' I admitted, somewhat ruefully.

'Now, Richard . . .' Amelia was upset.

I was leaving a trail of misery behind me, and saw even more ahead. 'We now know about Tessa and your brother, Mary,' I told her. I tried to dismiss this knowledge as something quite paltry. 'But I think there's more to it, still. And I believe you're the one who knows it.'

'I don't think I want to talk about it,' Mary said, turning away and barely breathing it.

I shrugged. 'You know how it is – a trouble shared is a trouble halved.'

'And *you* know – that isn't so. It's a stupid old saying. It isn't halved, it's doubled.'

'But . . .' Amelia was hesitant, darting glances from Mary's worried face to mine, which was equally concerned, I've no doubt. 'But if there's a trouble, Mary . . .' It was Mary whom Amelia wanted to help. But to me it seemed that so many other people were involved.

Mary made no reply. She seemed to find something of interest, out beyond the window.

'Did you know about Tessa's affair with your brother, Mary?' I asked, quite casually, once more perching myself on the bed.

'Oh no. Of course not. Not at the time. Of course not.' She'd turned to say this, but now returned her attention to the outside scene. 'Joe's here. That's his car.'

It seemed she was about to use this as an excuse to get out of her room and down to him and Jennie – away from me.

'He'll want to be alone with Jennie,' I said. 'And she with him.'

'Of course.' She smiled a slight admonition to herself.

'So now's the time for a good old chat,' I assured her. 'While we're alone.'

'Chat?' asked Mary cautiously.

'About yourself, and about Sir Rowland Searle.'

'No!' said Amelia flatly.

'If you think not, love,' I said equably. 'But I thought . . . talk it through and get it out of the way.'

'Out of the way?' Mary was confused.

'Before Phillips gets on to it,' I explained.

Mary frowned. The name hadn't registered. Amelia made a gesture. It seemed to be an angry one.

'Before the Chief Inspector starts digging deeper,' I amplified. 'I mean, he'll have all the physical details at his fingertips by now. All the clues and the circumstances. So he'll be nosing around for possible motives.'

'Motives!' Amelia was becoming agitated. 'Are you talking about Mary's motives?' There was a warning note in her voice. 'I've never heard anything so fantastic in my life.'

'Oh, come on, love. Nobody's even considering Mary. This is a man's crime. No . . . I meant, Mary's probably the key to it. What Mary knows.'

'But I know nothing!' It was a desperate appeal.

'It goes back quite a long way, you know. Not just what happened yesterday, or a month back . . . a year. I think it goes right back to your affair with Rowland, Mary. As far back as that.'

Mary tried a light laugh, rejecting such fantasies. 'Really, Richard!'

'I'm serious, Mary, believe me. And I want to peep into your memory.'

'Oh . . . really? What can I hope to remember that could be *that* much help to anybody?'

'Your affair with Rowland. You were very young, Mary. A girl. A servant girl. An attractive girl, I've no doubt at all, judging by Jennie.'

Amelia was moving around restlessly. She knew me, knew I didn't pry into personal matters unless I had to. I didn't think she fully realised, though, what it was costing me. It had to be done with a smile, that was the trouble, with a casual air that dismissed any suggestion that the discussion could be deadly serious. And now I felt that a smile might be physically painful. I dared not catch Amelia's eye; dared not even glance at a mirror, fearing what I might see.

There had been an extended pause, but Mary's attention had not wandered from my face for a second. Now she decided on her attitude; she would be lightly dismissive.

'Oh yes,' she said, 'I was young and silly, and Rowland . . . I can see him now. Looking back – I can realise he wasn't what you'd call a self-confident man. It was all on the surface. Poor Rowland. Rowley, he told me I must call him. But that was later, much later, when we sort of knew each other better.'

And Amelia, bless her, decided she must help me. 'I bet he was terribly handsome.'

'Oh yes . . . yes. But I was seeing him through a young girl's eyes. He was the master. We looked up to him – with awe. The real meaning of awful, I suppose. Or would it be awesome?' She was talking round it, sliding her mind away from the memory.

'But, I gather, he didn't act the part of the master?' I asked, leading her on.

'It was all on the surface, you know,' said Mary to my wife. 'That's all I ever saw. And he *did* think so much of himself. Poor Rowley, so weak and inoffensive, and he tried to act like a Regency . . . what's the word?'

'A Regency buck?' I suggested.

'Oh yes, that's it.' Mary smiled at Amelia, who would understand. 'He used to walk the grounds in his riding breeches and boots, so that he could slap them with his crop. But never a severe word. D'you know what I think, Richard?'

I shook my head. She was relaxing now, and lowered herself into the creaking chair. 'How could I guess?' I asked, when I already had.

'I think, inside, he was a very insecure man,' Mary went on. 'No self-confidence. He couldn't *give* orders, if you know what I mean. He asked. Will you do this, do that? I never saw him angry. Worried and confused, yes. But never angry. And he always smiled at me. Whenever we met in the house . . . that smile! "And how are we today?" he would ask. Meaning me. And, "No, no, my girl," when I gave him one of my curtsies. Mrs Hughes trained us to curtsy. And he'd reach over and put a finger beneath my chin and lift me to my full height, then stand back and say, "A beautiful young woman should stand firm, with pride." And I could do no more than smile. I was absolutely tongue-tied.'

Amelia flicked me a quick restraining glance. It was women's talk. 'Not the thing to be said by the master to a serving girl, Mary,' she suggested.

'It wasn't the normal thing at all,' Mary murmured. But her eyes were not focused on anything in that room; she was way back in her youth. And her eyes shone. 'Of course, I was madly in love with him,' she went on. 'I'd read all the latest romances, and I knew how it would be. He would snatch me away in his coach-and-four, and we'd fly abroad . . . all the nonsense that goes through a young girl's mind. And there was no coach-and-four. There was the Rolls Royce, and Perkins, the chauffeur, and there was no romance in that, and no possibility of Rowland taking me away. I knew that. Knew it. But a young girl lives on her dreams.'

She was caught in them now. There were no secrets to be restrained.

'Go on,' Amelia whispered.

'Well . . . Amelia . . . it had to come to an end, or a beginning. I saw that in his eyes. "We cannot talk here, in this corridor," he would say, and he was quite right about that. We could not. I would have been dismissed on the spot if any such . . . intimacy should have been detected. But he said, "I will arrange something." And that something was the gamekeeper's lodge. My own brother's home! And now, when I look back to it – the risks you take! But I was way beyond thinking about risks. Or if I did, it only increased the thrill of it. There was a word for it. I found it in one of my books. Clandestine, that's it. I was thrilled, and afraid, and flattered, I suppose, the master *wanting* me. And this – now I come to remember it, think about it – good heavens,

Amelia, this would have been about 1950. We were living in the past. But the whole estate, the Park, it seemed to be in its own little world, cut off from the reality outside. I didn't care about that . . . I had my Rowland, my Rowley, my lover.'

She was breathless, the words having poured from her so fluently, so fast. She was lost in it. Still was, I realised, that sad smile on her face stripping the years from her.

'But Charlie must have known,' I said. 'Must have.'

'Oh yes. I realised that. I don't know what Rowley did – sent him off to a far corner of the estate, I suppose, to feed the grouse, or whatever he was supposed to do with them. With a crackly pound note in his pocket, perhaps. But what did I care about that? I was insanely in love with Rowley.' She shook her head. 'And then there was Jennie on the way.'

'That would've been a shock,' murmured Amelia.

'I don't know . . . don't know what it was I felt. Really, I was just a stupid, ignorant girl. I didn't know what to do. I was frightened and confused, frantically excited . . . oh, I don't know. I had these wild dreams, you see, that now he would *have* to go away with me, take me away, where we could live . . . together.'

'But nothing's ever like your dreams,' said Amelia softly. 'Poor Mary, you must have felt absolutely lost.'

There was a silence. Mary seemed unable to go on. Then she said, 'And suddenly he was a stranger, a man I'd never seen before. I was going to have his child, and he didn't know what to do about it. And the love went out of his eyes. If that was what it'd been – love. By then, I was becoming doubtful. Had it been love? I'd suddenly grown up, I suppose.'

'Yes,' said Amelia softly.

Mary looked out of the window. 'He's been here a long while,' she commented.

'Pardon?' I glanced at Amelia, who hadn't heard the last remark.

'Joe. He's been here a long while – and they haven't come up to see me.'

At that point I nearly surrendered, nearly called an end to it. Mary so desperately needed her daughter's happiness, to reach out and touch it, to retrieve a little something from the past.

'They'll be along, Mary,' I said. 'But you haven't said . . . is that when you first found the *Lady Chatterley* in Tessa's drawer?'

Amelia turned and stared at me. I shrugged. I couldn't even try to explain.

'About that time,' said Mary, her voice now empty of all emotion.

'So the two came together, your reading of bits of *Lady Chatterley*, and the realisation that you were going to have Rowland's baby?'

'Yes. Together. Almost. But it took me quite a while to understand what it meant.'

'Until you put it all together,' I helped her along.

Mary sighed. 'Yes, Richard. As you have, I see.'

And Amelia was looking at me with hard, cold eyes. How dared I link the two!

But I had by no means put it all together. It was no more than a multiple trickle of background facts, not quite meeting into a single stream of logic.

'Mary,' I asked her, 'when did you realise that Jeremy is your brother's child?'

Amelia made an explosive sound of protest. I didn't respond. I was talking intimately with Mary, whose eyes were wild.

'But it's my secret,' she whispered. I had stolen it from her.

'It's a secret that's become far too obvious, I'm afraid. Your mistress, Mary, had been reliving *Lady Chatterley*. And she had her own husband's gamekeeper to pad out the illusion.'

'That's quite ridiculous, Richard,' said Mary, but there was no conviction in her voice. 'What on earth could she have seen in our Charlie?'

I almost laughed at that, but it would have been inappropriate, even insulting. 'Mary,' I said, 'you might better ask yourself what she saw in Rowland. It was an arranged marriage. She might very well have disliked the partner who'd been chosen for her, right from the day of the marriage. If only because he hadn't been her choice. And Rowland – what did she see but a weak and ineffectual man, lost in his own futile dreams that he was the squire, the lord of his little Penhavon Park – and unable to live up to it? That's what she saw in her husband, somebody beneath contempt. And there was Charlie, completely the opposite, uncouth, almost a savage, and you must admit that. She *chose* him, Mary, probably nearly instructed him to be her lover, simply because he was her dream of what a man should be. To take her and to use her. Old-fashioned language, Mary, but everybody's living in the past around here. And the union resulted in Jeremy. *She* would be certain of that – but would Rowland? Would he be sufficiently certain to disavow the child? Would he have been able to assert himself so forcefully? No. I think not.'

Amelia said sharply, 'Are you saying that Jeremy can't inherit the baronetcy, Richard? That he isn't Sir Jeremy?'

'No. I think that's all right. It's too late now to dispute it. He's been accepted all these years as a child of the marriage. It's too late at this time to do a thing about it.'

'Then why are you making so much of it?'

I shook my head.

Amelia was staring at me blankly, coldly. 'Then how does it affect anything?' she demanded.

I said nothing. I nodded towards Mary, whose hands were clasped over her face. She was weeping wildly.

'*Now* look what you've done!' Amelia cried, anger in her voice, and she rushed to Mary, putting her arms round her. 'Mary, love, Mary . . .'

I waited miserably. I wasn't wanted around there any more. At last the sobbing ceased. Mary sniffed herself to silence. Then she made a great effort, stiffened her shoulders, and stared straight ahead of her at the opposite wall.

In the end, she recovered some of her composure. 'You still don't really understand, do you, Richard?' she asked quietly. 'In some way, you know, I knew Rowley had no resolution in him. I could just about manage to excuse him, that he did so little for me – in the end. Adopting Jennie, that was as far as he would help me. Help, he called it! When she was born. His little girl. Then, he tried, but not much. But her adoption didn't help me, did it? If he'd tried to help me leave, but with Jennie in my arms, and with somewhere we could live, with a roof over our heads, and a little money to live on . . . Then, I could've forgiven him, and perhaps loved him still. But you see, I'd found that book. *That* book . . .'

'You said you were sixteen, Mary, at that time.'

'Yes, Richard.' Mary was impatient with me now, that I would not listen to what she had to say, only to what I wanted her to hear. 'When I found the book, I didn't understand it at first. The pencil notes, they meant nothing to me. And, you see, they were in pencil, and pencil doesn't fade. At first, I thought they were quite recent. Well . . . the book was there, in the bedside table. I thought; she must be reading a little every night . . . and was making notes. But gradually I came to understand. Oh, Amelia, I was so slow, so silly.'

180

'Just young, Mary. You wouldn't understand.'

'And then, it gradually came to me. The notes must have been written long before. Since before Jeremy's birth. And all those nods that Charlie gave me, all the winks, all the dirty grins . . . suddenly they made sense. My wonderful, beautiful mistress had had an affair with my own brother! With Charlie! And Charlie, I knew, had a reputation all round the district. And Lady Theresa Searle had had an affair with *him*! And Jeremy was the result. You've only got to think . . . the tempers, the unreasonable behaviour. Oh yes, Jeremy was Charlie's lad. And that meant . . .'

She faltered, biting her lip to silence it before it betrayed her. Then she took a deep breath, and sighed heavily. We waited.

'It meant', said Mary in a small flat voice, 'that everything Rowland had whispered in my ear was false, and every touch he'd given me had been unfeelingly given. I was his revenge. He just hadn't had the courage to face her, his Tessa, face her and charge her with it. He'd smiled and accepted it, and then he'd used me as a kind of . . . of rebound. There's a word. I knew it once. Oh yes. Rancour. That's what he'd used on me, when the object of it was really Tessa. *That* was what did it for me. *That* was what upset me most, so that I couldn't think of anything logically any more for the distress, and couldn't think of a better thing to do but get away from there – from him – even if I had to leave without Jennie. Even that!'

Then she buried her face in her hands and wept hysterically.

Amelia turned and stared directly at me. Could I be blamed for this? I thought not. Mary had volunteered it. But I knew that expression. It meant: leave this to me, and I'll be having a word with you, later.

'I'll be a minute,' I said quietly, and if Amelia saw me pick up the *Lady Chatterley*, she said nothing, certainly gave no sign of understanding what I intended.

I closed the door quietly behind me and stood in the corridor, my mind racing. It was difficult to decide how to tackle what I now had to do.

Then, resolutely, as befitted a big, tough ex-copper, I went along and tapped gently on Tessa's door.

She called out, 'If that's Richard, please come in.'

I did so. She was standing at her window, which overlooked the rear of the house, the view embracing the whole, magnificent spread of the valley, the Park that she would share with Geoffrey Russell, which then, apparently, would no longer be a prison.

She was now in complete control of herself, was even mildly amused at my persistence.

'Somehow, I thought you would be back,' she said. 'So now you know the sordid truth. Mary will have told you. *Know* it, I mean, not guess it.'

'Most of the truth.'

'As she knows it, or as she's imagined it?' She nodded to herself. 'What gems of knowledge has she trusted you with? Tell me, Richard. I can't wait to hear.' There was arrogance in that, even contempt.

It was something of a relief to realise that I was not going to have to force it from her. It was with a touch of dismay that I felt I was going to hear more than I could easily digest, and that she was going to thrust it at me with pride.

'I know now that Jeremy is Charlie Pinson's son,' I told her flatly.

'And you're finding that difficult to accept?' She spoke derisively, but whether the contempt was for me or for Rowland I couldn't be certain. 'What part of it do you find difficult to accept, I wonder? That I could force myself to any sort of intimacy with a foul animal like that?'

'That thought occurred to me.'

'But that was the whole point of the exercise, Richard.' She lifted her chin. 'And it *was* an exercise. An experiment. I had to know that my secret dreams could after all become reality, and that I wouldn't recoil from them. Recoil! Can you believe it if I tell you I welcomed every physical approach that Charlie, the animal, made to me? Yearned for them – joined him in experimenting in every foul deviation he could conjure up! But no . . . you could never imagine that. You would've needed to know my Rowland first. *My* Rowland! I'd barely met him before I found myself engaged to marry him. It was such a *good* match, I was told. Oh dear me, yes. But he was no man, believe me. He was a paltry imitation of a man. Ineffectual, incompetent, impotent. He could face nothing, only retreat to that weak smile of his. His every action, gesture, comment, everything was an apology. He was forever apologising for pretending to be a proper husband.'

'I don't think I want —'

'D'you imagine that poor creature could have fathered the son I wanted?'

'He fathered Paul.' I said that very quietly, now praying it should be true.

'Oh yes. But he'd had a bit of practice by then.' It was delivered like a whiplash, viciously cracking.

Could she possibly be referring to Mary? Of course not. Paul was two years older than Jennie. No – there must have been another maid before Mary. Or maids. Heavens, I'd better not allow Mary to know that. If it were true, of course.

'But no . . .' Tessa was saying. 'I wanted the son Charles Pinson might give me. With all his multiple faults.'

'And Rowland knew this?' I asked quietly. 'Knew that Jeremy was not his own child?'

'I don't think he had the gumption to realise.'

Yet poor Mary had been caught up in the middle of it, and she'd had to live with the result of Rowland's knowledge, his rancour. Oh yes, he had known.

'Of course he knew,' I said impatiently. 'Your wonderful animal, Charles Pinson, he would have known, too. D'you imagine that wasn't what he'd hoped for? Just think what that meant to Charlie – the power it gave him, the confidence. The future Sir Jeremy Searle would be the next baronet, and he was illegitimate. How he would dangle that beneath Rowland's nose! Almost jeering at him. I'm surprised Rowland didn't disavow Jeremy. But it gave Charlie something of a lever, power. How he would dangle that beneath Rowland's nose!'

'As you've said,' she put in sourly.

'Yes, I've already said it. Dangle it, and use it for blackmail. On and on, through the years. Until at last, poor Rowland, older now and perhaps a little more confident, would have had to do something about it.'

'Are you trying to tell *me* what happened, Richard? As though I haven't been here, all the time! Of course I knew Charlie was blackmailing him. A little at a time – which he no doubt drank away or gambled away. But Rowland – tcha! Can you imagine him facing Charlie? Face to face! Never. No guts, that was my husband . . .' Her eyes narrowed, a frown traced itself across her brow.

I wondered what had caused her to pause. To pause and think. I waited.

'I can't understand it,' she said at last. 'We used to go away for a month for the winter sports. Val d'Isère. And Rowland was a skier. Quite expert. He used to take place in the downhill racing.

183

That, surely, must have taken some nerve. Can you understand *that*? I can't.'

'Yes. I think I can.'

'Then please explain.' This was an instruction.

I shrugged. 'How can I? Two different kinds of opposition, physical and emotional. Something like that, perhaps.'

'I don't understand you.' There was impatience now. Was I to blame for her lack of understanding, now and in the past?

'Perhaps he was a man who was concerned about giving offence,' I suggested. 'About creating trouble, about the smooth passage of human relationships.' I watched, but there was no lightening of her fixed distaste. 'I'm sorry, I can't explain what I mean. But something does occur to me.'

'Yes?' She was suspicious.

'A man who's done downhill racing on skis would surely not break his neck by falling downstairs. His natural reactions would save him.'

She tilted her head at me, giving me a sour smile. 'It wasn't like that,' she said calmly.

'Then how *was* it, for heaven's sake?' How many versions had she kept in reserve?

Now her smile was delicate, secret, for her own amusement. 'It was Rowland, at last working himself into a fury. Oh, it was so strange to see that! He was tired of the Mary business being flung at him – not by me, of course – and tired of the Jeremy business being dangled in front of his nose by Charlie. And I knew it was an empty threat, after all these years.'

'What was?' I asked, because we'd got to get this straight.

'The acceptance of Jeremy as a child of the marriage. After so long, that threat meant nothing.' She smiled again. 'Geoffrey told me that.'

'You consulted *him*?'

'Well, yes. He was the family's solicitor, after all. And the man I wanted to marry. *And* who was my personal solicitor. Who else would I think of approaching? Do try to use your imagination, please. And Geoffrey told me there was nothing for me to worry about. And that Rowland had nothing to worry about. So I told him he hadn't, and that he'd be quite safe to tell Charlie to go to hell.'

I sat down abruptly in the creaky chair, and to hell with the conventions. The chair well-nigh collapsed. How many more facets of this woman's strange personality was I to uncover?

'You told Rowland that you'd confided in Geoffrey Russell?' I stared at my hands, feeling it to be better to hide my expression.

'I did. He'd got to face the facts some time.'

'And he therefore faced them?'

'In his own way. The farm where Pinson works – worked – belongs to us. It's part of the estate.'

'Don Martin —'

But she didn't allow me to say anything. 'It's rented. And Rowland applied pressure on Martin. Quietly, you see. No confrontations. Don Martin was told that he'd got to dismiss Pinson, as simple as that. Charlie was going to be hounded out of the district. Out of Rowland's life.' Again she managed a thin smile. 'As Mary was.'

I didn't dare to allow myself to be sidetracked. 'So it was Charlie doing the shouting downstairs, on that day?'

'Yes. He knew, as well as I did and Rowland did, that there was nobody else in the house.'

I nodded, not intending to interrupt, but Jeremy had said he was there. Not that he'd seen something, just that he'd been in the house.

'I had to urge him,' she went. 'I told you that. And he slipped. Silly man. You would think – a skier – that he'd be able to keep his feet. As you've pointed out. But he slipped and knocked himself out.'

I took a deep breath. 'I just cannot accept that he slipped.'

'He had no hand free for the banister.'

'How . . .'

'He was carrying a shotgun, with both barrels loaded, and both intended for Charlie. Rowland had some idea he could get away with that, as Charlie was, after all, an intruder. He'd gone over the brink, Rowland had. And *he* was the one doing the most shouting – filthy language. I do believe he'd had a few drinks . . . Anyway, he was shouting, and he ran, actually ran down the stairs. He had no hand free, you see. And he slipped . . .'

'And knocked himself unconscious?'

She nodded portentously. 'Slipped and fell. Unconscious, yes.'

'And so . . .'

'His head', she said distantly, 'was lying against the bottom stair.'

'Yes.'

'And Charlie stamped on his back. It was over in a second.'

185

I got to my feet. She was standing there at the window, nodding, nodding to herself, a smile flickering across her lips, disappearing, appearing again.

'So Charlie was still a bit of a threat,' I suggested. 'The thing had to be covered up. The doctor to issue the certificate, and perhaps Geoffrey to tell the right story to the Coroner?'

'That's how it was.'

'But it . . . it was murder!'

'I know. But it's all right now. Charlie Pinson's dead.'

'Yes, yes, it's all right now,' I mumbled, my mind racing away, trying to tie up ends, trying to find ends to be tied.

I got to my feet, my legs strangely stiff. There seemed nothing more to be said. If I spent hours talking to her, I would never satisfy myself that I understood her. But I had to tell myself that the emotions had been hammered out of her over the years. They had hit their peak when she'd struggled in Charlie's arms, in his cottage. From then, it had all seeped away, until now there were only the dregs she could offer to Geoffrey Russell. I had to hope that would suffice. For both of them. But at least, he would have his letterhead, though perhaps he would regret the price he would have to pay for it.

I was hesitating at the door, turning to see whether she had anything more to say – and meeting only a meaningless smile – when I heard shouts from the corridor.

'Nanna! Nanna!'

Flinging open the door, I ran out.

16

I followed Jennie into Mary's room, and caught the door as it was closing. Jennie, in great distress, was trying to talk through her tears, her back to me.

'They've ... they've arrested ... oh, oh, oh ... they've arrested Joe.'

'Now, now,' I said, coming up behind her in a perfect position to slip my arm round her shoulders.

She half-turned to me. 'They took him out to their car. I ran out after them. They were taking him away ...' she wailed.

'Probably only for questioning,' I comforted her.

But that wouldn't be for a short stay, I knew. Phillips could have done his own casual questioning in the drawing-room. This would be more intense, in a proper interrogation room.

'And he shouted ... shouted out, "The dogs, the dogs." And I don't know what to *do*. The dogs don't know me yet, and I'm ... I'm scared of them. Oh ... what am I going to do?'

She clung to me, as being the largest, chunkiest thing in the room to cling to. 'We'll look after the dogs. You don't have to worry, Jen.' I caught a glimpse of Amelia's expression, her eyebrows almost in her hair. She didn't like the sound of this at all.

Then Mary, who had gone white, and had seemed to be paralysed, finally came to life. She came over and took Jennie from me, to be replaced by Amelia, frantically clutching at my elbow and whispering tensely, 'But they're Dobermanns, Richard. They frighten me.'

'Nonsense. It's how you talk to them. Joe told me that.'

'It's all right for him to talk, but by the time you find out you're not talking their language, they'll have you on your back with their teeth in your arm. If not worse.'

I noticed that I'd been elected to this task. It didn't cheer me in the least.

'I'll go and see Phillips,' I said. Promised. Three pairs of eyes were looking to me as their saviour. 'The man doesn't know what he's doing. Why isn't he up there at the cottage? I'll go and find out what he thinks he's playing at. In any event, Joe's probably got a kennelmaid. Or something.'

'Oh no,' said Jennie, still not through with the sobbing. 'He does it all himself.'

'All right.' He would . . . I might have guessed. 'I'll go and see the DCI, right now. I'll be back as quickly as I can.'

Already I was planning alternatives. Joe had mentioned a friend. A breeder friend. I could get Phillips, at least, to find out that friend's phone number. Yes, it was sounding better now. He'd need to do no more than phone his station.

'I'll be back,' I repeated. Then I was out in the corridor, and I took that staircase three at a time. Try killing me, buster, I said to myself. It didn't. I arrived, a little short of breath, in front of the DC at the door. A different one.

'I want a word with DCI Phillips,' I said briskly.

'Name, sir?'

'Richard Patton.'

'If you'll wait a moment.' He slid through the barely open door like a sinuous draught, and was back in a few moments. He said I could go right in.

The room seemed little changed. Phillips still occupied the same chair, but was slumped deeper down in it, and seemed smaller, as though he might have sweated off twenty pounds or so, simply from the exercise of his brain. I knew that there would have been no reason for his presence up at the lodge, in fact he would not have been welcome. The Scene of Crimes team would take over – had taken over – each one an expert in his or her own field, and their reports would have been sent to Phillips, as and when sifted and cross-checked. He had only to conduct interviews, and wait. This was his Operations Room.

Before him, their chairs fanned so that each was facing him head on, were Jeremy and Paul. That he had them together was not surprising. There had been conflict between them, and it might have been possible to play one against the other in order to extract vital information. All three looked completely bored. Jeremy tinted his boredom with a shade of red on his cheeks, flaunting it like a warning flag. It was terribly obvious, his awareness that he was now Sir Jeremy Searle having penetrated his conscious mind, that with it had come a shade of confidence, something that added to his attitude a certain aura of condescension.

Beside him, Paul seemed to be relaxed and slightly amused, possibly at Jeremy's transformation into authority. The two suitcases were there and looking exactly as I had last seen them, but were now between their two chairs. Paul's right hand rested on the handle of one of them, a casual gesture, but it conveyed a sense of possession. Not the cases themselves, of course, those would belong to Jeremy. His cases. But Jeremy was not touching them.

Phillips lifted his head to watch me approaching. He leaned across and whispered something into the microphone, then switched off his recorder.

'What the hell d'you think you're playing at, Phillips?' I demanded. Perhaps my voice was a little strained. It was certainly close to a shout.

'My job,' said Phillips placidly.

'You've arrested Joe . . .'

Observing my hesitation, he helped me out. 'Torrance.'

'Torrance?' I asked stupidly.

'Gladys's nephew,' Paul offered, hating to see me confused.

'And he's not arrested or charged. He's been taken in for questioning,' Phillips said flatly.

'Damned stupid!'

'Is it, Mr Patton? Is it? Wasn't it you who told him how to explain *why* he was there at the lodge – cottage, whatever? Oh, a very plausible reason. I believe it. Oh, I do. But it hardly alters the fact that he *was* there. He could have gone inside —'

'He couldn't have done that. He didn't know where the spare key was kept.'

'Didn't he? How can you know that? Nobody can be certain about a negative.' He raised his palms, exonerating himself from defective reasoning. 'And he had a motive. If he'd gone in there – just to gloat over what he might be owning, someday not too far away – and he was using a torch, then Pinson could have spotted him. We've checked that possibility. And Joseph Torrance had a motive. He'd already had one set-to in the Red Lion with Pinson.'

The two brothers had been sitting woodenly, listening to this. Only Paul felt that Joe might merit support.

'So what?' he asked angrily.

'We have evidence that Pinson spoke to him about Jennie. Spoke insultingly.'

'What'd he say?' Paul demanded, leaning forward.

'That she was a bastard.'

'I'd have flattened him,' Paul declared.

'He'd better not say it in *my* presence,' put in Jeremy, who was in much the same situation as Jennie.

'He's dead, Jerry, dead,' Paul reminded him.

'Oh . . . yes.'

Phillips waited until they were silent, then he went on, speaking directly to me. 'So he's under interrogation. If he's got good answers, he'll be released.'

'Have you found the missing key?' I asked angrily. He was beginning to annoy me.

'No. Unfortunately not. We've done a crawl search. Nothing within throwing distance.'

'Or a weapon?' I insisted. 'It would have to be something the murderer was carrying.'

'Or something Pinson was carrying,' said Phillips mildly. 'Just imagine it. Pinson spots the light. Ah – an intruder, he thinks. Could be dangerous. So he picks up a rock or something, and takes that with him, to investigate.'

'You've already covered that,' I reminded him. 'And it looks as though he did pick up something – that chunk of rock with the dirt and the grass stuck to it. But you told me that hadn't been the murder weapon.'

'Quite so. And the man with the torch managed to club him behind the ear with something else.' Phillips was quite placid about it.

'Not while Pinson had his eye on him, you can be sure of that,' I said. 'And Pinson certainly wouldn't have turned his back.'

There was a short silence, while Phillips pretended to think about that. 'All right. So he took his eyes off him.'

'Why?' I demanded. 'What else was there to look at?'

Phillips smiled. 'Look, Mr Patton – are you trying to prove something?'

'Just helping with the old visualising act,' I assured him, though a little impatiently. 'I'm trying to imagine Joe Torrance there, facing Pinson, who'd got a chunk of rock in his fist, and somehow managing to belt him one with something heavy and hard, which hasn't appeared yet as an item of evidence . . . Oh, come on, Phillips, it's just not on.'

'He's a tough character, that Joseph Torrance.'

'Tough enough to have overcome Charlie Pinson, who'd already got his own weapon? All right, you'll say. A quick right to the chin . . . and Pinson's unconscious on the floor. Then what? Why take it any further? Why not simply walk away and leave him to recover? So where's your murder weapon? Show me a murder weapon. That room was completely bare when I saw it. You've already admitted it couldn't have been Pinson's chunk of rock.'

'That', said Phillips complacently, 'is why we've got Torrance in for questioning.'

'Hoping he'll admit he'd gone to that cottage, hoping Jennie might come along to say goodnight – with something heavy and hard in his pocket? You're crazy, Phillips. Pure bonkers.'

'Nevertheless,' he said placidly, 'we're questioning him. And we're holding him until we get some reasonable answers.'

It was clear that I was getting nowhere with my mission. I made an angry gesture. 'Then phone the station. They can ask him for the phone number of his friend who breeds Dobermanns. It's somebody out Leominster way.'

'And break into the interrogation?' Phillips was openly scornful.

'But he's worried about his dogs.'

He spread his palms. 'Fine. Then he'll give us straight answers all the sooner.'

I stared at him in anger, and he smiled back. I stared at the other two, who shrugged.

'Oh, to hell with you, then,' I said, and rushed out, almost walking over the constable outside.

Amelia and Jennie were hovering in the hall. They pounced on me.

'They're holding him for now,' I told them.

'Then what're we going to *do*?' asked Jennie, her eyes wide and her face all distorted with distress.

'It's not really anything to get upset about,' I assured her. 'The dogs are probably fed only once a day, and they won't starve, because Joe's sure to be released soon.' Sometimes I can lie quite smoothly.

'But they might not have had their one meal, today,' Jennie pointed out logically. 'The poor things, they'll be ravenous.'

191

And only waiting for me to chew at?

I was feeling a little peckish myself. But I didn't say so. It was unlikely that their one meal would be at this time, anyway. I glanced at my watch. Eleven twenty. Damn it – perhaps Joe fed them at noon.

Jennie tried to get it across to me. 'He shouted, "The dogs . . . the dogs!" Please. It must matter.'

I glanced at Amelia, who was frowning. At my lack of eager response? At my slightest hesitation? I sighed.

'He was here earlier,' I reminded Jennie. 'He came back. If it's just the feeding you're worried about, that's probably what he went to do.'

It in no way penetrated her distress. 'He probably went to the butcher's.' At my no doubt blank response, she went on, 'To get their meat. Oh . . . what are we going to do? They'll be starving!'

Amelia's gaze was darting from one to the other of us, unable to decide in which direction to focus her concern. To the dogs . . . or to me?

'How far is it?' I asked.

'It's only just the other side of the village.' She was all eagerness now. 'It'd only take a few minutes.'

To look at them? To judge whether they looked ravenous? Amelia said, 'It'll do no harm to go and see.'

But Joe was undergoing nothing worse than a difficult interrogation. They couldn't hold him for long without making a charge. At that time, if his stay became extended, we might need to start worrying.

'Oh yes,' said Jennie eagerly. 'We could go . . . and see.'

'Let's get in the car, then,' I said. Anything for a bit of peace.

'Can we take Sheba and Jake?' Amelia suggested.

'Oh heavens, no. Surely not. They'd smell the others and start barking, and that'd set the Dobermanns off . . . Oh no.'

'The poor dears.' It didn't seem that Jen meant the Dobermanns. 'They're not getting their exercise.'

I slammed the door. Jennie was in the back. 'They'll have to wait, then, won't they!' I said over my shoulder.

Jennie breathed in my ear. 'When we get back, I'll take them for you.'

It was an offer, in repayment for a very minor service. I grunted. I enjoyed going out with our dogs. It was now part of my life. 'If you insist,' I said equably. Now committed, I felt more relaxed.

It seemed strange, driving away from the scene of all the activity. Anything that meant anything had to be discovered back at Penhavon Park. And I was driving away from it. Yet, deep down, there was this niggling urge to continue to drive away from it, and forget the whole unpleasant tangle. If it wasn't for Mary . . . and for Jennie.

'There's a turning along here,' said Jennie. I hadn't noticed we'd run through the village. 'On the right there. There. There, look. Opposite that gate. On the right.'

'Yes, yes. I see it.'

'It isn't much of a place,' she said dubiously, so that we should not be disappointed. 'Joe's renting it now, and the bit of land.'

It was set back where high banks, topped with thorn hedges, lined the lane. Into this had been hacked a gap, and behind it there was a climbing driveway up to the cottage. Beyond this was the dog-run. High chain-link fencing – Dobermanns are very agile – behind it a glimpse of a row of hutments, then we had to draw to a halt. There was no further we could proceed. The cottage was beside us. One bedroom, one living-room, a tiny kitchen. But it was much less than half the age of Jennie's cottage, and in much better repair.

They could have married and lived there. But Joe had said nothing about Jennie's assumption that they would move over and live in the gamekeeper's lodge, which, although it had more land to go with it, was hardly a jewel. He had observed her delight, that she could present him with that treasure. Although he would be faced with a vast amount of work and worry, he'd not hesitated, but had reacted with pleasure.

Jennie was tumbling out of the car. 'We've got to go round the back,' she shouted, and she'd reached there before I'd slammed my door.

The dogs, seeing strangers, were going wild. At this time they were in their little huts, which might have been miniature Swiss cottages if it had not been for the frontage of vertical bars. Maybe it was delight in welcoming a friend, maybe their stomachs told them it could mean food. I didn't know anything, except that I wasn't the friend, and hopefully not the food.

The compound itself had an inset gate. This had a hasp, but with a padlock hanging in it. To keep the dogs in, not burglars out. Who'd nick a couple of Dobermanns? Jennie opened the gate, waited for us to follow, then fastened it again. Routine, I supposed, for when they were running free. I started praying she'd not be opening the kennel doors with such abandon.

We had to shout. The clamour was deafening.

'They're starving!' cried Jennie, in almost a scream.

'They look very thin to me,' shouted Amelia, reaching up towards my ear.

'They're naturally slim dogs. All muscle.'

'And teeth!'

'Pardon?'

'And teeth,' she shouted.

Muzzles were thrust between the bars, which had a three-inch spacing. Tongues flicked out.

'They're thirsty!' shouted Jennie.

'Nonsense. There's water in that one's bowl. And that one . . .'

'They drink from that trough over there.' Jennie waved an arm.

I looked round. The trough in question was at the side of the compound. 'You're not going to let them out?' I shouted.

The clamour was dying down now. Jennie shook her head violently. 'I'm scared.'

One of them put out a muzzle, and reached a tongue through. I bent down and offered the back of my hand. It no doubt smelt of dogs. It was licked avidly. I put a hand on its nose, and retained all my fingers. 'I think we could risk it,' I called out, as they'd moved further along. But the dogs had relaxed into anxious whines.

'Oh no!' Amelia rushed back and caught at my arm. 'No, Richard.'

'I'm sure they're hungry,' said Jennie. She was almost in tears again. 'Look how thin they are.'

'Healthy.'

'I'm sure he feeds them about now.' She drew in her lower lip. 'Oh . . . what are we going to do?'

Her distress seemed excessive, considering that they would eventually be no more than an hour or two late with their food. But Joe had trusted her to do something. But what? That was the point.

'We could risk it,' I suggested. 'One at a time.'

'No, Richard . . .'

'What are we going to *do*?' wailed Jennie. The dogs howled back. 'Poor things.'

For Jennie, to put an end to her wails, and for the dogs, to put an end to their whines, I was willing to take a few risks. 'Where can we buy dog food?' I asked Jennie, moving close to her, close enough to detect she was shaking.

'He doesn't let them have tinned food.'

'Then what?'

'He gets meat at the butcher's. I told you that. Lights and things.' She grimaced. Her head was hunting from side to side.

'Then where do we get —'

'It'll be in the cottage. In his deep-freeze. He boils it.'

'Yes, yes. But how do we get in? Do you have a key, Jennie?'

'No.'

I groaned. She was moving from foot to foot with agitation, swinging her arms. Very soon, she'd not be able to say an intelligible word.

'Isn't there a spare?' I demanded, loudly and firmly, so that she'd not mistake me.

'Oh yes! Yes . . . of *course*.' She flashed a quick glance at me, sudden release in it, sudden joy. 'Of course. Silly . . .' She meant herself.

'And where's it kept?'

'Under the flowerpot,' she said.

And, standing in the frame of the open gate, there was Detective Sergeant Tate. He was smiling . . . grinning. 'Well, fancy that.' He winked.

Then he was gone. He would be using his car radio inside a few seconds, and there would be a long wait for the Dobermanns before Joe fed them again, because they would charge him at once. For a spare key, Joe would look under a flowerpot.

Jennie didn't realise the significance and stared after him blankly. I asked her . . . had to shake her arm, 'Do you know the name of Joe's breeder friend?'

She turned up a vacant face to me. 'I don't know. Geoff – something. I think.'

'Let's get inside.'

Yes, there was a spare key underneath the upside-down flowerpot. Yes, it opened the side door. I found Joe's phone, with a pad beside it, and Geoff's number written down. Amelia and Jennie were investigating the contents of the deep-freeze, which nearly filled the kitchen, as I dialled the number.

'Are you Joe Torrance's friend, who breeds Dobermanns?'
I asked.

'Yes. If he hasn't got one that suits you, I can —'

'It's not that,' I cut in. 'We're in difficulties, here. I'm a friend of
Joe's and of Jennie. At the moment he's at the police station,
being questioned. Very soon, he's going to be charged.'

'Gerrout! What with?'

'Murder.'

There was a pause, then, 'Not Joe, matey. Not Joe. A broken
jaw, a rib or two, a leg – and I'd believe it. But he couldn't kill a
rabbit if his dogs were starving.'

'That's what we're all worrying about, here. We don't know
what to do about his dogs. Jennie's in a panic, and heaven knows
when Joe'll be able to get home.'

'Leave it to me. Tell Jennie to leave the key under the flowerpot. I'll be right over.'

'The flowerpot . . .' But he'd rung off.

17

I drove carefully. This was not because the concern for Joe's dogs had now been lifted, not because I wasn't hungry, but so that I could concentrate. It availed me nothing. I was tracking through the same old facts, visualising the same scenes. There was nothing new. I saw it all with clarity, the images flickering from one frame to the next, like a slide projector gone insane. The body on the floor. And the key. The murderer leaving, locking the door, and taking away the murder weapon. And the key . . .

The key, the key!

Why had it been thrown away, or taken away?

I saw Tessa, leaning back against her pillow, her feet bare beside me. Dainty feet, pink feet, not hardened from unnecessary walking, for the walking to the lodge to meet her lover had been years ago. Add a year to Jeremy's age. Then she faded to become a vague shadow of a passionate woman – to the present.

I saw Jeremy's agony at the reading of the will – his delight as it became certain that the weight was lifted when he was introduced to the Impressionists' sketches. Then a flash of image – *Lady Chatterley* sliding along the table, to be caught by Mary.

But the key! The key!

And I saw Joe, denying he knew where the key had been kept, the spare key – when he need not have known. He would simply have reached for it by instinct.

But the key! The key! Why had it been taken away?

It made no sense. It would have been a deliberate act, for a purpose, when an easier deliberate act would have been to replace it beneath the flowerpot.

Then I was getting out of the car and Paul was standing at the door.

'They've charged Joe,' he said. 'He's under arrest.'

Jennie was whimpering, Mary clinging to her, whispering to her, and Paul was saying something about Gladys waiting to serve lunch.

Lunch? Lunch? Jennie wanted to be taken to see Joe, but I knew she would be refused access to him. I didn't say so, just shook my head. 'Later, Jen, later,' I said. But any time later than now was too late to stem the tears.

'Lunch,' said Amelia, tugging at my arm, but my mind was in another section of another day. Darkness. Night, with a torch glow streaming across the floor. The key still in the door lock. Surely it would have been left there, in order to draw the door shut on leaving? It *had* been drawn shut.

But the key! Why throw it away, or take it away?

'Lunch?' I said. 'I'm not hungry.' Only for understanding.

'Nonsense, Richard.' Amelia took my arm, and led me to the dining-room, like a blind man. Because, indeed, I saw nothing but the tantalising images.

If Gladys served the lunch, I was aware of her only as a presence. Joe was her nephew; she moved in a stiff agony of concern. I think I ate, but what I saw on my plate was images. Not food for the inner man. Food for the brain, which was the maker of the images. I watched them as they came and went . . .

Jeremy with his hot face streaming with sweat, near collapse on the suitcases he'd strained himself to bring there. 'It's locked.' The sun streaming through the trees, winking at me on the bare, frost-clothed branches. Or from a key that had been thrown there? For why, necessarily, throw it from the cottage door? Why not on the way home?

The key, the key!

And . . . home? Was I assuming something there? On whose way home? For who – if this house was 'home' – would walk that night-time path between the trees, a rusted key in his hand?

But of course . . . a rusted key would not glint in the sun.

I think I smiled ruefully to myself. It had shattered my images. An incorrect image, because it was not in the frame of logic.

Home? With the key?

But why – oh heavens why?

'Richard?' Amelia was saying. 'Make up your mind.'

We were standing outside on the front drive, I realised. The sun was weak now, hiding behind immature, fleecy clouds.

I was aware that Jennie was standing and watching me, haunting me. Wherever I looked, there was Jennie, staring at me with pitiful hope. I was in some way letting her down, failing to measure to her expectations of me. I must wave a magic wand, and produce the key to Joe's freedom. That stare! Why me?

'Richard!' Amelia jerked my arm. 'Do make up your mind.'

'What about?'

'We can't just stand here.'

'I've got to think. Shall we take the dogs?'

'Oh yes. We've been neglecting them,' she said.

She made me feel guilty. 'I think better when I'm walking,' I said.

But she had already hurried away, and in any event it had been a lie. I see too much, sharp, clear, unquestionably real things, a much more solid image than the ones I was trying to capture in my mind.

The key! I saw someone standing there, at the cottage door, the key in his hand. Deciding. Working it out . . . to leave or not to leave? Then the image raised an arm, hesitated, made up its mind . . . and took it away to discard elsewhere. Never to be found.

But why? Why?

Then the dogs were upon me, leads trailing. I crouched to them and they thrust at each other for the pleasure of licking the care from my face. I laughed . . . foolish creatures! They'd thought they had lost . . . lost what?

The key? No, he had not lost that blasted, stupid, stubborn key.

Amelia said, 'We've only seen the smallest part of the Park. There are acres of it behind the house.'

We walked round the house, but I remember none of the acres. Down to the river. I called the dogs to heel. At home . . . the same water, perhaps. There they swam and disported themselves. Otters lived there, had lived there, but fewer now, their food depleted by humanity's pollution. I called them to heel for the sake of Gladys Torrance's kitchen. We stared at the water. It was much the same as any other water.

Pinson walking into the cottage. He wondered what the light was. And a voice whispered: Kill. Kill now. And imprison him for ever in a cell of death, from which he could not be released. Especially if you throw away the key.

I said, 'It's cold here, down by the water.'

'Yes,' Amelia agreed.

We turned, and made our way back to the front.

Jennie stood on the front terrace, watching my activities worriedly. She could see no action, no progress.

'Shall we walk up to the cottage?' I asked Amelia.

'What is there at the cottage?' she asked, but she shrugged, and we headed that way. Suddenly Jennie was at my elbow. She said nothing.

Her anxious reliance on me was like a knife left in its wound. I could not shake it free. I felt her presence, and could do nothing to ease her desperate worry. Joe had been arrested. Only proof by production of the real killer would free him.

Proof? And I had nothing.

Pinson – Jennie's uncle? – walking into the cottage. Silence as they faced each other. 'Wondered what the light was.' That from Pinson. Then: 'Oh – it's you.'

But to whom had he been speaking? Speaking his last words? Possibly. Unlikely. There would've had to be provocation. It could not have been a sudden, unexpected attack.

The dogs were now running free. Amelia led the way. She walked down the four stone steps, making a new set of footprints in the mud at top and bottom.

My foot had almost covered her footprint at the top, when I stopped. It was as though I had walked into a wall. Even, I was slightly giddy for a moment. The dogs made whining sounds. Why had I stopped? I hissed, and they were silent, seated one each side of me.

'Richard,' said Amelia, 'what is it?' She was standing below me, looking up.

I could manage no more than a whisper. I pointed. 'Look.'

Jeremy's original footprints, pointing away from the house, were still there, frozen in the mud. A right foot at the top, the level surface. Beside it was Amelia's right footprint, impressed in the mud. At the foot of the steps was Jeremy's left – beside it Amelia's right.

'Hold the dogs,' I managed to get out. I tossed her the leads. She called them in, and fastened their leads. 'Don't move from there,' I said. 'Please, stay exactly where you are. I'll be a minute.'

Then I turned and ran past Jennie to the house. 'Stay here,' I shouted. There were barks from both the dogs, who hated to see someone running when they were not. I took the terrace steps in two strides and burst into the hall.

200

The DC said, 'You can't go in there, sir.' But I was already in, and had the door shut behind me.

Phillips eyed me approaching, and was suddenly alert. Jeremy and Paul were still there. They stirred, but said nothing.

I spoke reasonably calmly, proud of my restraint. 'I know where the weapon is. I know what happened. Come on . . . I'll show you.'

He was not impressed. 'Sit down and relax,' he said placidly. 'I wanted a word with you, anyway.'

'There's something —'

But he wouldn't allow me to get on with it. He was aglow with an awareness of his own acumen, and in a boastful mood. 'Sit down. Draw up a chair.' He gestured.

I wasn't going to do that. Couldn't have done. 'There's something you've got to see.'

He flicked a finger at cigarette ash on the chair arm. 'I went and let you lead me astray. Images. Visualisations. Tcha! And there we were, trying to build a picture to explain why the key was taken away.'

'So?' I could barely contain my impatience.

'The obvious, man, the obvious. Never ignore the obvious. What's the simplest reason you can imagine for removing a key from its usual place?'

I sighed. 'I don't know. Listen —'

He laughed. 'Why . . . to prevent somebody else from using it. Nobody can use a key that isn't there. Get it?' He cocked his head. 'Get yourself a chair.'

'No. Finish what you're saying, then come outside.'

He shook his head. He was still thinking about the damned key. 'But who'd do that? Just look at it from the other direction. Who was it that the removal of the key would stop from getting in? It'd have to be somebody who hadn't got a key of his own, but would know there was one under the flowerpot. Or ought to be. There's only one person who fits *that*, our friend here, Jeremy.' He inclined his head to Jeremy, who scowled at him, clearly having heard this before. 'And one person who didn't want him to get in, because Jeremy had said he intended to, and that was Paul, there.'

Paul grimaced, and I said, 'So?'

'So that gives Paul a reason for being there at the cottage last night. And maybe he took a torch, to check his paintings were all right – or some such reason. But he could have been there, and

Pinson could have spotted *his* torch. *Now* do you see? It puts Paul at the scene of the crime.'

I couldn't see what Phillips was playing at. He surely couldn't have become so desperate that he was blindly casting his hook in all directions, clumsily hoping for a catch.

'No motive!' I dismissed it with a flick of my hand. 'I can *show* you . . .'

'Oh – what a pity. I thought for one moment you'd jump in and claim it let Joe Torrance off the hook.' One of his hooks in one of his directions. 'But as you say – no motive. If we pursue that —'

'If', I cut in heavily, 'you will come outside, I can probably cure your headache a bit. Phillips, you're overworking your brain.'

Paul hauled himself to his feet. 'I've told him that. I'm getting out of here.'

'Oh no.' Phillips smiled crookedly.

'Oh yes,' I said definitely. 'I've got something. Come outside and I'll show you.'

Phillips gave this his serious consideration. Then he reached across and switched off his recorder. 'I hope this is worth seeing.'

'It is. You'll like it.'

He managed to get himself to his feet, but he was stiff. Paul and Jeremy stared at each other, then Jeremy too stood up.

'Not you,' Phillips told them.

'It's all right.' I ran my hands over my hair. 'They can watch.'

'Watch what?' asked Paul.

'You'll see. Oh . . . and we'd better take along the suitcases.'

I went over to them, moved one sideways so that I could stand between them, and then picked them off the floor. I tried to make this a nonchalant action, as though it was nothing to me, but in fact I had to summon up a few muscles that I didn't know I had.

'Right,' I said. 'Let's go.'

Jeremy stood aside and watched me. 'How far d'you intend to take 'em, Mr Patton?'

'Not far.'

'I'll take one of them,' he offered, as to an old and broken man.

'No, no. I'm all right. It helps, if only to get an idea of how you managed it. Anyway . . . I want you fresh and relaxed. Lead the way, Mr Phillips, if you please.'

He was eyeing me from beneath his eyebrows suspiciously. 'What're you up to?'

'It's only an experiment.'

Outside in the hall, Phillips nodded to his DC, who held open the front door for us.

The terrace steps were a little difficult, as they caught the back edges of the cases as I went down. I had to bend my arms to hold them clear. There was already a pain across the back of my neck, and my right knee ached.

'How far d'you expect to keep this up?' Phillips asked.

'Not far. Just to the steps.'

'Ah!' But Phillips probably hadn't even seen the steps.

Paul said, 'You'll do yourself a mischief.'

'Oh . . . I don't think so. After all, Jeremy managed it – and all the way to the cottage.'

'I'm fitter'n you,' said Jeremy shortly. 'And it just about knackered me, anyway.'

I managed it by fastening my eyes on the top of the steps, with Amelia's face low down beyond them, and by simply keeping one leg moving after the other. It felt as though my shoulder-blades were coming apart.

Six feet short of the steps, I stopped, put them down, straightened my back, and sighed.

'Well?' demanded Phillips.

Jeremy and Paul were beside me, one at each shoulder. Jennie hovered a few yards back.

I pointed. 'My wife's footprints. The ones with the smooth soles. She'd just walked down. D'you see them? She started off from her right foot, and she came down into the soft surface at the bottom with her right. Same foot. Four steps, so it'd be: start from the right, then – left, right, left, right. Okay?'

Phillips mumbled something.

'And these', I said, 'are Jeremy's prints, also coming down. They were made this morning when he carried the cases up to the cottage, and they're still nice and clear. A bit deeper than Amelia's. Naturally. They're his trainers, with the cleated soles. And what do we get? A right footprint next to Amelia's at the top – both right. But at the bottom, from Jeremy . . . another right print? No. It's a left one. Now . . . ask yourself. How could that have happened? No – we'll ask Jeremy himself. Still got the same trainers on? Ah, I see you have. A bit muddy, aren't they, for inside the house? Never mind. Now look . . . here're the cases. So you just pick 'em up, Jerry, and show us all how you did it. Come on. Give it a try.'

He looked round him, studying each face. He must have seen only what I saw myself – puzzlement. It assisted me with my own decision.

'No.' It was a flat rejection.

'Why not? All right. I'll show you, then.'

I picked them up again and stood, my right foot beside Jeremy's right footprint. And I walked down. But these steps were even more difficult than the terrace had been, being steeper. I had to lift the cases clear of the steps behind, the whole weight taken by my biceps. I felt a flash of hot pain across my neck. As I knew would happen, I came down at the bottom on my right foot, beside Jeremy's left footprint.

I put them down, and turned. They were all three staring at me, bewildered.

'All right?' I asked. 'Can you tell me how you managed to switch feet, Jerry? How did you manage to land on the bottom surface with your left?'

Nobody said anything. I sighed. Now came the difficult part – carrying them back.

But in fact it was a little less difficult, as I had to tip only the forward edges, and I could watch it happening. All the same, I was breathing deeply when I put them down in front of Jeremy.

'Well?' demanded Phillips, annoyed with himself that he couldn't see what I was trying to put across.

'I want Jeremy to demonstrate how it happened.'

'For God's sake!' Phillips burst out. 'What *is* this, a test of strength?'

'You could call it that,' I conceded. 'Well, Jerry, how did you do it?'

He shook his head. 'Just did. D'you think I was worrying what foot went where?'

I slapped him on the shoulder. 'Of course you weren't. But – you see – there *is* a way you'd take off from your right foot and land on your left at the bottom. That's if you jumped it. In one go, missing out the steps altogether.'

'Gerraway,' said Paul.

I smiled at him. 'He must've taken the steps in one big running stride. A leap!' I explained.

'That's impossible,' said Jeremy flatly.

'No, no,' I told him encouragingly. 'You managed to do it once. Well, here're the cases, exactly as they were. Try it once more. For me. Just to show me how you did it.'

204

Phillips came across to me and took my place, tried lifting the cases, and shook his head. 'Impossible. Even running at all with 'em ... that'd be something. A great big running jump? Nah! He'd break a leg or an ankle or something. How could he have been running?'

'I rather hoped Jeremy would show us,' I said. 'Aren't you going to try it?' I asked him.

He turned away.

'All right, then,' I said. 'I'll have a go at guessing at it. He'd have *had* to be running. He couldn't have done that leap without a run at it. And he *could* have started running, and nobody realise he had, the moment he was out of sight of the house. Once hidden by the hedge, and it would have been a flat run – and he took the steps in one single bound.'

'Carrying damn near a hundredweight?' asked Phillips. There was no sign of scepticism in his voice now. His eyes were bright.

'No,' I said. 'Not that. He was carrying empty suitcases.'

There was a silence. Then Jeremy said, 'Like to try it, mate? Try it with two heavy cases.'

'But that was the point,' I said. 'They weren't heavy, they were empty. You pretended they were heavy. Once you'd seen you'd been noticed, you thumped along with your arms hanging straight. But the second you were out of sight it was one desperate run. When we got up to the cottage, you were exhausted. But that wasn't from the weight, that came from having to run up the slope to the cottage. And you could have got there five, perhaps eight minutes before anybody would've expected you to.'

'You were watching this?' Phillips demanded.

'We had to go up the drive in the car,' I told him. 'We didn't hurry, because I assumed he'd have to take it slowly. But he wasn't going slowly at all. He was running. In that way he'd have reached the cottage minutes before we did. It gave him the time to do something he desperately had to do. That was to go inside and pack the masks back inside the cases, lock the door after him when he got them outside – and be found in exhaustion, sitting on full cases with the door locked – and no key available to open up again.'

'I don't believe this,' said Paul, his voice uncertain. I glanced at Jeremy. His face was set, his eyes glazed. I'd hoped he would carry it on from there. But apparently not.

205

I shrugged. 'I'm having to guess,' I apologised. 'But the way I see it is that he must have left the masks in there, the night before. He'd taken them up there – as he'd said he would, but he was interrupted. By Charlie Pinson. What did he say to you, Jerry? What?'

I turned to him. He was shivering, but not from the cold. He shook his head, so I had to carry it on.

'Did he greet you as Sir Jeremy? Did he say he had news for you, because you weren't Sir Jeremy, but plain mister? And that Sir Rowland had not been your father?' Jennie made a sharp sound of protest, but I had to ignore her.

'You'd dipped into *Lady Chatterley*, hadn't you, Jerry?' I asked. No response. 'It was tucked away on the shelves in the library, but you'd come across it, and you spotted the pencilled notes. In your mother's writing. And gradually, you came to suspect what those notes meant, and you put one or two things together in your mind – your father's obvious dislike of you, for one thing. Until in the end you'd got to believe it. Your own mother! But there – in front of you – was the living proof. Charlie Pinson. Jeremy! If you'd only called his bluff. Told him to go to hell.'

Jeremy made a wretched sound, perhaps intended as a laugh of derision.

'But did he offer to shake hands, Jerry? Shake hands with your father, son!'

'Oh no!' Paul whispered.

But I wasn't taking my eyes from Jeremy. 'And the appalling knowledge that you'd have to live with this creature as a perpetual burden, a special personal nightmare. And how could you face your mother . . .'

'Stop it!' shouted Paul, and Jennie whimpered.

I turned to Phillips. 'Your weapon's been with you all day,' I told him. 'It'll have been one of the stone masks. There they would've been, Jeremy busy unloading them on to the floor. And perhaps one of them was still in his hand – as Charlie gave him the glad news that he was his father. He probably, from blind instinct, struck out in fury —'

'No!' cut in Jeremy abruptly. His voice wasn't strong. 'It wasn't like that. It's all very clever, but it wasn't like you say. Oh yes, he walked in on me. Near gave me a heart attack, he did. There I was, the torch on the floor, and laying out the masks . . . oh, you don't have to worry, Paul . . .'

'Who's bloody worrying about the soddin' masks?'

Jeremy gave him a thin, sardonic smile. 'Well, I *was* being careful, and I'd just about finished, the last one in my hand, and all of a sudden, there he was. Said he'd seen the torchlight, and he was glad to get the chance of meeting me, because there were things I ought to know.'

'But as I said, I expect you already knew,' I said quietly.

'Guessed.' Jeremy was dismissive, disgust flattening his tone. ' "Meet your dad, son," he said. Or words to that effect. "Shake hands with your real father." Christ!'

'And you lashed out at him?' asked Phillips.

'No! No, I didn't. I told him he could get stuffed, and he could do as he bloody well liked. It was all so long ago, see. Who'd believe him, anyway? I laughed in his face – what I could see of it. I told him I'd see he got hounded out of the district . . . and he had a go at me. By God, the temper he'd got! There was something in his hand . . . a lump of rock or the like. It was so damned stupid – that's the point. Stupid! I could've disabled him in a second. Killed him, even.'

Phillips clearly didn't understand this. I said quickly, 'He's trained in martial arts.'

'Ah.' Phillips nodded.

Jeremy glanced at him, and licked his lips. 'But it didn't occur to me. He was . . . oh, I don't know . . . all of a sudden he seemed damned pitiful. Just a drunken lout. I reckon I laughed at him, and he swung his rock at me . . . well, I blocked that easily enough, and I sort of swung back, and that stone mask was in my hand – and he went down. Then, when I . . . when I checked, he was dead.' He looked frantically from one face to the other. 'Oh Lord, I'd killed him.'

Then he was silent, staring away into the distance. I took it up for him.

'Can you see it?' I asked Phillips. 'You and your damned images, do you see that one?'

He stared at me. Eventually, he nodded.

'Right,' I went on. 'So there was sure to have been panic. Jeremy would've had to get away from there. Couldn't wait to load the masks back into the cases – and of course, he didn't dare to abandon them.'

Jeremy cleared his throat. 'I had to get away. I couldn't bear to bend over him and load the masks back in the cases, and didn't want to toss 'em back, willy-nilly. Didn't want them chipped . . . for Paul. But I just couldn't wait. Couldn't. I grabbed up the cases, threw the torch inside, and took out of there like a rocket. You bet. I couldn't get away fast enough.'

'And you left the door open?' I asked quietly.

'Yes.' Jeremy shook his head, wanting to get it straight. 'And d'you think I got any sleep? Not on your life. I had to work out how to do it, 'cause I didn't dare to have the masks found, right there by him, and I couldn't face it till it was light. So . . . the empty cases. Run up there, as you said. And *still* I didn't have to throw the masks in. I was ever so careful, Paul. Honest. But I had enough time. Just. Got the door locked behind me just as I heard the car arrive.'

He was silent, licking his dry lips. Then, silently, he produced the missing key from his pocket. Jennie was coming up quietly behind him, and Amelia was beside me now, with the dogs.

'And there's your answer to the question about the key,' I told Phillips. 'The key *had* to be missing, to show that he couldn't get in – and therefore hadn't *been* in. It was a very neat inversion. Don't you think?'

He grunted. 'So it's all been a bloody waste of time. And I bet it'll go down on the file as self-defence.'

I nodded. I was sure it would. 'If you'll phone ahead, and tell me where to go, we'll run along and fetch Joe home. All right?'

He nodded morosely.

Jerry stared at us, his mouth gaping, then his splendidly fit body went limp and he collapsed to his knees in the mud, covering his face in his hands.

The dogs, hating to see distress so close to them, pushed in and frantically slobbered all over his distorted face. Jeremy howled in distress, not recognising the only genuine and unqualified affection he'd received in his life. Until Jennie joined them, kneeling in the mud, joined them in the affection proceedings with her own comforting hugs. Because after all, they were really in the same situation, not quite brother and sister. And Sir Jeremy Searle would probably return home from the station, his title undisputed.

Jennie looked back at me over her shoulder. '*Now* look what you've done,' she said severely.